Also by Max Travis

The Thunder Bay Seiner Series

Rocky Bay

Res Bay

K Bay

Windy Bay

Taylor Bay

Aialik Bay

Aurora Bay

Secret Bay

Midnight Bay

Aialik Bay

an Inside Alaska novel

The Thunder Bay Seiner Series
Book 6

Max Travis

Inside Alaska

Aialik Bay

Copyright © 2024 by Max Travis

This is a work of fiction. Names, characters, businesses, places, events, locales, and incidents are either the products of the author's imagination or used in a fictitious manner. Any resemblance to actual persons, living or dead, or actual events is purely coincidental.

All rights reserved.

No part of this book may be reproduced in any form or by any electronic or mechanical means, including information storage and retrieval systems, without written permission from the author, except for the use of brief quotations in a book review.

ISBN Print 978-1-936826-65-0

ISBN ePub 978-1-936826-66-7

Published by Inside Alaska

www.inside-alaska.com

78701.120424

Introduction
Thunder Bay Seiners Prequel

This short story takes place the summer before **Rocky Bay,** which is book one in the ongoing Thunder Bay Seiners Series.

While this book is a work of fiction, it is based on actual places in Alaska and uses many terms common to commercial seine fishing for salmon in the Southcentral area of Alaska.

I invite you to visit the publisher's website at www.inside-alaska.com for details about the names, places, and terms used, and to view photos and videos showing Alaska, fishing, seine boats, and much more. Thank you for reading, *Max Travis.*

The saga continues! Sign up for Max's Newsletter at

http://www.inside-alaska.com/authors/

Introduction

Local pronunciation of Aialik sounds like: eye-<u>Al</u>-ick

This is book six in The Seiner Series. *It begins at the same time and place that Taylor Bay ended, with very little backstory.* For the best reading experience please start with Rocky Bay, Res Bay, K Bay, Windy Bay, and Taylor Bay.

While this book is a work of fiction, it is based on actual places in Alaska and uses many terms common to commercial seine fishing for salmon in the Southcentral area of Alaska.

I invite you to visit the publisher's website at www.inside-alaska.com for details about the names, places, and terms used, and to view photos and videos showing Alaska, fishing, seine boats and much more.

Thank you for reading The Seiner Series,
Max Travis

1

Mid-September Campfire

Justin watched Hattie return the small birchbark basket to Nell's palms as if it were a chick fallen from the nest, cradling it gently as Ginny cooed over it. Standing beside Ginny, he scanned the rest of the group in the campfire clearing, his gaze stopping on his twin, who was uncharacteristically quiet as he, too, watched the women.

"It's beautiful," Hattie gushed as the bowl left her fingers. Nell exuded confidence as she described how she'd peeled the bark, folded it, then secured the corners to make the basket she'd just finished creating. She continued to talk about the nature of birchbark, but no one seemed to be listening.

Handing the cup to Ginny, who looked like she was afraid she might break the small creation, Nell laughed, then explained that birchbark was one of the strongest choices for a basket. Native Alaskans used to cook and boil water in birchbark baskets, she told them.

Excusing herself to check on the boys playing in the gravel pile, Hattie chatted with the kids for a moment, then wandered closer to the campfire to see what Mack, Pete, and Wade were laughing about.

Justin nudged Ginny, then looked at Nell. "We need to clean up. Your fruit salad was delicious. Thanks for bringing it, and your little cup is nice." Ginny gave the small basket one last look, handing it to Case, then she followed Justin as they gathered buns, hotdogs, drinks, and other leftovers from their end-of-season cookout and campfire.

Hattie turned away from talking to Mack and Pete, giving Justin her *I told you so* look, and he sighed. His aunt had been right yet again. He'd let jealousy overtake him as he watched Ginny greet his twin, then laugh with him as they talked and touched like reunited lovers.

"Hattie asked if we'd make s'mores with the kids," Justin said, putting sacks of groceries and leftover cookout food into the back of Hattie's car. "Here's the bag of stuff." He handed it to Ginny, who'd put her armload of groceries into the car. "I'll go round up a couple of sticks," he offered.

They gathered the boys and helped them spear marshmallows, roast them, and sandwich them between graham crackers and chocolate bar squares, then took them through the alders and trees and into the house to get their sticky hands cleaned up.

"Case seems to be pretty impressed by our co-worker," Hattie said dryly, noticing Pete's concerned looks in his son's direction.

"She knows how to get what she wants," Pete commented and continued to monitor them as they moved closer together. His son was also used to getting his way with the opposite sex, but he was several years younger than the striking Nell. He also didn't believe that Case was nearly as experienced as he pretended to be. His gut clenched, watching Case return the small basket to Nell's hands. *He'll be on the train in the morning, back to Fairbanks and school,* Pete reassured himself. But he couldn't shake the feeling of apprehension as Nell blatantly set her sights on Case.

Pete returned to his conversation with Hattie about rearranging rooms in his house to give Justin and Ginny their own space and was surprised at her quick approval. He left the campfire clearing, walking through the wooded area back to his house to talk to Justin about the idea.

Case hadn't planned on coming home to Seward after starting his third year of college in Fairbanks a month ago, even though Mack's after-season campfires were a long-standing family tradition. It was an annual affair that he could live without at this point in his life, he'd decided. But a friend happened to be driving home on the same weekend, and it seemed meant to be. He'd gone along on a whim, planning to surprise everyone, then take the train back the next morning, and study on the long return trip north.

He loved the delighted looks on everyone's faces as he'd wandered down the driveway and into the campfire circle, Ginny's most of all. He rarely had a chance to talk to her alone and he was looking forward to teasing her, knowing she'd ask about Viv, who he'd bumped into in Fairbanks the week before.

Meeting Nell changed everything. His growing feeling of being a pawn on a checkerboard, of being guided by invisible forces intent on winning—as if things were meant to happen exactly as they were—grew stronger the closer she came.

She was electrifying and magnetic. He felt a jolt with every glance she sent his way, overpowering any effort he might exert to restrain himself, but he entertained no such thoughts. Watching her every move, smelling the earthy scent from her hands after working the birchbark, knowing her aura was pulling him, he let his body respond, enjoying the sharp pangs that raced up his spine and out to every nerve. Anticipation teased from her slanted eyes, and he was eager to give her whatever she wanted.

"That looks like trouble," Mack muttered to Hattie as they walked toward her car. She'd checked on the younger boys, who were spending the night with Pete, before offering Case a ride to wherever he was staying for the night. Nell had smoothly offered to drop Case off, after culling him from everyone at the campfire.

It put Hattie's mother-bear senses on high alert, and she had to fight her instincts to protect her outgoing nephew, who she knew would not appreciate any such efforts on her part. "I was looking forward to asking him what he thought about the weirs he'd visited this summer," Mack complained.

"Looks like you missed that chance. I hope it's nothing more than a flirtation between two very attractive people," she said quietly, filled with qualms about the woman she'd helped hire.

"Let's hope," Mack replied. "Doesn't look like she's letting him up for air," he mumbled, watching them walk into the trees together.

"There are blueberries all over this property," Case said, then wondered why he'd blurted that out. "Your cup..." He looked at her and stopped talking as her face filled with passion, lips filling, as she leaned closer. He was floating in a timeless existence of nothing but the heat radiating from her.

"Let's fill it up," she suggested with a slow smile. She held out her hands, and he placed his, still cupping her creation, in hers. It felt like a ceremony. Her hands touched his gently, lingering and caressing, and he saw sparks flickering—the lightning strikes within him jerking his senses. Time seemed to stop as he watched his own hands spread, easing the basket to hers.

She looked up at him playfully, voice teasing, eyes piercing his soul. "You should fill it."

His heart pounded, and his blood surged in a wave as his fingers tingled and twitched. His body ached, wanting to fill far more than her little cup. He could only stare as her lips curved into a smile. She took his hand, heading for a nearby spruce among the trees circling the clearing.

"It's pretty late in the season for blueberries, but crowberries love to grow big under the strong spruce trees. They ripen right about now. You know that, right?" Her eyes searched his face.

Never had he needed to rein himself in with such rugged force. Case hadn't heard a word she'd said—his whole body was throbbing to relentless beats: *I want you. I feel you burning for me.*

Waking up to Case's phone alarm at five a.m., Nell rolled closer as Case twisted to turn it off. Pressing her body against his, running her hand over him, she instantly felt the reaction she sought.

"You're not going anywhere," she purred.

"I'm supposed to—oh," his voice caught as she tightened her grip on him, "be on the train. Leaves at six."

"I'll drive you to Anchorage. You can fly from there," she told him, sliding on top of him, molding herself to him as she reached for the nightstand. Grabbing another of the small packages piled there, tearing it open with her teeth, she added the wrapper to the pile on the floor by her bed. Before rolling off him, she whispered, "Later. Much later," against his lips

2

Ginny unlocked the door to the Smith's house, holding it open for Justin, who carried a small sack of leftovers from the campfire, an unfinished bottle of wine, and a couple of glass baking pans in need of washing. He went into the kitchen, setting everything on the large granite island. He loved the modern look of the kitchen and had already made a mental note of several things he'd love to have in a kitchen of his own, starting with a pot filler. Ginny often made soups, and he loved pasta. They'd use it every day. No longer under pressure to feed three hungry crew anymore, Justin was enjoying cooking and trying new recipes.

After receiving Hattie's invitation to the family campfire, Justin had said he wanted to try making lasagna. It had been his favorite food growing up, and he'd found his mother's recipe.

"I'll clean any mess you make, captain," Gin had teased him.

"You're on, and don't forget you said that, either." There was nothing but sauce and some caked-on cheese left in both pans now.

. . .

Moving from one house-sitting gig to another, they were each developing must-have lists. At the top of Ginny's was a woodstove.

"Want a fire? Ah, probably not since we were just sitting at one. Movie?" he asked her, putting the pans in the sink, filling them with warm water.

"I'm almost done with a great book…"

"Okay, I'm gonna start measuring stuff. Beds, dressers," he added at her curious look. "I want to see what we can fit into that room at dad's. Besides a bed, I think we need a desk, or maybe two. Anything else you can think of?"

Ginny took a wineglass from the cupboard and poured from the open bottle. Watching her, waiting for a response, Justin went to the fridge and took out a beer. He followed her to the living room, waiting as she picked up her tablet and settled into the sofa, then sat as close to her as he could.

"You want a desk and chair, don't you? Maybe we can find something that fits two laptops." She didn't reply, staring into the red wine like it was a crystal ball. "Gin?"

"I just…" she waved her free hand, and he waited, knowing it normally took her forever to be able to say what was bothering her.

"You want to stay there, at least for now, right?"

"Yes," she replied quickly.

"But?"

"I'm not used to planning out my own space," she admitted. "Like in the dorm, stuff's where they put it. And on the boat…"

"Well, we need a bed and a dresser, minimum. And I want a desk—hey, let's go to Anchorage. I bet we can get everything we want at Costco, and if not, we'll hit some furniture stores."

"What if he changes his mind?" she blurted out. "I mean, Candi…"

"Ugh, don't even say that name, Jesus. He won't, but," Justin stiffened, "if he does, we'll rent a place. Seriously. I was ready to do it before he offered to let us live there. I never even thought about staying there or swapping rooms, but the playroom is bigger than I'd thought."

Ginny sighed and relaxed, sipping the wine. "A desk would be nice," she said softly, her eyes still staring into the deep red wine. Justin kept quiet, letting her imagine having her own space, wondering if she'd ever really had a room to herself. Growing up in foster homes—probably not, and he didn't want to ask. She was smiling; that was good enough for now.

He leaned back, taking a swig of beer, planning. They'd take the truck to Anchorage. Take some straps and tarps in case it rained. He started a mental list, thinking about what they'd need, then stopped. First, we need to move the stuff out of the playroom. Get the kids involved, so they won't feel—

Shit. That woman. The boys said they were scared of her when Gin started her bedtime saga, and he didn't think it was because of her facial markings. The simple dots down her chin weren't scary. She came across as being friendly, open. His dad worked with her. Case had looked like he was instantly smitten with her.

Nell.

Justin glanced at Ginny, then went back to looking at his beer. He hadn't seen Nell go anywhere near the kids.

Why are they scared of her?

"Gin, have you figured out why Robbie and Mickey are scared of Nell?"

She sat up straighter and set the glass she was holding down on the table beside her, dropping her tablet into her lap. "No. I don't get it. And I don't remember her even talking to them. The first time they've ever seen her must have been today." Her eyes met his, her mouth tightening. "What do you think the story is? Those tattoos?"

He shook his head. "Nope. They're harmless. Just dots, really."

She swallowed. "I trust kids," she said, her voice rough.

"Me too. I'm gonna—no, you and I will talk to my dad about it tomorrow. You up for cleaning and moving stuff tomorrow? Then Monday, head to Anchorage for a bed and desks... and whatever else we need?"

Her smile said everything, and Justin watched her melt. He put his beer on the coffee table and reached for her as she set her tablet aside, then crawled into his lap.

This.

This is everything.

He held her, brushing curls off her cheek, kissing her. It was going to be wonderful, having their own space together. He could hardly wait. She'd have a room to call her own. He'd let her pick the bed, sheets, blankets, and a desk, too. A good chair, he added to his mental list as his hand absently stroked her arm. Another kiss. She held it longer, teasing, twisting in his lap, breasts brushing his arm, pressing against him. The list was obliterated from his thoughts as his hands took over.

Sitting at the kitchen island the next morning, Justin texted his dad, pushing his empty coffee mug further away with the back of one hand.

JUSTIN

We had breakfast here. Ready to move stuff. Need anything before we come out?

PETE

No, all good here. Kids are up, already
sorting toys

Justin dismantled the twin bed he'd slept in for years, putting it in the living room. He emptied his dresser drawers, taking out all the clothes that were too small for him now, then carried it to the living room. With the bedroom nearly empty, he and Pete stood in it wondering where things should go.

Ginny walked in, the two boys behind her. "I think some bookshelves would be good in here," she suggested. "Maybe a table for homework? Or for drawing?" In her eyes, the kids still lived here. She couldn't make herself think of Hattie's house as being permanent for them. Pete looked at her with gratitude, and Justin reached for the tape measure he'd clipped to his jeans.

"Bookshelf here? In this nook?" He measured between the window and the end of the closet. Forty-two inches. He wrote it on the paper he'd stuffed into his pocket, then surveyed faces. "Is that a yes?"

"I think that's good. What about putting the table under the window? For light," Ginny suggested.

"That sounds good," a hesitant Robbie offered quietly.

"Sounds good," Mickey agreed, moving closer to Robbie.

"Maybe put up a corkboard next to the window for your drawings?" Ginny pointed to the wall above where she proposed the table, and both boys nodded, then looked at Pete.

"I like it, Gin. Keep going," Pete encouraged.

"Fifty-inch plasma screen TV, coupla recliners..." Justin offered, and the boys jumped up and down, pumping their fists, while Ginny and Pete laughed.

"Yeah, no. But, maybe a better TV. With a wall mount. I think we could do that," Pete offered. "Maybe make one shelf for DVDs?" he asked Justin.

"Sure. I'm pretty sure Mack has some scrap lumber, too. I can build some shelves, and we can get cork tiles or something like that in Anchorage. I have a list started..."

"Okay," Pete clapped his hands, "Let's see what we want to move in here." The kids raced down the hall to their old playroom, and he turned to Justin. "Buy what you think is right when you go to Anchorage. Give me the total when you get home. Maybe twenty-five inches or so for the TV? And a DVD player?"

"Will do," Justin agreed, adding them to his growing mental list.

3

"Are you sure you want them for another night?" Hattie asked Pete, wondering what she'd do for another day with no kids. Two days in a row. She hadn't had that since last winter, when Ginny had offered to stay with the boys all weekend, giving her more time for herself and with Mack.

"Yes. They want to stay; I mean, if it's okay with you. I said we had to call first and ask. I can have them home early afternoon tomorrow, so they'll be ready for school Monday." Pete hesitated, knowing it wasn't like her to ponder much.

I'm asking too much, too soon.

He felt his heart rate increase and took a deep breath. "The thing is, um, Justin and Gin are here, and we're moving the playroom, and the boys are helping sort out toys they don't play with anymore. Baby stuff. Justin's gonna build some shelves—" he rushed out.

"No, it's fine Pete, honest. I just don't know what I'll do with myself," she laughed, "but believe me, I'll find some-thing," she added quickly. "It's all good," she reassured him gently, hearing the apprehension in his voice. "Ah, plan on dinner here tomorrow. You too, okay? Early-ish. Say, four or five? Something like that? Tell Justin and Gin they're invited too."

"Okay, thanks. Let me know if you want me to bring anything."

"Will do. Bye for now." She pressed the button on her phone after Pete said goodbye.

"Two whole days?" Mack said, sitting next to her on the sofa.

"Yeah, I can't believe it. Oh, thank God! I want that soaking tub, man!"

"Hey, I get a break too, ya know," he complained. "No more remodeling, dammit."

"We'll see about that." She stood up and stretched, sighing, then gave him a very suggestive smile while she reached for her design notebook.

He groaned and grabbed the book from her with one hand, flinging it onto the floor, and pulled her onto his lap, holding her struggling body tight, rubbing his stubbly chin on her neck as she laughed.

"Let's go back to bed," he suggested, his hands loosening.

She quit pretending to struggle, tipping her head onto his shoulder as a large, calloused hand slid up her side. She kissed his neck, then took his earlobe between her lips, and he groaned and pushed her up. Standing quickly, he grabbed her hand as her laughter deepened.

Pulling her behind him, he threatened, "You're gonna pay for doing that." His voice was its deepest, sending shivers of anticipation through her core, and she laughed again. After more than twenty years, he could still tighten her strings like a virtuoso, her body eager to play.

With her living room transformed into a dining room on Sunday afternoon, Hattie glowed with satisfaction, watching everyone serve themselves at the new counter she called her buffet. Even the younger boys could see to choose what they wanted. She'd roasted two chickens, the pans loaded with carrots, potatoes, and onions, and then had boiled, mashed, and whipped more potatoes because the kids loved them.

"So, am I spilling any beans if I say the word *tender*?" she asked after everyone had served themselves, looking at Justin, who grinned.

"Ever since Elliot said he was selling out, it's been on my mind," he confessed between bites as Mack and Pete stopped eating, staring at him. Pete looked stricken and Hattie guessed he wanted all the details but didn't want to grill his son. And, she suddenly remembered, Justin had a lot of money that may still bring up bad memories for Pete. She wished she'd kept her mouth shut.

Mack, however, never had qualms about voicing his opinion. "Yes! Dammit, our own tender!"

"He'd have to go wherever the cannery sent him," Pete countered. "That's how the contracts work. You know that, right?" Justin nodded.

"Have you looked at other boats?" Hattie wanted to know, hoping he wasn't basing everything on one boat.

"Um, I'm thinking about going to the boat show in November, then looking at boats in Seattle—"

"Yes," Mack interrupted, excitement jetting out of him. "Good idea. Do that."

Justin looked at his dad, who nodded agreement. "That's a good start. Walk the drydock yards. There's so much to learn there. You really need a good engineer and a back-up skipper for steering. It's not a one-man job."

"Yeah, I think Gary from the Lady Luck might be available. He wants to stay with the boat, but if it doesn't sell, and he wants to work..."

"He's a great guy," Mack agreed.

"I'm thinking about getting my hundred-ton license, too," he added, which stopped all conversation and turned all eyes on him, with the exception of Ginny, who'd already heard it.

"That's a good idea, too," Pete murmured, returning to his dinner, then asking, "What about you, Gin? What do you think about all this? You're going to the boat show too, right?"

Ginny hesitated, and Mack jumped right in. "You gotta go. You'll love it. All kinds of stuff there. Seattle's fun."

She hadn't said yes to Justin yet. She glanced at Hattie, then Pete. They were both nodding in agreement with Mack. "Yeah, I guess I'll go."

"Good. Don't let him buy too big a boat," Pete said, winking at her.

"How big's the Lady Luck? Like, eighty-five or so?" Mack asked.

"Ninety," Justin said. "Built in nineteen eighty-eight. A hundred and seventy-five tons. Packs two-thirty with a fifty-ton RSW."

"Whoa," Mack said, leaning back, grinning from ear to ear.

"But there's a smaller one, listed out of Seattle, asking eight-hundred." He looked around the table. "Might be more my speed."

"Ah, you're making me want to go fishing again," Pete said, his voice dripping with envy as he pretended to be sad, and everyone laughed. The conversation, manipulated by Hattie, turned to Pete's work, and Ginny listened avidly, missing the weekly meetings and the excitement of hearing everyone's updates on their projects.

Hattie took the boys downstairs for a shower while Ginny cleared the table, then stood at the counter picking chicken from the bones, filling a stock pot. The guys were deep into comparisons of boats, hold capacities, and what to look for in a tender.

"Oh, thanks for doing that. Chicken soup tomorrow, that's for sure," Hattie said, coming upstairs. "I've given them ten more minutes. They asked if you'd finish a story you started?"

"Sure. This won't take long, then I'll go dry them off."

"Thanks. Their pajamas are on their beds," Hattie said, pouring herself a little more wine, then walking around the extended counter.

"Um," Ginny started, and Hattie turned around. When she didn't continue, Hattie went to stand next to her. "What's up?"

Ginny lowered her voice. "Have the kids said anything to you about Nell?"

Hattie shook her head, furrowing her eyebrows questioningly.

"Well, I made up this goofy, convoluted story about superheroes. I started it when you and Mack went to Vegas last winter, and, um, when I tried to add Nell in, they said they were scared of her."

Hattie's mouth fell open. She put the wineglass down. "What? When did that happen?"

"After the campfire Friday. I think it's the first time they've ever seen her."

"No. We bumped into each other at the grocery store last week. She tried to hug Mickey, and he pulled away, and Robbie hid behind me. I had no idea what was going on." Hattie watched Ginny picking small bits of chicken off the bones, then she started wrenching the bones apart.

"Do you have any ideas?" Hattie asked. The situation was obviously upsetting Gin.

"No, but I trust kids. I don't force them to like people

they don't want to like," she said tightly, throwing the bones into the pot, catching Hattie's concerned look.

"Me neither. Thanks for letting me know. They won't cross paths again," Hattie reassured her.

"But what's causing it?" Ginny blurted out, her frustration growing. "We hired her—"

"Yeah, we thought she was pretty cool. Well, something's odd. I think I'll—"

"Hun," Mack called out. "We're goin' across the bay to look at boats."

"Who's driving?" Hattie asked, running a hand across Ginny's back gently before she went into the living-dining room.

"Me," Pete said. "Only drank water," he added.

Ginny turned from washing her hands in the kitchen sink as the three men trooped behind her, heading for the garage. Justin stopped to ask if she wanted to come along. "We won't be long—"

"Nope. Story time, downstairs."

"Damn. I'm gonna miss it," he said, kissing her quickly on the cheek. She promised to give him the update later.

4

Feeling better than he had all year, Pete went to work early Monday, taking the stairs two at a time, turning the corner to see a strange woman sitting on the floor, leaning against the office door as she scrawled quickly on a page in a huge binder. He stopped short, waiting for her to notice him, but her head was down, and she showed no indication she knew he was there. He wondered if she had headphones on, those tiny ones he never seemed to notice until the person started speaking to some unseen voice.

"Hello," he said, backing up, hoping he didn't startle her.

"Yeah, one sec," she mumbled, continuing to write. Pete leaned against the opposite wall, looking her over. Tousled, wavy, longer than shoulder-length hair, not blonde but not brown, and looking like she'd just stepped off a working boat. She wore a wildly colored scarf wrapped around her neck, draped down the front of her, a few tassel string ends laying on the hall carpet. Sneakers, dusted with the grey silt that came from every glacial beach, faded khaki pants, her notebook propped on raised knees. She turned the page and kept going.

18

"I'll open the door so you can get comfortable. We have desks and chairs you can use," he offered.

"I'm good."

He waited, taking in her fierce concentration, adjusting his reaction from surprised irritation to amused curiosity. He gave her another full minute before speaking again. "I'd like to get inside, and you're blocking the door."

"Jesus. Fine." She slapped the notebook shut and stood. Pete could almost hear her bones creaking. Standing, she was less than five and a half feet, if that. At over six feet, he towered above her. She's wiry, he noticed, as she bent over to pick up her basket-woven tote, then looked up at him. "Well, I thought you wanted in," she said, standing in front of the door.

Pete smiled at how silly the whole thing was and immediately regretted it.

"Something funny?" she asked, stiffening, offense radiating from her.

"You're blocking the door," he said gently. "I can't go through you," he added, just to see how far he could push her, trying to force the smile off his face.

"Pffhhht," she blew bangs off her face and stepped sideways a few inches.

Pete sidled in, sticking the key out as far as his arm could reach, inserted and turned it. Leaving his keys hanging, he pushed the lever down and eased the solid wood door open, then stepped back, swooping his arm as an invitation to enter.

Without glancing at him, she walked in as if she owned the place, heading straight to the conference room, where she plopped her bag and started emptying it. Pens, well-used notepads of all sizes, stapled reports, and a small laptop. She pulled out a chair and sat, opened the laptop, waited a moment, tapped something, and started typing. Pete watched her through the glass wall and open doorway, then went into the small break room to make coffee.

"Turn the router on," she called out. He finished pouring the water into the machine, then flipped a nearby power switch, watching the tiny lights of their router blink on and flicker.

When the coffee machine gave its customary huff of steam at the end of its brewing cycle, the woman fetched herself a cup, then returned to her laptop. Pete's desk was angled to see both the office entry door and the conference room, and he hid his smile as he watched her.

Nell came in, singing hello as she went to fill her mug, twisting quickly at seeing someone in their conference room. She shot Pete a questioning look, and he shrugged, then shook his head. Nell stepped inside the conference room doorway. "Hi, I'm Nell. Is there something I can help you with?"

The woman looked up quickly, then stared at Nell for half a minute, studying her.

"No."

The stranger refocused on her laptop, typing away, and Nell backed up, easing toward the break room, but as she hesitated, the main office door swung open.

Al walked in, smiling. "Greetings from the lower forty-eight. Ah, I see Tessa beat me here. We hoped to use your conference room. We've needed to connect in person for quite some time," he continued, turning between Pete and Nell as he spoke, "and found last night that we'd both be in Seward today. I hope it's not an inconvenience—"

"Of course not," Pete chimed in quickly, wondering why Nell looked so stiff, her eyes slitted, mouth pinched, shoulders back.

"You're always welcome here, Al," Nell agreed slowly, then moved toward Al's former office—her office now.

"Thanks. Oh, good. I don't see anyone scheduled on the

board for the conference room today. That's great. This may be an all-day session," he said, going into the room, closing the door.

"Who the hell's the supermodel?" Tessa asked, not looking up.

"Oh, I'm sorry, I thought you'd met. I should introduce you—"

"Don't bother. I hate fakes. Not interested."

"Tessa—"

"Let's get started," she blurted, interrupting him. "Things are really coming together. Whoever this P.E.N. is has really dug deep. It's made all the difference. Stop dithering. Come here and sit down. I didn't come all this way to waste time. We have a lot to go over."

Pete left for his afternoon medical appointment, hoping that Al would still be in the office when he returned. There was so much he wanted to tell Al that didn't seem to come out right in the emails he typed, then deleted. Half-reclined on the paper-covered slab, with the electronic leeches attached, Pete tried not to feel depressed.

He and Hattie had gone over some of his watch's health readings while he'd helped her load the dishwasher after they'd come back from looking at tenders last night. Hattie seemed to think the readings showed good things, which had cheered him up.

He'd peeked at the boys, asleep downstairs, afraid he'd feel resentment or loneliness at leaving them there after having them all weekend, surprised that he'd only felt relieved. They were happy; they were safe; they were in a home where they were loved. He'd sighed, gone upstairs, thanked Hattie again with a hug and called goodnight to his brother, son, and Ginny, then headed home for a long, hot shower.

Pete had been relieved when Justin had eagerly accepted the offer to continue living at home, in between house-sitting gigs, bringing Ginny with him.

It'll be almost like having the twins home again—maybe?

He smiled through the entire shower and again, while reading a book in bed, hearing them come home from the house-sitting gig after feeding the cats and leaving the keys. They'd be using the boys' room for the night, then head to Anchorage in the morning to pick out their own furnishings.

I won't be alone.

"So, Mister—"

"Pete," he interrupted. Great, another new face. Here we go again.

"Right, Pete. I'm Camille, and I specialize in cardiology. And you have atrial fibrillation. So, I don't see any meds here. Your diagnosis is paroxysmal... No script?"

"No, I'm treating it with diet and supplements—" he started, then was interrupted as she put his folder on the counter, crossed her arms, and stared at him, cutting him off quickly.

"That's good, to be pro-active, but in my experience—"

Pete sat up, sending the monitor into a spasm of its own, then started pulling the small tabs off his body. The ECG technician had taken his readings but left him connected, for some reason, and he'd had enough. "Look, been there, done that. If all you're going to do is push meds, we're done here."

"Hey, now," she put her hand on his knee. "Sure, let's get those things off and just chat for a moment, okay?" She peeled, apologizing for pulling off chest hair, turned off the monitor, and leaned back against the wall. "So, let's start over, can we?"

Pete nodded warily, pulling his shirt back on. He'd give her three minutes, maybe two, then he was leaving.

"I know traditional medicine is all about pills, and I get that people don't want them—"

"The side effects are worse than the heart issue."

"With A-Fib, there are a lot of factors to consider. Each person is different. If you feel you're controlling it, let's keep monitoring things for the next six months. So, no recent episodes?"

"One. It was like a flutter. As soon as I felt it, I calmed myself down with some deep breathing, drank some really cold water, and went for a long walk."

"Vagal," she murmured, opening the file, making a few quick notes. "That's good, Pete. Really," she added at his skeptical glance. She leaned against the counter, her arms folded again, but her tone much more congenial.

"I'm supposed to offer you the meds. It's protocol for your age, health, all that. You probably already know that. What I'm going to suggest is called pill-in-the-pocket. I'll give you a script for a few pills. If your methods of converting don't work, I want you to take the meds exactly as I describe. They should return you to sinus rhythm within hours and prevent another cardioversion. Many people are good with this method, as long as you understand that the condition will most likely deteriorate over time."

"I'm doing all I can to make sure I don't make things worse," Pete said, standing up. Her three minutes were up. "But I'll do that. I'll take the pills if it doesn't work."

"But if the pills don't work, I need you to come in for cardioversion. Do not go for more than twenty-four hours in A-Fib. Do we have an agreement?" She held out her hand, and Pete forced himself to shake it.

"Sure."

· · ·

Pete nodded to Connor as he came into the office, then saw Al alone in the conference room. He hurried in. "Oh, Al. I'm so glad you're still here. Do you have time to talk? Are you overwhelmed?" he asked, seeing Al's faraway gaze finally focus on him as he closed the door.

"Pete. Good to see you. Yes, let's chat. It's just that Tessa—you know what it's like to talk to Tessa, right?" Pete's eyes widened, and he shook slightly with an involuntary tremor as he nodded, finally connecting the unknown woman with the voice on the phone that sent him off-planet every time they talked.

Al choked and laughed quietly. "Anyway, she's writing an expose that leaves my hair standing on end. But," he waved a hand, "sit. Let's chat. Aha, you must be the P.E.N. of the reports Tessa was referring to?"

Pete nodded again. "My initials. I put them on my drafts, to let me know it's only a draft. How did she—"

"Let me tell you where she's going with this. It may answer some questions for you, although, by all that's holy, it raises a lot more. But first, let's start with you. What's on your mind?"

"Well, I don't want to be difficult, but um, it's about Nell. I'm having a hard time getting the information I need from her."

"You are not the first person to tell me that, and it's becoming a priority. Tell me everything."

5

The annual Alaska Coalition of Tribes gathering in October was the most exciting event Al attended, *and I've been to Hollywood*, he thought, amused by the contrast. But since arriving, everything seemed to be putting a smile on his face.

Joy.

That's what I feel right now. The same feeling of joy when I get to see my kids.

Family.

These are all people I can relate to. People I am related to by blood and spirit.

We are all family.

Unity vibrated through the building like music, wafting in the air like smoke curing salmon for winter, exciting everyone. *Well, unity among people who have differences, just like everyone else on earth*, he qualified.

The gorgeous and varied kuspuks were all worn proudly, some as everyday clothing, others ceremonial in design and material. Seeing them put a huge grin on his face. Add some beadwork, adorning faces he treasured, and he was in heaven.

He searched those faces for Nell, standing where they'd agreed to meet.

"No kuspuk?" he asked when she finally arrived, ten minutes late.

"No, I, ah, spilled coffee on it," she said, looking away.

He looked at her closely. She seemed uncomfortable, and her face was flushed. "Let's find a quiet corner. Something's come up. We need to talk."

They settled into an upper-floor corner, outside a closed conference room, sitting cross-legged on the carpet, and Al started. "I was just invited to an important meeting in Sitka, regarding hatcheries. We need to book tickets today. Let's see what flights are available, leaving tonight or tomorrow."

Nell stiffened. "I, um, wasn't aware we'd be going anywhere. I, ah, have plans—"

"I'm afraid you'll have to change them," Al said, tapping his phone for Alaska Airlines. When she didn't move or reach for her phone, he took a hard look at her. "This is critical to our tribe's goals. As the tribal representative, you need to be there. I'm sorry that it conflicts with your plans, but this is an opportunity that isn't to be missed. Things are changing very quickly. We need to stay on the crest, leading the way. This is everything I've been working toward for the past few years. You'll be talking about how we closed the weir, implemented the fish ladder, and partnered with the stream-keepers."

She still didn't move or reach for her phone. "You'll be there," she said assertively, her face a stiff mask, her voice authoritative. "I'm sure you'll describe everything perfectly and keep us posted."

"No. I don't represent the tribe anymore," he said firmly. "That's your job. You knew that when you accepted it."

"But Al," her voice softened, her head tilting, her lips

attempting a smile. She touched his arm. "This is rather a personal thing. A commitment I made to someone special," she whispered.

Al hated being played by a woman who was using her looks to do it. Either she was committed to the work or she wasn't. He said so. Surprised that he needed to go further, he mentioned the names of a few other attendees who'd confirmed that they'd be there. The people who'd hired her. People, he said, who would want to know why she wasn't there. He hoped her excuses would stand up to their scrutiny, he finished. Standing up and giving her a look that clearly said *get your act together*, he walked away, turning back to say he'd email her the details of the meeting time and place.

Nell squinted as her large eyes followed Al down the corridor, her mouth turned down. She pulled out her phone and looked at her text messages. Two new ones from Case, who had flown in from Fairbanks and was in her hotel room. He'd sent an image of himself that had her blood running hot in seconds. She messaged that she was on her way, then stood and stretched. She left the convention center, throwing the schedule in the trash before leaving the building, unaware that Al was watching her.

"Keeping an eye on the beauty queen?" Tessa asked, coming up behind Al. She'd seen him come downstairs, but she'd been in the middle of a conversation. She'd kept an eye on him while she finished, then followed him discreetly when she saw that he was following someone else.

"She's refusing to come to the meeting," Al said, disgusted.

"I thought you hired from inside the tribe," Tessa pushed angrily. She'd worked too long and too hard to have a vital meeting ignored by the one tribe that had a chance of leading others out of the hatchery fiasco, and said so. Vehemently.

"Nell's a tribal member. Haida, I think she said," Al replied, agreeing with her on everything else.

"Bullshit. Eyebrows don't lie. Plus, she nearly tackled me after I left your office one time. That sound right to you? Not me. Not one bit. Fake, fake, fake. I'm going for a coffee. Come with me."

"No, thank you. I think I need to do some research of a different nature," he said quietly. "And there are three more sessions I want to attend today. They're important. She should be in all of them. One's running now," he finished, turning toward the conference center.

"Good. Go find that P.E.N. gal and hire her. I can read passion in every word she writes—in every document you forward to me."

That's another thing, Al thought as he walked back inside, not bothering to correct Tessa on P.E.N.'s identity. Pete emailed him far more than Nell did, sending specifics as Al requested, often including more than he'd asked for but always very relevant data to Al's inquiries. Nell's messages were vague and flowery, and he often had to repeat his requests for details.

Six weeks later, Pete wasn't sure if he would ever get used to the revolving door at his house. Justin and Ginny were at another house-sitting gig, and the boys had spent the weekend with Hattie. Alone, he'd spent most of the weekend eating leftovers and working at his dining table. His only break had been moving his car to a spot in front of the warehouse, then shoveling four inches of early snow from his driveway.

His breakthrough last night—well, at one in the morning, had left him speechless, unable to sleep. He'd watched a movie until he'd finally fallen asleep on the sofa. He emailed work at three a.m. to say he'd be coming in late, then crawled into bed.

Waking at 10:30 and taking a quick shower, he'd walked out of his bathroom and into his bedroom to find Evie there, tugging the sheets off the bed. She'd screamed, and he'd backed up quickly, grabbing his wet towel off its hook by the door. Pacing the tiny bathroom in a near panic, willing his heart to return to its normal level, he splashed cold water on his face and neck and focused on deep breathing while wondering what she was doing there.

Eventually, he cracked the bathroom door open, looking around, listening carefully. Scanning the room, he exited and dressed as fast as he could, hoping Evie had left.

Walking down the hallway cautiously, smelling coffee, he debated trying to sneak out of the house, pretending the whole thing had never happened. But he had to walk either past or through the kitchen to get out of the house, and the damned floors creaked with every other step.

Who designed this house, dammit!

He peeked around the corner and saw Evie sitting at the small kitchen table, her back to him.

"Pete, I'm so sorry," she said, then laughed and covered her mouth, not turning around. He smiled. Under any other circumstances... well, she was a lovely woman.

"Ah, Evie, I, ah—"

"No, I should have warned you that I was swapping days. I told Hattie, but that was dumb. Really," she turned halfway toward him, "it's my fault." She waved him into the room.

He stepped into the kitchen and poured coffee into the mug she'd left next to the pot, taking it to the table and sitting down with his head down, wishing that they could keep this short and reasonable. They were both adults; they both had kids and had seen a good portion of life. He smiled at her quickly, then focused on the hot coffee.

"You clean my house," he said after taking a sip, then putting the mug on the table. "It's like we know each other but don't know each other," he continued, and she laughed as if it had been exactly what she'd been thinking.

Evie had been cleaning for Pete since July and thought she had a good feel for the kind of guy he was. Plus, she got the inside scoop on him from Hattie when they met at the playground, watching their boys play while they gossiped. Pete had let his older son and the son's girlfriend move back into the house with him, Hattie had told her. Plus, he'd redone the playroom for the little boys who didn't even live with him. It didn't look like he spent a dime on himself. He left notes, thanking her, along with cash for payment.

She wished her husband had been the kind of man Pete seemed to be, not the abusive bastard he'd become.

Seeing Pete—*barely*—she smiled while lifting her coffee mug, had only startled her because she was always on alert for a man popping up unexpectedly. If the whole thing hadn't been so surprising, she'd have taken advantage of the situation. She laughed when he said they didn't know each other while she contemplated getting to know him better. *Much better.* She looked into her coffee, searching for the words to turn this around.

"I'd just started a load of laundry and was pulling the sheets up off the bed. You startled me, that's all. I never even heard the shower, and your car's not in the driveway." She stood up, going to the coffeepot and setting her mug down.

Pete gulped the warm coffee while she talked, then stood, moving to put his mug in the sink. She reached over and put her hand on his arm, looking into his eyes. "Let's not feel awkward around each other? I've been looking forward to meeting you." She looked at his chest, smiling. "Maybe not in such—"

"An embarrassing way?" he finished for her, and she let out a light laugh.

"Aw, Pete, don't. It's a little awkward, that's all. I barely saw you. I was focused on pulling up the sheets. Really. From what I saw, you're a good-looking guy. I'd nominate you anytime for that calendar they do of hunky Alaskan guys," she said, squeezing his arm.

He turned slightly, looking away. "Oh, God. I'd never live it down."

"You'd have a fan club," she gushed, hoping he'd look at her.

"Yeah, no. With what, no fans? No, thank you."

He finally met her eyes, and she held his gaze, hoping he saw the invitation there and heard it in her voice. "You have a fan, right here." She slid her hand up his arm, squeezing as his biceps tightened, beaming with playful anticipation as her eyes danced over his mouth.

"I hope I'm not getting this all wrong," he said, moving closer, his eyes searching her face.

She continued to slide her hand up as his head lowered. "Oh, I think you're getting it right," she said as his lips touched hers. Pressing harder, he wrapped his arms around her, deepening the kiss.

6

"I can't believe it's this warm here, in November. There are flowers still blooming," Ginny gushed, riding the hotel elevator to their floor. "I should pay for at least some of this," she said, dragging her carry-on into the small room, slinging her backpack onto the bed.

"It's all a write-off, especially if I buy another boat." Justin closed the door and scanned the room. They'd already planned where they wanted to eat, then they wanted to go wander the Seattle waterfront. "Are you tired? Changed your mind about walking? Want to stay in?" he asked, settling his suitcase on a folding rack. "Chug that water. You'll feel better."

She tipped the bottle, drank a good portion, then swirled the dregs of the electrolyte powder that Hattie had added, and finished it. "Yeah, that's probably what I needed most," she admitted, then pulled the curtains aside and looked out the window at the view of the wharf. "I still want to go wander before it gets too dark, plus I'm starving."

"Good, me too. Take only what you need. Let's go," he urged, as his stomach rumbled.

. . .

"Oh, man, my feet are killing me," Ginny gasped, sitting on the floor of the conference center. They'd been walking the aisles all day, standing and talking to so many vendors. Learning, watching videos, listening to sales pitches about the newest in RSW systems, slush ice makers, brailer bags, and so much more. The non-stop voices and tremendous volume of noise in the huge event center had given her a headache. She pulled a bottle of water from her backpack, then had to re-stuff a pile of pamphlets that fell out. She passed the bottle to Justin, sitting next to her, leaning against the wall.

"A quiet night tonight. No walking," he said, his eyes closed.

"Hey! Justin. Ginny, hey guys, it's great to see you," Gabe said, coming down the aisle, tugging a woman by the hand. They sat, collapsing, laughing, and Gabe introduced his wife, Zoey. "These guys helped save my dad's life," he told her. "I'll never forget that. Where's Case?" Gabe asked, scanning the crowd.

"We did what you'd have done if it had been Mack or my dad, you know that," Justin said. "Case's at school, in Fairbanks. He said he was coming, then had to change plans at the last minute."

"Oh, bummer. So, what's brought you here? Everything working okay on the Calypso? I heard you guys had a good season."

"We had a good year. Heard you did, too," Justin said. "Ah, everything's working okay on the boat, but you know, it's good to see what else is out there—see what's new. I've been seining on the same boat since I was a kid. I bet you have been, too."

"Nope. My mom wouldn't let me go. I finally jumped on someone else's boat. He made me *work*," Gabe laughed. "But I loved it. We had a really good season, and I started saving for my own boat. So, you're just looking around at stuff?"

"You heard that the Lady Luck's up for sale?"

Gabe's mouth dropped open. "No way," he barely whispered.

"I'm just thinking at this point. We wanted to walk the Expo, then go walk drydock. Maybe see what else is available."

"No shit," Gabe croaked.

"What about you?" Ginny asked. "What's your big draw here?"

Gabe took a moment to regroup and drink from his own water bottle. "Ah, this might seem off base to you guys, but I'm looking at direct marketing." Ginny and Justin both looked at him expectantly, then Justin shook his head. "You know. Catch, process, sell."

"Seriously?" Justin asked, his brows drawn together.

"Yeah, it's big and we think," Gabe looked at Zoey, who nodded and smiled, "well, we think we can pull it off. Zoe's gonna do the fulfillment. She's been studying marketing—"

"But who's gonna process? And *what*? Pinks?"

Justin tried to smooth his puzzled face, wondering if Gabe had lost it. Big companies like Trident, Peter Pan, and Ocean Beauty controlled processing. There were smaller ones, and recently there had been some interesting partnerships made, but he and Gabe were seiners—*catchers*—not processors.

"That's just it. We think we can market it all. We're looking at supplying some of the shops and restaurants on the Spit, starting small, then seeing where we can go with it," Zoey said eagerly. "Here, look at our graphics," she said, reaching into her tote bag, pulling out a folder. She handed it to Ginny, who opened it and leaned toward Justin.

"Wow, this is nice," Ginny said, turning the pages on graphic designs for labels and packaging. "Is your website up?"

"Not yet," Zoey said, watching both of their reactions carefully.

"Are you—have you already started processing? Where are you storing everything? Are you freezing and canning?" Justin asked. "I have a million questions," he said, looking from Gabe to Zoey.

"I want to tell you all about it," Gabe answered eagerly. "Are you walking the docks today?"

"Oh, hell, no," Ginny gasped. "No way. I'm walked out."

"Good. Where are you staying? Order in and talk?" Gabe suggested, and Justin grinned.

The couples talked through dinner, with a bottle of wine shared by the women and a couple of craft beers ordered by the guys. They shared desserts and herbal tea ordered by Ginny, who said she'd need it to get to sleep. "This is exciting," she gushed, half-way through her dinner, then had to stop and catch her breath when Gabe suggested that she and Justin consider doing it, too.

"Seriously. It's not a closed market, and after what we've learned here, it might be better for us to focus on a specific area."

"That sounds smart," Justin said. "Have you picked something specific?"

"No," Zoey answered. "We're here looking at what others have done, are doing, and most of all, what they stopped trying to do."

"So, tomorrow... want to meet up and walk the show with us? Are you interested? Or still leaning toward a tender? I mean," Gabe said quickly, "there's nothing wrong with that. Especially if you can find something that could be a tender-processor."

"Let me sleep on it," Justin said. "But let's trade phone numbers and meet up, one way or another."

"Perfect. You staying through the weekend?" Gabe asked.

"We hadn't planned on it, but let's see how things go. Gin's filling in at the tribal offices next week. We have to get home by Sunday night."

"Let's do the show tomorrow, then maybe walk the docks the next day?" Gabe suggested.

"Sure. Sounds like a plan," Justin agreed.

～

"You know, I still stay in touch with Al after that fiasco in Res Bay," Gabe said to Justin the next morning as they lined up to enter the Expo.

"I work with him," Ginny interjected quickly.

"Really?" Gabe mused, then turned to Justin again. "And he's your uncle, right?"

Justin nodded, saying, "He's a great guy. He's doing a lot to protect the natural runs."

"Exactly. We're talking about how to get rid of the hatchery in K Bay now, which is a total frigging mess."

"What a surprise," Ginny said sarcastically.

"Right?" Gabe agreed. "That organization's a menace to salmon. They gave up the special harvest areas but held onto the hatchery. That was a worthless move. There's no way it can continue—"

"What are you thinking? Of using the hatchery for processing or something like that?" Gin asked as they worked their way through the throngs of attendees.

"Nope. Never. It's outdated, and I don't trust it not to be filled with viruses, either. No, I want to see it closed down forever. I was at a meeting a month ago that Al held, and he made it pretty clear that shutting it down was at the top of his list. He's working on putting a stop to the new one first—the one that's supposed to be built in the village outside of K Bay."

"Kicarwik," Ginny said. "Yeah, he's been working on that for a while, but I didn't know about one in K Bay."

"They kill more fry than they release, and there's not enough fresh water in the lagoon for their net pens. It's in a federal park and should never have been built or permitted in the first place. It's been an ongoing battle for years. Just like the lake by you guys—they take way too many fish for brood-stock, and what's worse is, their take isn't factored into the escapement numbers."

Justin stopped walking, staring at Gabe. "Wait a minute. I think Mack's been saying that for years, but I never really got it until now. Under-escapement *and* a huge harvest of salmon by the enhancement program for their hatchery projects leaves what? Nothing? No fish to spawn? I never knew that their *take* was from the escaped fish! Who the hell approved that? That's guaranteed to kill a run."

"Exactly!" Ginny exclaimed. "That's how they justify," she air-quoted, "being needed to *enhance* the run. It's bullshit. They're actively *killing* the run," she said, then noticed people turning to look at her.

"I agree, Gin. Total bullshit. Anyway, I just wanted to see if we're on the same page here. This is important to me, like, really important. I can't even think about processing fish if there aren't going to be any to harvest. And the year the virus was found? That did me in. No income. I'm working with a couple of other organizations that want the hatchery gone for their own reasons, but..." Gabe paused, looking uncomfortable, "well, I heard that your brother was working for them and..." he shrugged, looking from Justin to Ginny, "I wanted to talk to him about this stuff."

"Good for you. Believe me, I'm totally against them. And

Case was only working there to get the inside scoop," Justin explained.

"I even did it for a few weeks," Gin said, and Justin jumped in quickly.

"Right. He's not supporting them. I'm sure about that. Let us know if we can help," he offered, then changed the subject. "So, what are you looking for here today?"

"Processing equipment. Pin bone pullers, packaging, anything like that. Want to split up and compare notes tonight?" Gabe suggested.

Ginny grinned as Justin said, "Sure. Text me when you're done here. There's a tender-processor for sale that I want to look at, and we have an appointment early tomorrow to see it, then we fly out tomorrow afternoon. I'll send you the details if you want to see it, too."

"Yeah, I do. Okay, see you later," Gabe said with a smile. Taking Zoey's hand, they headed in the opposite direction.

"God, I wish Case was here," Justin mumbled as they aimed for the far corner of the show.

"What did his message say? He's got a lot going on?"

"Yeah. That's all he said," Justin replied, shaking his head, wishing he could talk to his brother, wondering what he'd think of this new idea. Case was smart and had sharp instincts, often seeing connections that other people missed. Going direct would be a huge endeavor. If he could get Case excited about it, maybe he'd want to be part of it—they could work together again.

Underlying his thoughts, Justin knew, was the ongoing emptiness inside him, the feeling that part of him was missing. Having Ginny with him eased the pain, but he couldn't help wondering if Case was going through the same thing.

Passing on meeting again for dinner, because they'd be touring the tender together in the morning, Justin and Gin picked up takeout and ate in their room. "So, what do you think about what Gabe's up to? You think it'll work?" Justin asked.

"I don't know anything about it. Seriously, I barely get the whole picture of seining, and I still can't get over the idea of the processor deciding how much the product's worth. Like, I wish I could choose my prices when I go grocery shopping."

Justin had grown up with that business model, always wondering what prices the cannery would pay for salmon. When there was a glut of fish, they lowered the prices to the point that it wasn't worth fishing, making that announcement after the season had already started, groceries bought, fuel tanks filled. With rising costs—of everything from groceries, to fuel, to insurance—fishermen were squeezed in the middle. When the glut exceeded their capacity to process, they limited how much they'd buy from the seiners or cut the fleet off completely.

"What are you thinking?" Ginny asked, watching his frown growing. He told her, and she told him about her first season with Mack, when that's exactly what had happened. They'd been put on limits, then cut off. It wasn't until the wild stocks had been declared virus-free that they'd been called back to Rocky Bay to fish the wild runs, and the prices had been outstanding as the processors competed for their catch.

"If I buy a tender, it's a little different. I'm not sure if you know how that works," Justin said, finishing his dinner.

"Nope. I thought it was the same as for us. I mean, for the seiners."

"No. They get a flat contract for the whole season."

Ginny thought about that, then asked, "Fish or no fish, they get paid?"

"Yup. But," her head popped up as she scooped the last of her fried rice, "a contract isn't guaranteed," he said, watching to see if she understood. She shook her head. "If they have plenty of tenders, they use their own first, then if they think it's going to be a good year, they contract with others."

"You're shitting me," she gasped. "A million-dollar boat, and no contract? No fishing at all? No way..." she swallowed, her eyes blinking rapidly. "Jesus. I'd have a heart attack."

Justin tipped his head, wondering if that kind of stress was the reason the Lady Luck was up for sale. "But, back to Gabe. He wants to catch, process, and sell straight to consumers..."

Ginny shrugged. "I just don't know. I still don't know if I get it. Why would that be better than seining?"

"Yeah. I want to see how many other fishermen are doing it and if they're making enough to survive. In other fisheries. Lobster, crab, shrimpers..."

Ginny picked up their empty food containers, cramming everything back into the bag and clearing the small table. She went to her backpack, pulling out her iPad, and started searching the internet.

7

Sleeping on the flight back, then doing a big shopping trip at Costco for groceries, kept Justin and Ginny from discussing Gabe's enterprise, but as they wandered Costco's wide aisles, Ginny stopped, pointing to an item on the shelf. Canned Alaskan salmon. Her mouth made an O as she considered that she might have actually caught the fish in those cans. Looking at Justin, she could see he was thinking the same thing. They looked closer at the label, then moved away, watching the customers who added it to their cart.

On the drive to Seward, Justin eagerly brought up the subject again, and they compared their impressions. He couldn't wait to talk to Mack and his dad. Ginny thought she'd love to hear Hattie's take on the whole idea of direct marketing, and she planned on chatting with her sometime when they could talk privately. She missed their lunchtime walks and quiet conversations about the large and small details of everyday life.

. . .

Ginny walked into the tribal offices on Monday, surprised at how much she missed working there and how happy she felt to be back. It was strange, riding with Pete to work, then following him in as he unlocked the door. She'd only be there part time, answering phones and working on small projects, filling in while Nell took time off before Thanksgiving.

She was looking forward to seeing what Nell had done with the video footage Hattie'd taken, wondering if Nell had been able to relax the interviewees as well as Hattie could, maybe even more because of her looks and her facial markings.

After Nell had been hired, Ginny had immediately noticed that the beautiful woman was always adorned with multiple pieces of Alaskan jewelry. Her collection of quill and beaded earrings and highly decorative headbands and hair ornaments was extensive. She usually wore at least two silver bracelets, engraved with images similar to totem poles, and often had intricately beaded brooches pinned to her blouse. Her porcupine quill chokers stood out on her long neck, and she had a habit of touching her jewelry constantly, which brought even more attention to the traditional pieces.

Walking past her old desk, Ginny smiled. Connor sat there now, and he must like it crowded, she mused. He had photos and sticky notes everywhere. "Do you want Nell's office, Gin?" Pete asked. She followed him into the break room, thinking she'd clean it while he and Connor were at lunch.

"I guess. Do you still have a Monday morning confab, like Al did?" she asked, watching him make coffee.

"Not really. Not Nell's thing. But we can, if you want?"

"Sure, if you guys are up for it. I'd love to hear what you're both working on now, and maybe see what I can help with while I'm here."

"Sounds good." He flipped the internet router on, then stared at the sink full of mugs.

"Let me get that. It'll make me feel like I'm part of things again," she offered, edging toward the sink.

Pete still had a housekeeper coming to his home, a gal Hattie had hired, and it made Ginny feel weird, knowing that someone else was coming in and cleaning up their messes. Not that she left many, but the first time the bathroom she and Justin shared had been tidied up, Ginny had asked Pete to tell her not to do it anymore.

As soon as Connor arrived and poured himself coffee, they all met in the conference room where Ginny was waiting. She'd peeked into the interview room and seen that it was full of boxes, supplies, and what looked like surplus equipment.

"So, I'm just curious," she started, "about what you guys are doing and if there's any part that I can help with; plus, should I track you down for anyone, if they call?"

"Oh, Al, for sure," Pete said.

Connor added, "Probably Nell, if she checks in. Sometimes she's too busy..."

"Right. So, Connor, I'll need your cell number," she said, writing it down as he recited it.

"I'd love to flip you the follow-ups for bad addresses. Mail and email," Connor said. "Then I can concentrate on getting the next newsletter out and maybe make it better. I want to start linking to more resources and other tribal organizations and their projects. You know how it is, even in the same family, some are members of one tribe and some members of another."

"Okay, I'll be happy to do that."

"Kinda boring," Pete said quietly.

"Nope, right up my alley. Really. I'd rather do that than nothing. And maybe I'll clean up the interview room? Are we not doing interviews anymore?"

"Ah," Connor twisted in his chair, "well, Nell kinda put all that on the bottom of the priority list." He looked down at the table.

"What?" both Pete and Ginny said.

"Wait," Pete held his hand up, turning to Connor. "When did this happen? The grant was specifically for that project. I thought that she was putting in hours every day, editing or something."

Connor shrugged. "She told me to work on other stuff, about a week after she got promoted. She gave me those addresses and said to work on the newsletter. I'm supposed to do that, too, but I was supposed to be spending about an hour a day on video, from what I thought, replying to comments and sending links to other tribes, telling them what we've been doing."

Pete and Ginny shared a look, then quickly looked away. Pete said, "I'm still pulling reports and tying things together, but I'm through the major portion of it. I want to know where we stand with those video interviews. Gin, can you access the files and give me an update? Not today. Take your time. But at least start looking, okay? You know a lot more about that technology than I do. I'll check in with Al and see if there's been some change that we don't know about."

"Um, the addresses can wait, I guess—" Connor started, but Ginny interrupted.

"No. I'll go cross-eyed if I don't have at least one other project to work on. Hand it all over. Seriously," she assured him with a smile, remembering how much she had enjoyed his optimism and cheerful attitude. She wondered where it had gone.

JUSTIN

Hattie wants us for dinner. Ok with you?

Ginny imagined that Hattie was probably sick of listening to Justin and Mack talking about direct marketing by now. She looked up to see Pete coming into the interview room, his phone in hand, and she giggled. "You get summoned, too?" she asked, and he nodded.

"I'm thinking she wants me to weigh in on whatever brainstorm Mack's come up with now. He had his heart set on a tender," Pete said.

"Better say yes for both of us, then. I know I should be gone by now. I'm calling this my own time, but I can't *not* sort this out. We all put too much time and effort into this project," Gin explained.

"No problem. I'm sure it needs doing. Do whatever you think is right. Al's traveling today, and I haven't heard back from him yet, but I'll let you know as soon as I do."

She nodded, then returned to sorting out the microphones, camcorders, cords, and memory sticks, trying to control her anger and frustration, wondering how much to tell Hattie, who'd done so much work recording oral tribal traditions. They both had thought that work would continue with Nell when they'd interviewed and hired her. So far, Gin hadn't found a single new video file.

Hattie's blood's gonna boil worse than mine.

Gin never found a chance to get a word in edgewise. Mack dominated the conversation, asking about the tenders they'd looked at, wanting to see the photos she'd taken. His only comment on Gabe's idea had been, "Not a chance. You can't compete with the big guys."

Pete and Hattie had listened carefully, asking a few questions, but Mack was completely against the idea. He liked Gabe and respected all the work he'd done for the seiners a few years ago, and he liked fishing with him, but he didn't think

Gabe had the years behind him to make something like this work.

Hattie's only comment, and she had to stand up and threaten to put her hand over Mack's mouth to be heard, was that she was planning Thanksgiving dinner at her house. Ginny offered to make pies, saying she'd been asked to housesit a small home and take care of the owner's cats for the Thanksgiving weekend.

8

After inviting Evie and her boys to have Thanksgiving dinner with her family at the last minute, Hattie surveyed her dining area and realized that her house was too small to fit everyone. She called Pete to ask if they could have it at his house, promising to bring all the food and handle the cooking, only mentioning Evie as an afterthought at the end of the conversation. Pete easily agreed before she'd finished asking since the kids were already at his house. Hattie texted the change in plans to Ginny on Thanksgiving morning.

Walking into Pete's, the boys came running, eager to show Hattie something they'd created in their new playroom. She asked Mack, Justin, and Pete to haul the containers of food in from her car while she went with the boys. After admiring their creation and the playroom—for the hundredth time— she asked the boys to make table placemats for everyone, giving them the construction paper she'd brought, along with small scissors and a glue stick.

Heading into the kitchen, ordering everyone out except

Ginny, Hattie set to work, glad she'd done the prep work at home. Ginny had made two pies at the home she and Justin were house-sitting and was now trying to help, but there didn't seem to be much Hattie needed her for.

"Evie should be here soon. Can I talk you into keeping an eye on the kids? She has two boys, too. They all play together, and Robbie and Evan are in the same class this year."

"Man, we're so outnumbered."

"Yeah, we need Evie," Hattie said, putting the turkey in the oven. "Four and a half hours. Think they'll be done talking about fishing by then?" she asked and laughed.

"Never. Did I hear you say that Al's back in town?"

"No. I was hoping he would be, but he said he had a last-minute change and was staying in Anchorage or Juneau; I can't remember which. All good at work?"

"Oh, it's fun to be back. Um, kinda weird working with Pete and living here too, when we're here, but he really comes alive at work. It suits him."

"God, that's good to hear. I need to look at his watch and see his readings again."

"How do you manage that?"

Hattie smiled at her. "I remind him to charge his phone and watch, then I sit down at his desk and open the app."

"Hmmm. Good plan. I can start doing that, too."

"So, what are you working on in the office—"

"Hattie-mom, Eeeeevie's here!" Robbie yelled, and they could hear the four boys talking over each other, each excited to show the others something vitally important, crowding the entryway. Hattie sent them all to the playroom and took Evie by the hand to the kitchen, closing the narrow pocket door, which normally never came out of its slot.

"I'm pretty sure it's five o'clock on the East Coast," Hattie said, opening a bottle of Prosecco, then pouring three glasses.

She added sparkling water to her own, then passed glasses and bottles to Evie and Ginny, asking if they'd met before.

By four o'clock, the dining room table was set and loaded with food, and it only awaited the turkey that was resting on top of the stove on a platter. Hattie had saved a spot in front of Pete's place at the head of the table for the big bird but told him she'd be happy to carve if he didn't want to, and he readily agreed.

With everyone passing dishes, filling plates, helping a kid sitting next to them do the same, Hattie carved, and Pete circulated plates. No one heard the car pull up or the outside door open until Robbie yelled, "Big brother! My big brother's here!" and all eyes turned to Case, pulling his coat off, and Nell standing behind him.

Hattie's eyes widened, wondering where she'd put them both, and Ginny got up to get more plates. Pete went to the laundry room and pulled out a card table, turning around to see Justin behind him.

"I'll get the chairs. Do you remember the kids and Nell issue?" Justin asked.

"Yes. Let's set this up by the TV, then turn it on. Hopefully, it'll distract them," Pete said quickly, heading for the living room. They moved the kids, with Ginny and Hattie helping, while Case and Nell protested that they hadn't intended to disrupt things. Mack kept Case and Nell's attention as he described Gabe's interest in direct-marketing salmon, and the two were quickly integrated into the table, with Justin moving closer to Ginny, letting Case and Nell sit next to each other across the table from them.

. . .

Awkward was hardly a good enough word, Hattie thought with a sinking feeling, watching Nell touch Case's hand as they ate, sharing intimate glances through dinner. She was afraid that Mack had been right when he'd said, "That looks like trouble," a couple of months ago at their campfire. She whipped a quick glance at her husband, but he was absorbed in the conversation that Case was leaning into—about Gabe's idea of going direct to market with his catch. Hattie noticed Nell squeezing Case's hand to bring his attention back to her, and she quickly looked away.

Hattie put a hand on Pete's shoulder as Ginny leaned over him from his other side to pick up the remains of the turkey. "We've got this. It's too crowded in the kitchen for more people. Thanks for offering, though." They carried away the platters, bowls, and utensils as Mack, Pete, Justin, and Case debated the earning potential of a tender versus a direct-to-market enterprise.

Evie sent a questioning look Hattie's way, then stayed seated at Hattie's quick shake of her head. Glancing at the boys at the card table where Ginny was cleaning them up, Hattie nodded, then headed for the kitchen. Evie stood and went to the card table and started clearing the kid's plates as Ginny herded them toward the playroom.

Slicing pies, Hattie carried them out to the cleaned card table, along with a fresh pot of coffee and a pot of herbal tea. Bringing out a stack of plates and a handful of forks, she left them by the pies, then caught Pete's glance and smiled, pointing at the desserts as she headed for the playroom.

Knocking twice, she tried the knob, which was locked. Ginny opened the door and let her in, and Hattie shut it quietly behind her.

"Well, that was a surprise," she blurted out as Ginny and Evie moved into the corner of the room with her.

"I'm not leaving this room," Ginny said quickly, "and I told Evie why."

"Good. I knew you'd have things under control. I'll do my best to get rid of her. Promise the kids ice cream; no actually, promise them anything. You have your phone?" Ginny pulled it out to show her, then shoved it back into her pants pocket. "Good. Evie, the goal is to get Nell on her way."

"I can leave, if it makes things easier—"

"No way. The boys are distracted by having your kids here, plus *you* were invited. She wasn't. Follow my lead," Hattie said, leaving the room. She went down the hallway, past the living room entrance, entering the kitchen from its back doorway, to find Nell standing there.

"I hope you had dessert?" Hattie asked with her best forced smile, the one that was meant to look fake.

"I ah, did, yes. The strawberry-rhubarb. It was delicious. I thought maybe I could help in here?" she looked around at the tidy kitchen. "Or with the kids? I love kids," Nell smiled, and Hattie's skin crawled with the creep of goosebumps up her shoulders and the back of her neck.

Hattie exhaled dramatically. "Ah, this is sort of awkward because I love your facial markings, but somehow they've frightened the kids and we have to be especially careful with them. I know you're a kind soul, and you'll understand. They're deep into a new movie I promised they could watch," she lied. "They've been looking forward to it all week. Now," she moved forward, bodily crowding Nell toward the half-open pocket door, "let's go sit and relax, shall we?" She tightened her fake smile and reached around Nell to push the pocket door open. "I think Pete was hoping to talk to you for just a moment," Hattie urged.

She was desperate to find out exactly how Case and Nell

had managed to arrive together and planned on asking him. Shutting the pocket door behind her, she fixed her smile slightly, then saw Case heading for the arctic entry. She hurried over to hug him, whispering in a tight voice, "Honey—what on earth?" He returned her hug, then backed up, smiling down at her. She hated that he was so tall and handsome. It made him too vulnerable, in her opinion. He looked older than he actually was. "She's not—"

"Oh, don't go all Linda on me. We clicked the minute we met."

"You don't know—" Hattie started.

But Case leaned down, whispering in her ear, holding her shoulder. "I know all I need to know. Don't worry," he assured her, then let her go and pulled his coat off a hook. He shrugged it on, then grabbed Nell's. "I'm happy. Be happy for me," he said quietly. Hattie backed up slightly as Nell eased her way into the crowded entry. Holding out an arm like a model as Case held her coat open, she made a production of sliding into it and flipping her long hair out.

"Thank you for a lovely dinner. Happy Thanksgiving," Nell said, glowing.

Hattie swore she saw *I win* in her eyes. "I'm so glad you both came. Family is everything to us. It made things perfect to have Case here," Hattie replied.

Case opened the door and quickly gave his aunt his normal, confident look, then took Nell by the elbow as they walked to her car. Hattie eased the door closed, watching Nell grab Case by his coat front and pull him in for a kiss. Hattie recognized that the manipulative display was meant to be seen, lowering her opinion of Nell even further.

9

"Well, that was interesting," Evie said, with a slice of pie in one hand, a fork in the other, eavesdropping behind Hattie.

Turning around after finally shutting the door, Hattie growled, "Good thing I didn't have a fork in my hand."

Pete crowded the entry behind Evie. "What the living hell is my son doing with *her*?"

Evie spun around and backed up, her eyes widening at the depth of the anger in his voice. "I'll go tell Gin the coast is clear," she blurted out, easing away, heading for the playroom. Hattie leaned against the wall of the entryway, her eyes on fire.

Pete went into the kitchen and came back with three beers in one hand and a new bottle of Prosecco in the other. Hattie went to the kitchen for the glasses, bringing them to the table, as Evie came into the room.

"Pete, Ginny wants you to come talk to Robbie. About Nell," Evie said, looking worried.

Pete left the Prosecco bottle half opened and ran to the playroom, where Robbie sat in Ginny's lap. He knelt down. "She's gone. Door's locked. Hattie made sure, and I watched and checked it."

"Okay, dad." Robbie got up and hugged Pete. Ginny pressed play for the short cartoon they'd all chosen, and Robbie settled into a chair.

"Come get me when the second one is over," she reminded them as they sprawled in the four kid-sized pillow-chairs she'd bought.

Pete stood in the doorway, and she wriggled past him. He watched the kids intently for a minute, then closed the door silently.

"Okay, let's start from the beginning," Hattie said after downing half a glass of undiluted bubbly. They were all seated again at the dining table, and she'd urged everyone to keep their voices low.

"I think maybe you should start from the end. What she just pulled on Ginny," Evie said.

Hattie twisted to look at Evie, completely confused. "I told Nell the kids were intimidated by her markings and then said that they were watching a movie. I was pretty firm about it, too."

"I heard you tell her, and I watched her almost race to the playroom as soon as your back was turned. You were saying goodbye to Case," Evie explained.

Hattie's eyes widened, and her mouth dropped open. All three of the men at the table knew Hattie was worse than a bear when it came to kids. They shared glances and kept their mouths shut. The anger coming off her was like a volcanic cloud. Her iron gaze went to Ginny, and she waited.

"She didn't knock, just turned the knob. When it wouldn't open, she knocked. I opened the door a crack, and she said she wanted to say goodbye to the kids. I said they were winding down and needed quiet and kept my foot against the door as she pushed it. She said kids love her, and she wanted to give them a quick hug, and I said, not today. Then she looked at me with, argh… hate, just… total hate, and smiled. It made my skin crawl." Ginny rubbed her arms and shivered. Justin's mouth dropped open. He sat up quickly, and Mack kicked him under the table. Hattie closed her eyes and clamped her mouth shut, breathing heavily through her nose.

"Robbie must have been peeking behind me," Ginny continued, looking at Pete apologetically. "She tried to get in again and I shut the door. I heard her say, 'You won't be working with us anymore,' and I called her a word I don't use. Much," she finished, looking down, her hands in her lap, fidgeting. "I didn't want the kids to hear me, but I think maybe Robbie heard it," she finished with a whisper, looking down.

"Don't worry, I'll deal with that," Pete assured her. "Robbie and I are good. He's fine now. Thank you for keeping her out of there. My turn?" Everyone turned to him in surprise.

"I've been talking to Al. Nell's work is not what he expected, and he's talked to the tribe about it. They want him back and, hearing about the work she hasn't been doing, they want her gone. He's promised to keep me informed."

Ginny's mouth hung open in shock, but she recovered quickly. "I was waiting for the right time to tell you, but she hasn't done anything with our video footage," she said, looking at Hattie, whose face turned to granite.

"You gotta be kidding me," Justin let out, looking from Pete to Ginny, then leaning forward to look at Hattie. "What did you say to Case?"

"I tried to warn him that he might not know her as well as he thinks he does, but he said they, ah, were attracted to each other from the moment they met."

The dead silence, as each of them contemplated the situation, lasted for a few minutes. Beer was drunk, looks exchanged, more Prosecco poured and swallowed. Ginny stood and picked up her glass. "I'm gonna debone the turkey," she said. "I need something to do."

"I think I'll watch the rest of the cartoon with the kids, then get my boys home. It was a lovely dinner, Hattie... Pete. Thank you for including us. I'm sorry that woman disrupted your plans—"

"Wait. What's your impression here? You just met her, and it's obvious we have issues. I don't want to put you on the spot, but before all this bullshit after dinner, what did you think?" Hattie asked.

"She's beautiful, and she knows it. All I got from her was the expectation that everyone should love her. I thought it was me being an outsider. But from what Ginny said, I wouldn't trust her for one second around my kids. And, well, I've been fooled by first impressions before." She shared a sad, knowing look with Hattie, whispering, "I'm not the greatest judge of character." She stood up and headed for the playroom.

"You done?" Mack asked, sending his wife a piercing look.

Hattie took a deep breath. "For now, man. I'll finish putting things away." She stood up, poured the rest of the Prosecco in her glass, and went into the kitchen. Pete stood up and headed for the playroom. Justin and Mack looked at each other with slightly shell-shocked grimaces, then stood and started wrapping up the pies, putting them on the dining table, then folding up the card table and chairs.

At the end of the hallway, in the darkest corner, Evie leaned against the wall. Pete walked to her, standing so close they were touching, his hands at his sides, his voice low. "Are you okay?"

She put her hands on his chest, looking up at him. "I just... It's hard not to touch you in front of everyone. Then that chick—she made it worse. Can I have one kiss? The nice kind, not the make me hot kind," she whispered. He lowered his head, his fingertips touching her waist, and kissed her tenderly. "Well, that didn't work," she breathed, as he stepped back.

She kept one hand on his chest. "Maybe, sometime this week—"

"Tomorrow?" he suggested quickly. "Justin and Gin are house-sitting."

"Tomorrow morning. Early, before the kids are up. Before five."

"I can't wait."

Tracing the line of beard stubble across his cheek with her finger as he lay sprawled on her bed, still waking up, Nell said, "Let's spend tonight in Glenallen, on the way back to Fairbanks."

Case laughed. "Why the hell would we want to go there? It's a tiny bible town. They'd throw us out."

He propped himself up on his elbows, looking at her as she stretched out, completely naked. He loved that she didn't cover herself. She had no modesty and no inhibitions.

"We've fucked in Fairbanks, Anchorage, and Seward," she said, rolling onto her back.

"Keeping a list? Interesting tan lines, and your chin markings have faded."

"Mmmm. I hike up and strip whenever I can in the summer. The markings are an experiment. I'm trying to decide if I want to make them permanent." She rolled again, then climbed over him, supporting herself on her arms and knees, her muscles well defined.

"I need somewhere new."

"There's always North Pole," Case tried to choke out

while laughing. "You can sit on Santa's lap and wish for something," he barely got out, laughing harder. She wasn't amused.

"There's Chena, if you want to overshoot by an hour," he offered, after catching his breath.

"Chena?"

"The hot springs. Everyone knows Chena," he said, studying her curiously.

She lay down on him, then slid away, sitting up, running her fingers through her hair. "I'm from southeast, remember? And I'm hungry."

"I'll make you pancakes," he offered, propping himself up on one elbow, watching her.

"I'd rather go out." She stood up and crossed the one room cabin, took panties out of a drawer and pulled them on with the same finesse a stripper would use taking them off.

"Want to see if my brother can join us? You two didn't get to chat much at dinner last night, what with Mack hogging the conversation about tenders and other fishing crap."

"Maybe, if it was only him. Ginny was mean to me. I wanted to hug the kiddies goodbye, and she wouldn't let me. God! Why are women so jealous of me? I don't deserve it. I'm always sweet to them, and I work with her. Even your aunt made up some story, trying to hurt my feelings. At least kids love me," she pouted, pulling on a bra, adjusting her breasts, drawing it out as he watched her every move.

10

Dropped off by Justin on Friday morning, Ginny waited at the office door for Pete, who'd texted that he was on his way. She had her laptop and a large external hard drive in her tote bag and was determined to copy as much as she could, as fast as she could, from all the office computers she could access. If she needed to, she planned on asking Pete for his key and working through the weekend.

Pete came up the stairs two at a time, smiling, and quickly let her in while she told him her plan. She unpacked in the interview room and started hooking up cables while Pete started coffee and turned the router on.

Connor popped his head into the small room. "Hey Gin, Al's on the phone. He's coming in on Monday. He said to ask if you can come in too? Right at eight?"

"Sure," she looked at what she was doing and swallowed hard. "Sure thing," she repeated, afraid she'd panicked, misread everything, and was going overboard.

She'd talked to Hattie and Pete after Evie'd left, saying that she didn't trust all their work with Nell, and they'd both agreed it was a good idea when she offered to come in and copy Hattie's video files. Hattie had asked how many interviews were on the tribe's website, and when Ginny had said two, she'd gone coldly furious. They were the original two from almost a year ago.

At noon, Pete brought containers of leftovers into the interview room, closing the door, trailing the distinct aroma of warmed turkey. Ginny took a deep breath of the delicious smell and smiled gratefully. Pushing cables aside, she made room for his plate as he urged her to fill her plate first. "How's it going?"

"Good," she said, after swallowing turkey. "I think I'll be done in less than an hour, and I've got it all."

"Can I ask you to do mine too? I have a lot of research here, files, spreadsheets, reports. If I could have it all copied and kept somewhere safe, I'd sleep a whole lot better tonight."

Ginny looked up, surprised. "Sure, I can do that. There's still lots of room on the hard drive. Can I sit at your desk for a while? Or I can do it after—"

"I told Connor I have a doctor appointment at two this afternoon. I'll go for a walk. Text me when you're done. If he asks, tell him I asked you to run a back-up for me."

"Will do."

Connor swung around in his chair, facing Ginny as she hooked up the cables to Pete's computer. "Doin' a hard backup," he said. "That's good. I have some stuff too. Maybe, like the newsletters—addresses. Should you do them too?"

"Sure, Connor. I'll do yours next, okay?" She'd have to

think of something to tell Connor to keep him from mentioning it to Nell.

"I kinda miss Al," he admitted quietly.

"Yeah, me too. It'll be nice to see him Monday. I wonder where he's been lately. Any idea?"

"Lately, I don't know. He sends me pictures. By email. Hey, can you back those up too? I save them to a file I call Al's Pics."

"Sure thing."

"When he goes to the villages, he sends me pics of everybody. It's nice to see them."

"Homesick?" she gave him a sympathetic glance.

"Ah, sometimes. Village life. It's not like here."

Ginny took a closer look at him, guessing him to be about nineteen or twenty, but she couldn't be sure. "What did you do yesterday? You had family you were going to visit. In Eagle River, right?"

"I was, but the starter went out on my truck, and the shops were closed. So, I stayed home. I'm gonna order a new starter after work."

"You know how to replace it?"

"Sure. It's easy. Done lots of starters. You all done?" Ginny was unhooking the cables. Copying reports and PDFs took very little time. It was the video files that took the longest.

"Yup, comin' your way. Clear me a little space, okay? I'll give you my pumpkin pie." She grinned at him, then stood, stretched, and went into the interview room for the slice of pie Pete had brought her. She quickly texted Pete that she was finished at his desk.

"Scoot that extra chair over, then you can point to the files you want backed up, okay?" She put the pie and a clean fork in front of him, where he'd rolled off to the side of his desk. Turning his computer around, she started plugging in cords to connect the hard drive, then pushed it back and turned the monitor so they could both see. He'd pushed his rolling chair to her and pulled the extra one over for himself. His mouth full of pie, he pointed.

Ginny clicked to open the hard drive, and the screensaver changed, showing a photo of a group of people on a beach. "Hey, that's Kicarwick! That's Joe. There's Drew, oh wow, that's little Shayna."

"Hey, how do you know those guys? They're my cousins, sorta. You've been to the village?"

"Yeah, last year. We were helping Joe with his engine. I was on one of the seiners. Were you there?"

"Awwww. Nope. At a retreat. I heard all about it, though."

"That kid is all kinds of cute. I almost stole her," Ginny said wistfully.

"Oh, hey, don't say that. That's bad," his voice trembled. "You should know better, being—"

"Oh, shit. I'm sorry. What did I say? I didn't mean it. Really," she touched his hand, seeing him biting his lips, his face twitching. "Really. I'm so sorry."

"Well, it's okay, you being a girl and all. But you know. Stolen girls. Missing women. Bad, bad." He was fighting tears, and she put an arm around him as Pete walked into the office.

"Hey guys, what's wrong? Can I help?"

"Naw," Connor wiped his eyes. "Our missing girls. Makes me cry every time."

Walking to Connor's desk, Pete lay a hand on the young man's shoulder. "Angels of mercy, we ask you to bring them back to us, who love and miss them," Pete said, then let his hand slide away as he headed for his desk.

"Amen," Connor responded solemnly, then bounced back to his normal eagerness. "Here, I'll find a better pic of Shayna for you," he volunteered, taking the mouse. Ginny stole a quick glance at her watch. Not even three o'clock. Plenty of time. She'd gotten everything she'd wanted. She looked up at Connor's screen, waiting patiently.

"Be sure and do Nell's if you have the time," Pete said, readjusting the things on his desk that she'd moved.

"I, ah, I lost her password," Ginny replied, surprised by the request, wondering what he was thinking. Pete knew she didn't have Nell's passwords. Maybe he was only trying to make it sound like she was doing everyone's?

"Oh, I have it," Connor offered. The other two stared at him in surprise. "She wanted me to do some work in there a while ago, when she went to lunch, so she gave it to me and said to go in and do it. I'll get it for ya in a sec. There she is, look at that girly-girl. My cousin's kid," he beamed.

"She's so adorable. She was wandering around when we went to find Joe, and I picked her up. She let me," Ginny exclaimed, remembering the moment and the joy of holding the little girl, astonished that the child had come willingly into her arms.

"Yup, she loves everybody, that's for sure. We all love her too."

"She called me Sissy and said her name was Shay-Shay. Isn't that sweet?"

"Sissy?"

Ginny nodded, then pointed to a file, looking at Connor. "This one?"

He stared at her. "Sissy," he whispered.

Ginny glanced back at him after copying the file, waiting for him to point to another one, but he kept staring at her, and it gave her goosebumps. She decided to copy everything, dropping them into a folder she named Connor. Quickly finished, she said, "So, that password?" She stood up and started unhooking cables.

11

Pete poured another mug of coffee, then glanced at his watch for the fifteenth time. 7:45. He took the mug to Ginny as she paced the conference room, and they both jerked as the main office door opened, and Al walked in.

"Ah, good to see you both. Oh, coffee—wonderful. I'll just help myself, if you don't mind?"

Ginny tried as hard as she could to unfreeze her face and body. She was sure she was going to be confronted about running those backups. She had everything in her bag, ready to hand over.

She twitched, hearing the door open again, and her jaw dropped, seeing Hattie walk through, brushing fresh snow off her coat, then taking it off. She draped it over her arm and came into the conference room, smiling. Ginny closed her mouth quickly and counted chairs, doing a mental tally of who'd be there: Al, Nell, Pete, Connor, herself, and now Hattie... *Again with the freaking door!* She jerked, turning quickly to see who was coming in.

Connor held the door as a strange woman walked through. Seven people now, and there were five chairs around

64

the table. She walked to Pete's desk and grabbed his chair and then the spare, pulling them into the conference room, then busied herself rearranging things.

They were all seated around the oval table, sipping coffee, chatting about the snow and road conditions, when Nell walked in at 8:15.

"Oh my," she said, standing in the doorway, eyeing the one place open at the table, then meeting the eyes of Pete, then Al, glowing and preening as if she were accepting an award.

Al stood. "Please, get your coffee and join us," he gestured to the empty chair opposite him, which he'd specifically arranged. It wasn't until Al had asked everyone to leave that seat open that Ginny'd taken a truly deep breath.

"Of course," she purred. Tousling her hair while she poured the last of the coffee into a mug, she grinned, then toned her look down to satisfied amusement.

Bending down, placing her mug on the table, Nell eased gracefully into her chair and admired Al's handmade vest, complimenting him on the color.

"Thank you. It is definitely one of a kind, and I treasure it. I honor the woman who made it for me by wearing it with pride." He looked straight at Nell and no one else, as if they were alone, and she sat tall, her shoulders back, perfectly at ease.

"Nell Harris, this is Edna Fox from the personnel division of our umbrella consortium of tribes. I was asked by the consortium to meet with you this morning, regarding the grants funding your position—"

The rest was a blur of unmet expectations, requirements, and deadlines that buzzed past Ginny's ears as she watched Nell's face go from over-the-top show-off to dead fury as she froze in place. Ginny wanted to run from the room and puke.

She was shaking and deeply regretted ever wanting to be there, especially when Nell's gaze circled the faces at the table, stopping at each one, hate radiating from her eyes while one facial muscle near her eye twitched.

Nell twisted sideways, crossing her legs, then put on a mask of disdain as she replied that she'd been working diligently, describing her background while insinuating that perhaps Al was disappointed in his current position and would prefer to push her out rather than admit his own errors in judgment.

Oh, touché, you arrogant bitch, Pete thought, watching Nell's act. How unexpected that you'd go on the offense, he mused, sarcastically.

You're gonna sink that much faster.

He tried not to smile. He'd grown up competing against arrogant, obnoxious commercial fishermen. He recognized greed and over-confidence when he saw it.

I'm so glad Al's recording this. The man's a genius with the patience of a saint. It will be wonderful having him back.

Holy shit, Pete perked up, focusing, listening closer. She falsified her CV!

Wait, what?

Edna, from personnel, was asking for Nell's BIA information. What tribe, what date, born where, what percentage? And Nell was babbling! Like a losing quarterback on the ground, crawling for the one-yard-line, she was grasping, unable to nail it. Edna, in her low, carefully enunciating voice, repeated the questions.

"What's the bottom line here?" Nell oozed, her lips smiling, her eyes sending death-spikes to the stolid Edna.

"I'll take that, thank you so much, Ms. Fox." Al faced Nell. "We have been unable to confirm your accounting degree or your tribal enrollment, despite repeated attempts. Your employment by this tribe and its umbrella consortium, both of which fund your position, is terminated, effective immediately. You may remove your personal items now." He stood up, leaning down slightly as he closed his planner.

Ginny scooted back from the table as Nell stood and lashed out. Using very few words, she cut down Pete's performance, blaming his lack of cooperation for missed deadlines, and then started attacking Connor's competence.

"Enough," Al interrupted loudly, waving his hand toward the door. As Nell stalked out, he turned quickly, holding a hand up to everyone else but waving to Edna to come with him. She was already up, and Pete guessed that this wasn't her first rodeo. *An imposter. How did we let this happen?*

Pete stepped away from the big table, letting Edna by, then moved to the doorway, turning his phone camera onto video, holding it against the door frame to brace it, watching Nell as she tried to take things from the office and was ordered to leave them.

Al and Edna conferred quietly in Al's enclosed office after Nell finally cleared out her personal things and left. Ginny made a fresh pot of coffee, then rinsed her and Al's mugs, while Hattie pulled out a pie from the small fridge. She set it on the small dining table in their lunchroom with plates, forks, and a knife. Slicing herself a piece, then filling her mug, she returned to the conference room, and Ginny did the same.

Connor and Pete quickly served themselves, then took the same seats they'd had, eating, sipping, no one speaking. Al entered the room with his own slice and mug and settled at the head of the table as Edna pulled on her coat and left the office.

"Never easy, always distasteful. This pie will help clear our palate. Thank you very much for bringing it." He took a bite, sipped coffee, and leaned back, surveying the people in front of him.

"What I can tell you is that each of you are to be thanked for keeping me informed. Separately, your qualms may have seemed, ah," he searched for the right word, "non-critical. Together, however, they painted a distressing picture. Let's get this all out into the open now, shall we?"

Left speechless by Al's summation, Pete decided that it was Connor's experience that had been the most damaging to Nell. She had ignored repeated requests for information from personnel. They'd finally contacted him, asking if Nell was even there, and he'd contacted Al.

They'd all gone to Al, it seemed. Pete, with data and updates on projects that Nell should have been doing; Ginny, with her concern that only two of the video interviews were online. Only Hattie was out of the loop, and Pete wondered briefly why she was there.

"So, that's the gist. Now, going forward. I had personally put my name on these projects. I've made calls to each of the grant funding organizations, apologizing for the delay, assuring them that we are close to our goals. We have a short reprieve. I'm asking Hattie and Ginny to come back to work, if they can. Their hours can be flexible." He paused for a moment, letting everyone's thoughts cycle through, then continued.

"Pete, whether you know it or not, you've already been doing Nell's job." Al held his hand up quickly. "I know—you don't want it. But I have to ask you if you would do it, or if you would share it with Hattie. But our first choice is you, Pete. You're doing great work, and," he turned to Hattie, "that's no strike against you, merely an acknowledgment of how much Pete's done, far beyond what we expected."

Pete glanced at Hattie, knowing he didn't have to. "Let's share it. I need her guidance. I'd feel better having it. You manage the details, Al; I'm sure we both trust you." Al looked from one to the other, Hattie nodding.

"Good. I'll do that. I'll get you your deadlines and expectations. We'll resume our weekly sessions as time and travel allow. The consortium is bringing me back onboard, but only for this meeting today and for limited consulting. I wish," he waved his hand up again, "I wish I could do more at this time, but I'm tied up through January. We'll re-asses then.

Ginny, what I need from you and Hattie are how many hours a week you can give. If you can get that to me by this afternoon, I will finalize the schedule. It'll be a push into January, no doubt about it, and we'll be able to reassess then."

"I'm in, especially since the kids are back in school. I have a friend who I think can watch them during the Christmas break," Hattie said quickly.

"I've needed something to do for months. I keep seeing more and more news stories about the damage hatcheries are doing, about weirs being taken out, dams being demolished, and best of all about hatcheries that are being closed. You'd have to lock me out," Ginny said, grinning happily.

12

Entering Pete's house after work, right behind him, Ginny toed her snow boots off quickly and ran to the stove, turning it off. The steam was overwhelming. "Hey, I'm making soup," Justin protested.

"Babe, bring it to a boil, then simmer."

"Oh, I forgot that part." He kissed her, holding her tight, and Pete came into the kitchen saying, "Get a room," and they all laughed. It had become Pete's favorite line, now that they were living with him, and he said it happily at every opportunity, his eyes glowing, his mouth grinning.

"It wasn't boiling long, I promise. So? I got your texts and then nothing. What's the rest of the story? Jesus, I'm gonna have to watch soap operas to keep my brain alive."

"Good Lord, don't do that. Hattie and I are now job-sharing. Ginny's promised to work with us," Pete offered, raising his eyebrows with a smile at Gin, then he headed to his bedroom to change clothes.

"Vegetables turn to mush if they're overcooked. What are you going to add?" Ginny asked, lifting the lid on the pot. "Potatoes, pasta, rice?"

"All three," he said, easing behind her, running his hand over her back and down the curve of her bottom.

"No way," she said, then laughed, twisting out of his reach. "Too many carbs. Pick one and hands off."

"Dammit, I want everything," he said quietly, looking into her eyes.

"Mmmm hmmm. Later. I'm working again," she said excitedly, grinning, practically bouncing.

"Me too, maybe. I have an idea. Let's go somewhere private." She narrowed her eyes suspiciously, half-smiling, and he lowered his voice. "Not sex. Seriously. Something I've been thinking about. I want to ask you about it." He leaned in and whispered, "Just you, for now. Tell me what you think."

"Okay. Where? And don't say bedroom," she teased.

"Damn." He smiled back at her, reaching for her hand. "Come with me." He headed for the new playroom.

Watching Justin close the playroom door quietly, then sit on the floor cross-legged, Ginny wondered what was going on. They had all kinds of privacy at the house-sitting gigs, where they talked about anything and everything, and they'd just finished one. She sat down across from him, wrapping her arms around her legs, waiting.

"I don't even know where to start," he muttered, looking around the room, running his hand through his hair.

"You're scaring me. What's the bad news? Say it fast," she blurted out, stiffening and frowning.

"No bunny, not bad. I mean it." He reached for her hands and tugged. She scooted closer as he opened his legs, bringing her in, lifting her legs over his so that she faced him. She eased her feet behind him, searching his face, holding his hands.

"Look, we've never really talked that much about money. Ah... Do you remember that insurance policy?" She nodded, continuing to watch him closely. "Well, we got the money..." She gave him time, the same way he did for her when she couldn't choke out the words she needed. "It was a mil, divided by three. You remember that part?"

"You...?" Her eyes widened, and he nodded as her mouth dropped open.

"Yeah, but my dad didn't get a dime."

She froze, taking a deep breath. "Didn't you say he mortgaged the house?" she whispered, looking at the door.

"Yes. And here's what I want. I want to pay off the mortgage and give him part of that money. I think it's the fair thing to do," he said quickly, and her gaze returned to him, her eyes still wide. "But I also want to offer to help him fix this place up a little. It needs work," he finished quickly, and watched her exhale and relax. She smiled, and he waited for her reaction.

"Well?" he asked.

"Well, what?"

"What do *you* think?"

Surprise registered, and her smile grew. "I think you should do it. Of course."

"Okay, I've been thinking about it for a while, and I think I should give him about a hundred and thirty-three, and so should Case."

"And Robbie."

"Yeah, and Robbie, but that may be up to Mack and Hattie. I think they have his money in a separate account."

"They'll say yes," Ginny said quickly, then hesitated. "But Case..."

"Yeah. I'm not so sure. I hope he'll do it. That would give dad four hundred and each of us two. I can either pay off the mortgage and deposit the rest of the money in his account, or just write a check for all of it."

"Oh... pay off the mortgage and give the rest if there's any leftover, right? What's your gut say?"

"I was thinking that, too. Pay it off and put the papers inside a card for Christmas."

"Oh, wow. Yeah. Do that," she agreed, gazing off over his shoulder. "When are you gonna talk to Mack?"

"Tomorrow morning."

"So, about that trip to Arizona," Hattie said, sitting at her dining table. The boys had finished dinner and were playing in the front yard in the fresh snow. Mack put foil over the left-over chunks of halibut, leaving it on the table, then sat down again. She'd given him a brief rundown of the day's events while the kids were in school, but then needed to go pick them up, and they hadn't had any privacy since.

That was another reason for Mack's desire for a get-away. He'd already talked to Justin, who promised to talk to Ginny about watching the kids for at least a week. Two, if he could talk Hattie into going for that long. Pete had readily agreed to have them stay at his house. Now he just needed her to say yes.

"Work's gonna be a crunch. Several major projects are past their deadline."

"Yeah, you said that already. So, no way then?"

"How about we try for a week? Between Christmas and New Year's? Like last year?"

"Okay. So, I asked Pete already, and Justin. Waitin' on Gin, and you know she'll say yes."

"But she's working now too, hun," Hattie said gently. She knew he wanted time in the sun, and that he missed Arizona. The texts and photos Wade sent didn't help matters.

"Evie—" he started.

"Yup, I'm asking her next."

"Damned good soup, son. You're hired," Pete complimented Justin. Eating in the kitchen was crowded but convenient. Everything was within easy reach, including the half of a beer that Pete was treating himself to.

Ginny giggled. "You sound like Mack."

"Who do you think he got it from?" Pete asked, raising an eyebrow, and she laughed. He loved hearing laughter, especially hers. He looked around his kitchen, thinking about his second date with his nurse. There had been zero laughter, and Pete gauged his connection with women by their laugh.

Bumping into her in the grocery store, one thing had led to another, and Pete had asked her to dinner. He'd choked at the prices on the menu and realized it had been far too long since he'd dined out.

Their second date had been a salmon dinner here in his kitchen, and he was sure it was their last date. Barely polite, her small comments and questions had added up to a negative assessment of his home that made him look at it with fresh eyes. Compared to Hattie's new kitchen, his was past *dated* and deep into the *needs-work* category. The carpet in the living room and bedrooms was original, from when the twins had been born.

It hit him like a hammer. That was twenty years ago! He blinked several times, looking around again.

He wondered how much money a remodel would cost and braced himself to ask Mack about his own remodel. Mack had done the work himself, with Justin's help, but Pete would have to contract it all out. What he knew about house construction would fit on a sticky note.

. . .

Justin ate his soup and watched his dad look the kitchen over as if he'd never seen it before, which cinched his decision, especially after the conversation he'd just had with Gin. He'd started on this train of thought when Pete had confessed to having a date over for dinner. Justin had found his dad cleaning the second bathroom and wanted to know why. He'd helped with the cleaning and eagerly asked how it had gone the next day, when they'd returned from a house-sitting gig. Leaving Ginny to her bedtime storytelling—they'd had the kids that night—he'd quizzed his dad quietly in the living room.

Pete had insisted that he wanted to keep the experience between just the two of them. When Justin agreed, he confessed that it hadn't gone well. She wasn't impressed by his home and still thought he should be on drugs for his A-Fib, even after they promised not to talk about it. He wasn't in her league, Pete admitted. She had a house in one state, a cabin in another, and vacationed in Europe.

Pete didn't tell Justin that the date had ended with a peck on the cheek, and he'd had a whole beer afterward, praying that she rotated out of the job soon and that no one in his family would ever learn about it. Pete was sure that if Gin found out, Hattie'd hear about it. Then Evie would.

Pete loved Evie's laugh the minute he'd heard it, entering the kitchen after that embarrassing episode. Deep, affectionate, with a touch of mischief. Then she'd teased him, and he'd fallen like a rock into water, with a splash and a happy swirl, twisting, tumbling gently, enjoying every second of the wet trip down to the bottom of the well that had culminated in a dash to the bedroom for the intimacy they were both missing.

The dates with the nurse had been a test of his feelings and his desire to remain detached, and he'd failed miserably—or passed, whichever way you looked at it. He couldn't even remember the nurse's name.

13

Ginny had her own key to the office now, and Justin dropped her off at work early, telling Pete he was helping Mack with another project. He waited around the corner from Mack's until Hattie left to drop the kids off at school, then parked in their driveway.

Going in through the garage, he was amazed at how organized and clean it looked. As he entered the kitchen, where Mack was standing, he urged, "Call the police, man, someone broke into your house and stole all your crap," then busted up laughing.

"Jesus Christ, you're not kidding. I'll never be able to find anything again," he said, disgusted.

"Holy shit, seriously? Hattie did that? She's mad at you?" Justin didn't know whether he should laugh or cry. If Hattie was that mad—

"Nooooo," Mack said slowly, dragging it out. "I. Did. It."

Justin howled even louder at Mack's miserable tone, doubling up and eventually wiping his eyes, pulling out a chair to sit down.

"I'm sorry," he mumbled, still smiling.

"No, you're not," Mack said, scowling at him. "So, what's the secret?"

Mack had immediately told Hattie last night, after Justin texted, asking to talk to him alone, and her money was on an engagement ring and a spring wedding. Mack disagreed. His bet was a baby with a July birthday.

"Ah, it's about that insurance money and my dad's house, which needs work," he said, watching Mack grin. "I want to pay off the mortgage and give him some of the money." He let that sink in while he stood up and checked Hattie's coffee pot, pouring the dregs into a mug. He leaned against her new buffet counter, watching Mack contemplate what he'd proposed.

"How much?"

"I don't know what the mortgage is, but I want to give him a total of a hundred thirty-three."

Mack's eyebrows rose, and he went to the fridge for one of his sparkling water drinks, popping the top, chugging half of it. "You talk to Case about this?"

"Not yet. You first. Well, Gin first, then you. She said yes," he added at Mack's questioning look.

"That's a lot of money to let go of," Mack said slowly.

"Not my money. Family money. Jesus! She used the money he earned to pay for the fucking policy," he exploded, then quietly apologized. "Sorry."

"We talked about it when the checks came in, then things just got busy." He chugged the last of his drink and tossed the can into a recycling bin under the counter. "I agree. Hattie will too. We'll match that from Robbie's trust. If Case... well, that's up to him. That gives Pete two point six. I doubt the mortgage is for more than a hundred..." he was talking more to himself now, and Justin waited.

"There's more."

Mack's head popped up, his eyes going back to Justin.

Here it comes.

"I'm gonna offer to help him remodel. I'm not going for that Master's license after all. Or, well, maybe later. But I kinda liked the work we did here." He looked around at Hattie's new kitchen. "And the bathroom."

"She wants the downstairs bathroom done now, too." Mack stretched. "That's why I cleaned the garage. I said I was too busy—"

"Pffhhht," Justin spewed again, laughing. He could barely choke out, "An' how's that workin' out for ya?"

"Ah, fuck me. She's gonna get it. But, hey, if I say I'm working on Pete's place... hmmmm. That could buy me a few months, maybe even a year," he gloated, looking out the window. "Oh, yeah. Let's do that." He focused on his nephew again. "When are you gonna tell him?"

"Christmas? I thought about going to the bank and paying the mortgage, then depositing the difference into his account. What do you think?"

"Good idea. I like it. I'll run it past Hat, and we'll deposit a check too."

14

Case's phone vibrated as he walked between classes.

NELL

> I have time off! Coming to see you XXX

CASE

> Exams coming. Cramming a double load. Not a good time

NELL

> I'm lonely. I want to kiss you all over and feel your lips on me

CASE

> X-mas break, 4 wks

Already burning with anger, Case's reply notched Nell up to cold rage. She was accustomed to instant gratification. Four weeks might as well have been four years. Even the five-hour trip to Fairbanks, flying most of the way, would have pushed her limits. She hadn't wanted to repeat it, but she'd enjoyed the anticipation of seeing him. It thrilled her with how stunning he looked standing next to her. They were perfect together.

He needs a reminder of what he's missing.

She rubbed the dots off her chin with an alcohol pad, then added a dab of moisturizer. Painting her mascara dramatically, she admired her look in the large mirror, then teased her hair. Taking off bra and panties, she wiggled into her stretchiest skin-hugging dress. Slipping on her heels, she smiled with satisfaction and anticipation.

Her rental cabin wasn't far from the loudest bar in town, and the path through the woods made it a short walk. She took a couple of selfies and texted them to Case. She didn't bother taking a purse, ID, or money. Stashing her key outside, she headed out to let some fun find her, and it did.

She spent the next four weeks dancing, drinking, meeting men, going anywhere they wanted, and they did everything she demanded. She texted photos to Case whenever she remembered him.

Chelsea grabbed Case's phone the third time it vibrated, after hissing that she was going to smash it to bits the first two times. She stood up awkwardly, put it in a pocket of her heavy sweatpants, grabbed her books, notebook, laptop, pens, and winter coat while he lifted his head groggily.

"Don't," he croaked, and she hissed at him again.

"My place. Now."

Standing at the library table, she wondered why she'd ever agreed to go there in the first place. She never studied there. Not since Justin had left, anyway. The chairs were old and uncomfortable, and she barely fit in them. The vending machines were always empty, and no one, ever, waved or said hi or stopped to chat with her. Ever. But it was the last two days of exam week, before Christmas break, and she and Case were supposed to be cramming. And then he'd shown up stumbling drunk, bitching about some ignorant female who'd dumped him.

Using the table in the building's arctic entry foyer, she put down her pile and shrugged her big, heavy coat on and zipped it against the twenty-below-zero temperature outside. Shoving her pens into a pocket, she picked the rest of her things up as Case staggered behind her, mumbling demands to give his phone back. The cloud of alcohol fumes out of his mouth was enough to make her gag, and she was no stranger to tequila.

No coat. Goddammit. I'm not going back for it. He can hope it's still here when he sobers up.

She grabbed his arm and pulled him, heading to her car, shoving him into it, starting it, and turning the heater on, then went back inside for his coat. She hoped he'd stay awake long enough to get into her off-campus apartment without help, then get some coffee down his throat.

He probably didn't need to study, not as much as she did, but he sure as hell didn't need to be drunk, either. Stupid fucker. Stupid in-lust-with-a-slut fucker. She wanted to kick him so badly it hurt.

Leaving him slumped sideways on her sofa, she warned him not to puke, then made coffee. Pulling out a huge salad bowl that had never seen lettuce, she put it in his lap, putting his arm around it, but it kept sliding off. Giving up, she put it at his feet. Coming back with the coffee she'd cooled with an ice cube, she held it under his nose until he twitched. He'll either drink it or—she put the bowl in his lap just in time and braced it there, trying not to spill the coffee as he jerked, heaving his guts out.

"Christ, Chess, why do you put up with me?" he slurred.

She took the bowl to the bathroom, dumped it, rinsed it, then went back to him. "Up. Shower. You reek. The coffee's in the bathroom, drink it while you're in there. Go." She pulled his arm, but it was like trying to hold onto a jellyfish and lift it, too.

He made it up and into the bathroom, where she had to take his clothes off while he clung to the towel rack. Starting the water in the large shower, she turned it to hot. Holding his hand, she led him in, and he leaned against the stall wall. Aiming the spray at him, he doubled over, heaving. She closed the sliding door, and he eased down, holding the wall and sitting on the built-in bench, the one she loved for shaving her legs. He kept heaving, but as far as she could tell, nothing was coming out. She put the lid down on the toilet and sat there waiting, hoping he wouldn't pass out.

Case finally stood, holding the wall with one hand and the opaque door with the other, then moved under the shower head. She pulled his phone out of her pocket. Tapping in his code to unlock it, she looked at his texts. The last one was from a guy they'd gone to school with in Seward. Wally. Chelsea recognized the rowdy bar behind Wally in the photo he'd sent. He was kissing the slut on the cheek, one hand on a breast, and some other guy was kissing her on her other side. Nice threesome, Chelsea thought, then tapped the slut's name to see what she'd sent to Case and quickly closed the app and put the phone down.

Jesus.

What's the point of sending a pic like that? He knows what it looks like. In Chelsea's opinion, there should be tattoos on her thighs, like the danger signs on highways. Warning—Heavy Traffic Entering.

Chelsea laughed to herself quietly, instead of screaming and throwing things, which was what she was aching to do. She hated the woman. Not because she was beautiful. That only generated resentment and envy while stabbing at her own body-shame.

No, she'd love to choke the bitch until her eyes popped for hurting Case.

My Case.

But first she was gonna choke *him.*

"Turn the water off. I can't let go of the wall," he said softly.

She slid the door open, reached in, and turned it off, then grabbed a towel from the shelf and started drying him off as he kept one hand on the wall, the other on her shoulder, his head hanging.

Leaning back on the sofa, wrapped in two large towels, sipping his second cup of coffee, he ate a few bites of the toast she'd put next to him. She looked up from the dining table a few feet away, whenever she turned a page, to check on him.

Eventually, he slumped. She stood up and went to her bedroom. Grabbing a pillow, comforter, and a fleece throw, she dropped them on the sofa, then worked on taking the damp towels off him. He barely moved. When she had him stretched out on his side, she layered the fleece and comforter over him, brushing his hair off his face tenderly, then kissed his forehead.

"I'm gonna choke you if you don't straighten yourself out, Case. I mean it," she whispered, running her hand over his shoulder, tucking the blankets around him snugly.

She started a fresh pot of coffee, then gathered his clothes. After tossing them and her own laundry into the washing machine and starting it, she poured a fresh cup of coffee for herself and went back to studying.

15

Hailing a cab at the airport in Anchorage on the first day of Christmas break, Chelsea took Case by the hand, opening the taxi door and nudging him in.

Exiting the cab in front of the garage of her family's Anchorage condo, she left him standing outside as she retrieved the keys to the SUV from the safe inside the garage. Backing out, hitting the button to close the garage door, she tapped the app and re-armed the house security as Case got in.

Neither of them said a word. The fit she'd had, finding him drunk again that morning, had split his eardrums, according to his resentful, drunken bitching. She'd told him to shut the fuck up and threatened to push him into the Nenana River. He'd have realized what a worthless threat it was if he'd been sober. The Nenana had been frozen solid for over a month, like everything else in Fairbanks.

She'd locked up his room, dragged him to the airport with her, charged his ticket to his credit card, gotten him through TSA, then bought tea for herself and coffee for him. He'd drunk it before boarding and slept through the entire flight.

Case sobered up enough to try to apologize as they left

85

Anchorage, but she told him she'd had enough and to shut up. He did, reclining his seat and going to sleep for the first hour. It wasn't until she topped Turnagain Pass that he put the seat up, and she spent the next hour telling him off, feeling better with every word she bit out as she drove down the winding, snow-packed road.

Driving straight to the address that Justin had texted when she'd messaged him, saying that she was bringing his drunken brother home, she put the car in park, saying, "Justin said he's house-sitting here."

Case looked at her, then the house, then at her again. "Turn the car off."

"No. Get out. I'm going home. My dad's waiting for me."

"Come in. Say hi. Turn the car off," he repeated.

"Out. I'm done with you. You can tell Justin I said hi."

But Justin had heard the car and was walking down the driveway, his shoulders hunched against the cold night air. Chelsea rolled the window down.

"He's all yours. Good luck. I need to get home."

"Thanks for bringing him. Come on in. We have coffee or tea..." he urged, looking at her rigid face as she shook her head. He walked to the other door and opened it, then reached down for his brother's arm as Chelsea pressed the seatbelt release.

"I'm sobered up, dammit. I can do this shit for myself. Chess—"

"Out."

"Fuck it." He stood, wobbly, and Justin reached for him, but he pulled his arm away. "I been sittin' on a plane or in a car for hours. Lemme go."

Justin bent down as he closed the door, quietly saying, "Thanks, Chelsea," but she wouldn't meet his eyes. The brothers stepped away, and she put the car in reverse, backing out of the snowy driveway and onto the street, changing gears, and driving away. He watched the taillights, then said, "Looks like you've totally ticked her off."

Justin led the way to the bedroom in the B&B that they'd picked for Case, then noticed that he wasn't carrying his duffel bag or backpack. I'll have to check at dad's house for clothes, he thought. But it had been years since Case had lived there. No, he'll have to wear mine, he decided, watching Case fall into the bed and curl up.

"Leave me alone. I didn't wanna come here. Fuckin' Chess dragged me," he mumbled, burying his head under a pillow.

Justin left his brother alone, bringing in a bowl of soup and cornbread and leaving it as Case slept. He and Ginny had found the homeowner's supply of alcohol and hid it, hoping Case wouldn't go looking for it or leave the house while they slept.

Ginny gave Justin a quick kiss, running a finger over his chin and stubble, then sat up, reaching for her pinging phone. Scooting back against the headboard, she read the message from Pete about Christmas dinner at his house, then she typed one out to Hattie and received a reply quickly.

GINNY

I can drop the pies with you or bring them to Pete's. LMK what's best

HATTIE

Plan on dinner at Pete's. Not sure what time yet, bring pies there, thx

GINNY

Ok. Case is here. Alone.

"Hattie wants to see Case, too," Ginny said.

"Ah, good luck with that. We'll be lucky to keep him sober."

"I'm gonna go make muffins, unless you want to make pancakes? I want him loaded with coffee and carbs." She slid out of bed and started pulling on sweatpants.

"Pancakes. He likes them better. I'll cook. Did you bring any of our blueberries here?"

She grinned. "I sure did. A full bag. It's in the freezer."

Ginny watched Case fidget, drinking only coffee, pushing the pancakes away. He had barely greeted her last night or this morning. Unshaven, for what looked like several days—his eyes were puffy and his skin had a tinge of yellow. He shot her an angry look that said *quit staring at me*, then looked away again, staring out the window. Ginny finished her pancakes, stealing glances at him, and at Justin's back as he cooked at the stove.

"I'm not going anywhere. Chess should have left me in Fairbanks."

Justin sat across the small kitchen table from his miserable brother, looking from Case to his untouched plate of pancakes and bacon, then to Ginny, who eased up and refilled all of their coffee cups, sitting down again very quietly. Might as well give him something to bitch about, Justin decided.

"I'm giving dad a hundred and thirty-three thou, and so is Mack, from Robbie's trust," Justin said, between bites, watching Case's chest expand. "His money paid for the premium on that policy," he added, digging his point in deeper. "It's only fair. Gin, these blueberries are the best, aren't they? God, I'm really glad we picked so many of them."

"You... are a fucking asshole," Case blew. He picked up the mug and went to the bedroom they'd shown him to last night. They were house-sitting at a bed-and-breakfast with four nicely furnished rooms in addition to the owner's suite. Ginny and Justin had peeked into all of the rooms but were sleeping in the smallest guest room because it had the best southern exposure. They'd put Case in the room next to theirs, so they could hear if he needed anything or if he left the room.

Justin grinned, eating the last of his breakfast, then leaned back in the comfortable kitchen chair.

"Why're you picking on him?"

"Because he needs to let it out, babe. The longer he stews, the worse he's gonna get. That's why he's drowning himself. No one to talk to. Or, really, no one to listen to him. Chelsea probably told him to shove it. I'm goin' to poke the bear," he said, getting up and putting his plate in the sink. "Leave his plate there. Maybe he'll eat later."

"It's only me." Justin closed the door and sat on the bed. Case was on his side, his head under the pillow, his body shaking.

"She said she loved me," he sobbed under the pillow.

Justin swung a knee up onto the bed, getting comfortable, and rubbed his brother's back.

"She fucked worthless Wally and some guy at the bar, too, the same day she said she wanted to come to Fairbanks to see me," he choked out. It took all of Justin's willpower to keep from saying that she'd have done it sooner or later.

16

The plan, by mutual agreement, was to split Christmas day with the boys at Hattie's when they awoke, then at Pete's by lunchtime. Ginny and Justin were looking forward to Hattie's waffles for breakfast, then heading to Pete's, where they'd left their presents for the kids and each other as well as the card for Pete that included the mortgage payoff, deposit slip, and an offer to help remodel.

In a quiet conversation over coffee at the kitchen island in the bed-and-breakfast where they were house-sitting, Justin vented his frustration. "I didn't realize how big a deal it was until now. I..." He shrugged, looking away.

"You want to be there. To see his face. I know. It's a big deal. You go," Gin suggested, moving to stand in front of him. "I'll stay here and babysit," she offered, melting into his sad eyes.

But that's only half of it, he thought, his love for her surging with her offer. Saying he was going to try one more time to talk Case into going, Justin took a mug of coffee with him and headed to the bedroom they'd put Case in.

He was back within minutes. "Nope, and I don't want to

leave him alone. He'll go to dinner; I talked him into that, but not now, not for the presents."

"I'll get Hattie to video it, without Pete knowing," Gin offered, holding her phone. She texted her request, saying they were hesitant to leave Case alone and were letting him sleep but would drag him to his dad's later for dinner.

With Ginny carrying pies, Justin opened the door at Pete's. She walked in quickly, putting them on the dining room table. She stepped back, watching Pete hug Justin, then wipe his eyes as they whispered quietly near the door. Case slumped into a dining room chair, elbows on the table, his head in his hands, while Ginny headed for the kitchen.

"God, I miss my buffet," Hattie said, looking at the food that filled the small kitchen table and every available space on the counters. "Let's, ah, put most of it on the dining table, on one side. We'll all sit on the other side, and I'll get Mack to put up the card table for the kids."

"Fair warning. Case has been crying and bitching all day," Ginny said quietly, her back to the kitchen doorway.

Hattie nodded, pursing her lips, then slumped like a deflated balloon. "Oh, the poor kid." She sighed heavily. "God knows we've all been there." Taking a deep breath and straightening up, she picked up two bowls to carry into the dining area. "I'll warn Mack not to bait him. We don't need to make things worse."

Gin suddenly remembered that when she'd started working for Mack, he'd been divorced. When she'd spied Mack kissing Hattie by his campfire, Justin hadn't believed her, saying they hated each other. She watched through the kitchen doorway as Hattie put the bowls down and leaned on Mack's shoulder, whispering to him. He nodded, then wrapped an arm around her and squeezed, like he was going to pull her onto his lap, and she laughed, wriggling away, giving his shoulder a push. It was probably like pushing one of the huge cottonwood rounds in his campfire circle, Ginny thought. Solid, heavy, and practically immoveable.

Pete, Mack, Justin, and Case were sitting in a row at the dining room table, looking at and commenting on photos in magazines Hattie had brought with her, leftover from her own kitchen remodel last year. She had also brought a binder of the designs she'd liked best, which lay open on the dining room table. She set the bowls down, flopped the binder closed, picked it up, and dropped it on the sofa as she came back into the kitchen for more food to bring out.

Settling the kids in the playroom after letting them play outside after dinner, Hattie started the promised Christmas movie for them, then went to help Ginny take the last bowls from their big Christmas dinner to the kitchen and pack leftovers into containers.

As soon as the women cleared the kitchen doorway with the last of their meal, Justin stood up from the dining table and walked around it. Sitting down on the opposite side, facing Case, his dad, and Mack, his look was deadly serious.

Most of dinner had been spent dealing with Case and his miserable remarks—like threatening to drop out of school or disagreeing with any of the suggestion about the remodel planned for Pete's house—and they were all sick of hearing it. Case and Mack were still bickering about windows. What should have been a happy discussion, with his dad celebrating unexpected financial security and a promise of help to update his home, had turned into an afternoon of irritating verbal jabs as Case vented.

Growling, Justin leaned in, closing the gap across the table, facing Case.

"Shut. Up."

Bodies jerked straight and two mouths dropped open while Pete's clamped shut as Justin rapidly poured out what he needed to say in the same low, forceful voice.

"I have a ring in my pocket, and before this night is over, I'm asking Gin a question I'm only ever gonna ask a woman *once* in my life. You," he stared at his brother, "I'm sorry for what you're going through, but starting right now, you better think about Ginny and no one else. *I mean it.* Dad," his voice softened, "you know I've been thinking about this for months." Pete nodded, his eyes wide. Justin's eyes met Mack's next, and his uncle jerked to attention.

"Gonna behave. I swear," Mack blurted out, and his hands went up as he grinned from ear to ear.

Justin leaned back, turned to look at the two women in the kitchen who were deep in their own conversation, then returned his gaze to the three men facing him—watching grins growing as their expressions changed. He stood up slowly and walked casually back to his chair, sitting down with ease.

Ginny popped her head into the open kitchen doorway a few minutes later. "We're cutting pie. Who wants what? Apple or strawberry-rhubarb. Yes or no for ice cream." Mack and then Pete answered, trying to smother grins, looking anywhere but at her. Justin beamed at her while he asked for strawberry-rhubarb, adding yes, for ice cream.

"They're all grinning like they stole something," she told Hattie as she cut pie and put slices on plates while Hattie loaded the dishwasher.

"Oh, Lord, I can't keep up. They've been bitching all through dinner. God only knows what they're up to now. I live in fear. Go ahead, take yours and Justin's. I've got the rest."

Serving the other three, then sitting down next to Mack, Hattie savored the first bite of pie, then realized her husband was staring at her. She put her fork down on the plate and returned his stare, which turned into a shit-eating grin. He pulled out his phone and started typing a note, angling it so she could read what he tapped out.

set your phone to video & keep it in your hand

She read it, looked at him curiously, then watched him erase it, open the camera app, then set the phone on the table in front of his right hand. He grinned again, raised his eyebrows for a moment, then continued to wolf down his pie and ice cream, smiling the whole time.

Ginny put her plate on the table, then settled into her chair heavily, sighing. She leaned into Justin, whispering. "I'm so glad everyone looks happy for a change. Do you mind if we leave after this? I'm tired. I just wanna curl up and watch a movie or something."

He looked at her closely and said, "Sure, babe. We can do that. Mack said they're leaving right after dessert. They want to make sure they get to the airport in case there're any issues on the roads."

Ginny helped Hattie clear the table of the dessert plates, piling them in the sink. The dishwasher was already running noisily, and Ginny touched Hattie's arm. "We're leaving now, too. I'm tired," she told her.

"Go ahead. I just want to check on the kids, then we're heading to the airport. Bags are in the car. I can't wait to get through security and relax with a glass of wine."

"I hope you have a great time," Ginny said, giving her a hug. "Merry Christmas. See you New Year's Eve." Gin went straight to the entryway and started pulling her boots on. Justin roused Case, shook his head at his dad, saying quietly, "Gin's tired. We're calling it a night. Merry Christmas," he added, with a half-hearted smile.

"Have a great time in the desert, man. I wish I could do it," he said to Mack's disappointed look, then headed for the door.

Pete checked the kids, sleeping peacefully, then the doors. Sitting at the small desk in his bedroom, he pulled out the notes and envelopes he used to pay Evie. He wrote a short note telling her about the remodel, thanking her, and saying that he wouldn't need her help at home anymore because of the construction and that he appreciated everything she'd done. He added extra cash, although he'd already left her a nice bonus for the holidays. Closing it, he wrote: I don't know how long it will take. Total destruction, from what I hear. I'm turning it all over to my brother and son. All the best, Pete.

17

Pete was the last one to arrive at work on Monday, which was unusual for him. With Hattie gone for the rest of the week, it would be just him and Connor, he thought, loping up the stairs. Ginny was working on editing video footage at home, where she and Justin were taking turns babysitting for the last few days of Christmas break.

Pete walked into the open office to see Tessa and Al chatting. When Al turned to greet him, Tessa looked at him in surprise, throwing her hands in the air. "P.E.N!" she exclaimed, rushing to Pete and throwing her arms around him, and Pete stopped, frozen, staring at Al, who was smiling and shaking his head.

"She's very happy to finally meet you," he explained, waving toward the conference room. "Get your coffee and join us when you're ready. Tessa will be updating us and helping with planning as we move forward to close the local hatchery and set goals for next year."

He stepped closer to Tessa. "Come, come," he urged her. She let go of Pete and bounced into the room, where she'd already unloaded her bag and scattered her pads and laptop.

Pete chose a seat opposite Tessa, putting down his mug, pad, and pen, easing into the seat as Al started introductions.

Tessa cut him off. "We've met," and Al turned a confused but polite look Pete's way. "I came in early one time. I was meeting you here, and he let me in," she blurted out before Pete could even open his mouth. "Enough social stuff, let's hit it."

She steamrolled through multiple examples of weirs and dams being removed along the west coast and in other countries, then started on hatcheries, listing the viruses they were known for incubating, throwing letters around like alphabet soup, and Pete scribbled like a maniac, gasping as she threw out numbers in the millions of fry being created and destroyed, transplanted to systems that were foreign to them, and worse.

If she went off tangent, and she frequently did—although the data was relevant and useful, Al gently brought her back with a short comment or question.

Pete's coffee cup stayed full and went cold, and he wondered which natural geyser she harvested her energy from, wishing he could tap it too but afraid he'd end up a weaving whirlwind like her.

She constantly blew her wavy hair out of her face, and Pete wanted to buy her a bucket of barrettes. Then he sat up straight as she nailed the issue. "So, that's why you have to ask, if they're bumping the numbers up to feed pollock and keep pink prices low, *was that the plan from the start?* Is that why they grouped so many critical returns together in one huge area—to keep everyone fighting among themselves instead of seeing the big picture and fighting the ocean-raping trawlers? And then," she bulldozed on, exclaiming, "there's the reds!" as if that made any sense.

Pete stopped writing and looked at her, then glanced

quickly at Al, then back at her, and she continued as if she were explaining it to a toddler.

"Reds cannot be treated like this. It's been proven over and over and over. They are not a hatchery stock, and they don't flourish when transplanted to foreign ecosystems. So, why do it? Why keep doing it? Why apply for loans, spend the money on worthless attempts, torture the fish, tell people it might work next time, year after year, decade after decade, when it *isn't* working? Why?"

Pete blinked.

"Because it muddies the waters! You think they're gonna accomplish something, and they never do!" She slapped the table as she finished, then said, "I need to pee," and stood up, bounding out of the room.

Al looked up from his notes and laughed quietly at Pete's mouth hanging open.

"She's a dynamo, no doubt about that, but she knows the issues better than any other person in this vast state, and she's a tremendous asset to us. She loves salmon as if they were her own children. The mistakes being repeated cut her to her soul."

Pete shut his mouth, took his first sip of the coffee and realized it was disgustingly cold. Watching Pete grimace, Al said, "Let's get up and refill and stretch for a few minutes, shall we?"

The rest of Pete's week was spent summarizing data and doing intense planning with Al. Tessa came in once a day, answered questions, flooded them with more facts and examples, then ricocheted off, leaving Pete's jaw on the floor every single time.

After babysitting the two energetic boys during the day and putting up with Case and his misery at night, Ginny was not looking forward to more of it tonight at Pete's, where they were all going for New Year's Eve.

"My turn to poke the bear," she said to Justin as they loaded the dishwasher after breakfast.

"Brave girl," he replied, hoping his brother knew better than to tear into Gin, no matter what she did. "I'll fire up the woodstove and make hot choc," Justin offered.

Ginny watched as Justin started the fire, adjusted the damper, then went back to the kitchen.

"Come sit on the floor where it's warm," she urged Case, who was slumped on the sofa. She leaned back against the loveseat, gazing into the glass front of the woodstove, watching the flames brighten as the logs caught fire.

Justin came into the living room carrying three mugs of hot chocolate, handing one to Gin. Standing in front of Case, he urged, "C'mon, get closer to the fire. It's chilly in here." Ginny sipped from her steaming mug, watching them both as Case shot him a look of *go the fuck away*, then pushed himself off the edge of the sofa, sliding down, sitting cross-legged on the floor, his head hanging. Justin set Case's mug on a nearby table.

"You know that Nell fooled Hattie and me too, right?" Ginny said.

Case tensed, studying her like a panther ready to pounce on its victim, waiting for the right second, holding back only long enough to determine where to bite first.

"We were impressed with her interview and her background, which was complete bullshit."

"Did she kiss you and whisper how wonderful you were in your ear?" he attacked, his voice raking like claws down flesh.

"*Case*," Justin warned, sending his brother a threatening look of his own.

Ginny continued as if Case hadn't opened his mouth. "We were so excited, so happy, to have found someone who fit everything we were looking for; even more than we'd hoped for."

Case kept his response to a sustained dirty look, jaw tight, nostrils flared, swollen eyes narrowed at her.

"I thought she was one of the most beautiful women I've ever seen up close. I loved the markings on her chin."

"They're fake too," he choked out, then put his head down, shaking. Ginny's eyes widened with surprise, her look turning to disgust. Another sham by a consummate con artist. She took a long drink of her hot chocolate then put the mug down, all while watching Case cry silently, reminding her of all the times kids had been dropped into foster homes she'd been in. Sympathy for his loneliness flushed through her. She scooted sideways across the floor toward him. Pulling his legs open, she twisted, backing up to him. He lifted his head only enough to put his forehead on her back, still sobbing heavily. She picked up each of his wrists and brought them around her waist, and he clenched her tightly, rocking her with his wracking convulsions as he let loose.

Justin watched them both, meeting Ginny's sad eyes as she looked over at him. They waited minutes for him to run down. Eventually he did, his breath coming in gasps instead of heaves.

"When you left for school, the year mom went to Mexico, I lost it completely," Justin said. Case's head came up, looking at his brother, his mouth hanging open in surprise, his face a bold mess of swelling and misery. His bloodshot and saturated eyes widened.

"She let me cry on her," Justin added. Case blinked at the

compassion in his twin's eyes as his ragged breathing began to even. He swallowed with difficulty.

"I soaked her shirt," Justin continued, and Case pulled back to see Ginny's top was wet where he'd had his head pressed against her.

Ginny's eyes met Justin's, and she smiled, her eyes full of love, her face urging him to continue. He met Case's eyes again.

"She took it off."

Case's eyes widened even more, and his lips twitched into a slight grin.

"Little sister, you tease!" he gasped hoarsely, hugging her. "What a way to ease a guy's pain." Holding Justin's eyes, he asked, "An' how'd that work out for ya?"

"She's here, isn't she?" he answered, then laughed.

"Oh, dear. Look what I've done to your top," Case croaked out. "You better take that off," he garbled, half-laughing, rubbing his face on her back.

"You wish," Justin cut him off, his voice deepening, "and keep your hands on her *waist*." He stood up. "I'll get a towel for him and a clean shirt for you, hon."

"Your technique is perfect," Case whispered hoarsely in her ear, hugging her. "I can almost see it. I feel more tears coming—"

"That's all you're gonna do, Romeo. Imagine it. And I think you're all cried out," she whispered back, smiling while she pushed his arms from under her breasts to her waist. He loosened his hold on her, resting his hands on her hips, leaning back against the sofa with a heavy sigh.

He nudged Ginny gently and she scooted back to her spot by the loveseat, then Case reached for his mug, drinking his hot chocolate, looking into the woodstove.

•   •   •

"Can I borrow your truck? Not to go get alcohol. I don't want to go to dad's empty handed," Case asked quietly. "I'm going to take a shower, then run a quick errand."

"You're not going looking—"

"No. I'm done. It's over."

Justin reached into his jeans pocket, pulling out his keys while holding his brother's gaze.

Case tapped his credit card to pay, and the clerk's eyes widened as he scanned the three bar codes. "Dude. You've either got three girlfriends, or you've been really bad."

Taking the three bundles of long-stemmed red roses in one arm while sliding his wallet back into his pocket, Case replied, "Three sweethearts. And I've been an asshole. But I'm gonna make up for it." He grinned at the astonished clerk as he walked out of the store.

Sitting in Justin's truck, he wrote a short message on each of the cards, then put two of the bouquets in the back seat of the truck, wrapping them in a blanket Justin kept there.

Parked in the driveway of the B&B, he took the last bundle of roses into the house, found a vase and clipped the stems. Pulling off wilted petals and leaves, he arranged them. After adding water, he hid the vase in one of the unused bedrooms.

18

Case pulled out his phone, holding it under his dad's dining room table, texting Chelsea.

CASE

> Thank you for taking care of me. You're the best

CHELSEA

You're welcome. You're still at the top of my shit list

CASE

> Take me back to FBKS with you tmrw?

> Please

CHELSEA

I'm leaving early. You better be sober

CASE

> What are you doing tonight?

CHELSEA

Not much

Case stood up, looking first at Justin, then at his dad. Conversations slowed and stopped. "I'm sorry I've been such a pain in the ass. I didn't even buy presents..." he held his hands out, hanging his head, then looked at his dad. "But I went to the bank today and deposited my share into your bank account. I should have done it sooner," he finished quietly. He watched the smile grow on his dad's face—his eyes filled with admiration and pride. But it was the respect in Mack's eyes that surprised him. Hattie's look clearly said *I knew you'd do the right thing*, and his brother and Ginny were grinning with satisfaction.

Pete started to rise, but Case held up a hand. "Now, I *hope* that gets me a vote in the remodel." He barely suppressed a smile, and everyone started talking again, insisting their plan was best, with far more playful comments as the accumulated tensions eased into delight and relief.

"Is that what you two were smiling about before?" Ginny asked Justin, twisting to look at him.

"Yeah. Now he's just being a show-off about it. He's almost back to normal." His eyes shone as he pushed some of her curly hair off her forehead, then kissed it, thinking that what he and Case had been smiling about was Justin's quiet comment that he had the ring in his pocket again, hoping for the right moment.

Listening for it, Case heard the timid knock on the door and stood up quickly to let Chelsea in. Introducing her to everyone as Chessy, he slid a chair in between his and Justin's, and everyone readjusted to make space for her. Hattie brought in several more slices of pie, two of which were quickly grabbed by Mack and Justin.

Pete and Mack took turns getting up for something to drink. The lively conversation continued around countertop surfaces, with Chelsea adding her preference for a large wooden built-in cutting surface. The new idea elicited even more comments from everyone as they chatted, coming and going from the kitchen, helping themselves to food and drinks.

Ginny's eyes widened. "Oh, shit, shit, shit," she gasped quietly, looking down.

"What's wrong?" Justin whispered, turning away from the ongoing discussion of countertop materials.

"My period just started," she said, leaning close to him, whispering, "Dammit!" She groaned, "Of all the worst times. I gotta run." She got up from the table quickly, hoping the damage wasn't as bad as it felt. Going through the kitchen, into the hallway, she headed for the bathroom, surprised to see the door closed. Knocking quickly, she heard a female voice say, "One sec." The sounds of flushing, water running, made Ginny murmur, "Hurry, please," as both a prayer and a psychic push. The door opened and Ginny rushed in, expecting Hattie, who she could ask for help. Chelsea stepped back, recognizing urgency, then shut the door quickly.

"Oh, I'm sorry. I thought it was Hattie in here," Ginny said, her eyes darting to the small cupboard below the sink, knowing she'd taken all her supplies with her, hoping for a miracle.

"Emergency?" Chelsea asked, watching Ginny get down on her knees, holding the countertop with one hand, the other searching the cupboard. Her head hung, and Chelsea felt bad for her. "I have stuff in my bag..." she offered, and her heart melted looking into Ginny's eyes. Embarrassment, maybe a hint of shame. Chelsea hated that women felt that way. She put her hand on Ginny's on the counter as Ginny stayed kneeling, probably scared to stand up again. "Be right back. One sec." She eased out of the door and closed it, then went to her oversized purse in the entryway, groped through it, stuffed her pockets, and made a beeline back to the bathroom, entering while tapping on the door.

Chelsea emptied her pockets on the counter. "Take your pick. I always travel fully stocked."

"God, you're a lifesaver. I, ah, I'm gonna have to change." Ginny looked aside, obviously very embarrassed, and Chelsea took over.

"Is it shower-bad?"

Ginny nodded, looking for the robe she sometimes left hanging in the bathroom. No such luck. "I feel like I'm gonna flood the bathroom," Gin admitted quietly.

"Got any clothes here?"

Ginny tipped her head. "In the bedroom there."

"Got it. Don't wait. Get in there. Toss the clothes in the sink here, and I'll fill it with cold water." Seeing her hesitation, Chelsea added. "Been there, done that. Seriously. Girls gotta look out for each other, right? Get in and toss," she pulled the shower curtain back, then left the bathroom, closing the door quietly. Heading into the bedroom, she went straight to the closet.

Not a single dress.

She's so cute—why no dresses?

Chelsea pulled out the top drawer of the lone dresser. Justin's tee shirts. She continued through the drawers, finally finding Ginny's panties and some sweat pants. Taking one of each and one of Justin's T-shirts, she went back into the bathroom.

Settled comfortably on the sofa, the guys still discussing

remodeling ideas at the dining table while Hattie put the kids to bed, Chelsea leaned into a newly outfitted Ginny and said, "All Case has ever said is that Justin has a girlfriend." She was hoping for more details, and she watched Ginny blush. "How'd you meet him? And when?"

Ginny told her about being a deckhand for Mack, coming back the next season, then deciding to stay in Alaska. Chelsea listened, completely enthralled, asking a few questions as they talked, saying she loved Vermont when Ginny said she'd grown up there.

They went off on a tangent of places and travel. Then Ginny mentioned the season that Justin took over the boat and Case came back as skiffman.

"Right. He was working at the weir—hey! That's where I recognize you from. Man, it's been driving me nuts! The weir. I was there too, doing paperwork."

"No way. That was such a blur. I was worried about making any money that season, and Mack was so pissed off about the enhancement stuff—"

"Yeah, the shit they pull. Don't get me started. I don't blame him. So, you worked on Pete's boat, then stayed on when Justin bought it? You stayed the winter last year?"

Listening to Ginny, Chelsea was loving getting to know someone who didn't try to show off or put her down or worse —slide in cruel digs about her weight or how *unfortunately* skinny they were, wishing they could gain two pounds.

"I stayed working Mack's boat. Justin had Ben and Greg, same as the year before. Yeah, my first winter here was last year. It was as long as everyone warned me it would be," she laughed, visibly relaxing, which made Chelsea more at ease. They'd turned toward each other more as they'd chatted and were now facing each other, cross-legged.

Instead of looking over her shoulder, Ginny looked straight at Chelsea, smiling most of the time. Most women didn't even make eye contact when talking to Chelsea, never mind gossip with her. It didn't help that she'd always been a bit of a loner.

"How do you know them? From school in Fairbanks?" Ginny asked.

"Oh, no. We went to school together here. They're a year behind me."

Ginny's eyebrows rose. "No way. Me too."

Chelsea perked up, leaned closer, languidly lifted a hand, and gently pushed Ginny's shoulder. "Cradle robber."

They stared into each other's eyes and laughed like idiots.

"Jesus," Case mumbled, watching the two women on the sofa as they practically levitated, laughing and talking over each other. He was tired of arguing about floors and counter-tops, and his head was pounding.

"They're laughing at you, you know. Just sayin'. It's what they do. That's how they make friends with each other," Mack observed cheerfully.

"Asshole," Case shot back under his breath, putting his head on the table, groaning, while Mack laughed loudly.

Hattie came out of the kitchen carrying glasses and a bottle, then quickly retrieved the rest of the glasses needed, setting them on the dining table. Mack stood up and joined her, opening the bottle and pouring the bubbly, telling her, "You're gonna have to gaff those girls. They've been jabbering non-stop. I think they're glued together now."

Mack sent a questioning look to Justin, who was standing on the other side of Hattie, picking up two full glasses. Justin shook his head and whispered, "Another time," then brought glasses to Ginny and Chelsea.

Hattie organized everyone into a circle, and Case wormed himself between Justin and Chelsea, with Ginny on the other side of Justin. They held up their glasses and toasted, watching the countdown on TV, clinking glasses, singing out, "Happy New Year" while hugging whoever was beside them.

Mack and Hattie left first, right after the toast, saying their travel had worn them out, and they were looking forward to a night home in their own bed. Bundled up, Hattie aimed for the passenger side, letting Mack drive home. She reached in to put her purse on the floor and was stunned to see a bouquet of red roses on her seat. Mack slid in, shut the door, and turned to buckle up. "Where'd those come from? You got a boyfriend I don't know about?"

She climbed in, putting the roses on her lap, and shut her door. "Not you?"

He shook his head and started the car, and she flipped on a light to look for a card.

I love you. No signature.

"Hmmmm. I guess I do," she murmured, admiring them on the drive home.

Chelsea shared her contact info with Ginny, then headed for the door, and Case intercepted her. "Don't forget me, Chess," he whispered, watching her anxiously.

"I'll never forget you," she answered quietly, not meeting his eyes. She pulled on her heavy coat and left him staring at the door as she walked out.

Justin hugged his dad and whispered, "Bad timing. Talk to you later," then went for his coat, handing Ginny hers, telling Case to put his on.

Justin lay in bed, trying to place the noise that woke him up, when the noisy coffeemaker in the kitchen blew off another blast of steam. Easing out of bed, listening to Ginny's steady breathing, he pulled on sweats and left the bedroom quietly. "Hey," he said, coming into the kitchen.

Standing by the window and watching the driveway, Case turned, sipping coffee. "Tell Gin thanks for me. Chess'll be here any second."

Justin took his travel mug from the dish drainer, poured coffee into it, pressed the lid on, and handed it to his brother. "Take that with you. I never did ask about school."

"Double load. I'm done in May. Wish me luck; I'm not goin' back."

"Jesus."

"Yeah. She's here." Case put both mugs on the table and held out his arms, hugging his brother. "Thanks. I owe you." He turned quickly, grabbed the tall mug, opened the door, and walked out.

Justin moved into the doorway and watched as Case climbed into the passenger seat and buckled up, waving as Chelsea backed out of the driveway, turned, and drove away.

Again, Justin watched half of himself leave, feeling empty and alone. So many conversations he'd wanted to have. He desperately wanted to reach out and pull Case back. Easing the door closed, he turned to finish Case's cup of coffee and stopped.

Ginny stood in the kitchen doorway in her pajamas, holding a red rose, smiling. Running to him, she threw her arms around him, gushing, "Thank you! They're so beautiful! No one's ever bought me roses before."

She kissed his neck and played with his earlobe while running a hand over his bare chest, whispering, "Come back to bed."

19

February

Dropped off at the office by Justin on Monday morning, Ginny walked upstairs to work, smiling the entire way. She asked Connor about his long weekend, listening to him describe the weather he had to put up with while trying to get back to the village, which had culminated in a skiff ride from hell.

Smiling at Hattie, Ginny went into the interview room and unpacked her laptop and hard drives. She was ready to show Hattie and Al the first of the videos they'd been waiting for and introduce another project she'd been compelled to start after listening to Pete over dinner as he'd reminisced about growing up fishing with his dad. Moving her laptop to the conference room, she finished making the necessary connections as everyone gathered around the table.

"Let's go around the circle, shall we? Starting with you, Connor?" Al opened.

"Sure. Ginny helped clean up my mailing list, and that gave me time to expand our newsletter. I included a lot of upcoming nearby events and a list of save-the-date things. I'm going to learn to use one of the email services next and switch from PDF to a more flowable format. I understand that they give you the metrics to see how people are reading, and I'm really interested in knowing how many readers use phones and tablets for looking at our newsletter."

"Very nice."

"Thanks. My goal is to have a new service going by June."

"Perfect, thank you. Hattie? The videos?" Al looked at Ginny too.

"Ginny's been editing them and then uploading them so that only I can view them, and then she edits to a final version. She can tell you more about that, and when she's done, we have a proposal to talk about. Right now," Hattie clicked the power button on the TV remote, "I want to show you the first one."

She pressed play on the paused video, and Connor stood up and turned the lights off in the room. A video started of an elder sharing her memories. Small photos rolled over the screen as she spoke, some with transitions to a second camera for close-ups on her hands and some with transitions to clips taken outside somewhere. Each of the photos and short clips inset into the video related to topics the woman spoke about.

Hattie turned the power off, and Connor got the lights again. She looked around the room for reactions, asking, "Likes? Dislikes? Changes you'd make?"

"Wow," Connor said, smiling.

"What's the wow, Connor?" Al asked, but Connor shrugged. "Think on it. What's so unusual?"

"It was like sitting in the village. Like we were right there. The clips of the things she was talking about, and the things she picked up. Her hands. That's what I'd be looking at if I were talking to her, not looking into her eyes. She hardly ever looked right at the camera. And her words. In our language. I liked that you showed the word on the screen as she said it, then paused. That's good."

Al swung around, gazing at Hattie. "I think you nailed it."

"Thanks. We figured out that the cameras were making people uncomfortable, so Ginny and I hid them behind art in the room. One's behind a dream-catcher. I wanted two views, but I never thought of their hands until I tried to do close-ups. Then we mounted a camera above, but at an angle, to capture their hands and the things they held. We had all kinds of things on the table for them to touch. Ginny did the zooming in and, of course, swapping views as she edited."

"I'm impressed. How many are finished, like that one?"

Ginny answered, "Only that one so far, to be sure we're on the right track. But I have clips ready for the rest. The files are organized by each person's name, and all the graphics, intro, outro, are done and will stay the same. I've even started numbering the clips and photos, so I know where I want to drop them in as I edit. I think I can have the rest in two months, hopefully."

"Very nice. That grant's good through the end of April. You said you had a proposal?"

"Yes," Ginny said, and Hattie powered up the TV and forwarded the clip to the spot Ginny had asked for when they'd discussed doing this presentation. "Don't bother with the lights, Connor. This is short." Hattie pressed play, and they watched the clip, then she stopped it.

"That part—about how they used to fish and store it and relied on it year-round. There are parts like that in every single story. I'd like to put those clips together and maybe, I dunno, use that for the battle to get things back to the way they were for the salmon?"

"I love it," Al said, sitting up straight. "In fact," he paused again, bringing his fingers together, then continued, "I want more."

Hattie smiled and leaned forward. "I was hoping you'd say that. I'm ready to start interviewing again."

"Let me do this first..." he sat thinking for a moment, his fingers steepled. "Let's work on some specific questions. I want a day or two to think this over. This is excellent. Ginny, you managed to do all that prep-work and put together that video while alternating working here and working at home?" She nodded. "Feel free to work anywhere you want. If there's anything you need, let me know. Those clips may be the most impactful thing to push our agenda to completion this year, especially when they speak to the abundance they grew up with that we no longer see. Thank you both."

"Now, Pete. What do you need as we get closer to closing the hatchery? I'm working on those presentations," Al started.

"And I've got the reports. The more I meet with Tessa, the bigger the database grows, but I'm working on pulling out the most impactful data for you," Pete replied.

"Every analysis you send me helps so much. So, for my own update," Al said, looking around the room. "Now that the weir's demolished, we will be monitoring the stream and ladder, coordinating with the local stream-watcher organization. That's all in place for summer, and it includes five streams. We are committed to protecting all species, not just sockeyes. That means the number one priority now—taking on the gorilla—is getting the old hatchery closed down. I'll be doing more traveling, and we'll be hiring another intern by summer. Last, I'm still working with the seiner association and the state to split the area and end the tax on them that supports the enhancement program. I truly hope to have a resolution to those issues before this summer's commercial fishing season begins."

20

After weeks of measuring and drafting drawings of exact room sizes, wall lengths, and window heights and then tearing out pages of magazines to show ideas to his dad, with the cost of materials factored in—and everyone's opinions weighed—Justin was ready for Mack to arrive and demolition to start.

The kids wouldn't be coming to Pete's for weekends during the construction, and he and Ginny were done house-sitting for at least a month. He was glad to be home.

Sitting at the dining table, organizing pages, condensing his notes of questions for Mack, he started a separate list for his dad and then listed the stuff that everyone seemed to want to put their two cents in on but didn't agree on. The back-splash, of all things, was the one thing no one agreed upon. He wrote *dad* next to it on the list.

Leaning back, Justin finished the dregs of his coffee, looking around the combined living-dining room. He could clearly see what Hattie kept pressing: the kitchen was far too small, the living room too large. With the dining area between them, it was going to be construction dominoes. Make the living room smaller first by moving the dining area further into it. Expand the arctic entry—which was also too small— then they could start expanding and updating the kitchen, creating a better flow into the dining area.

With nothing to keep his mind on the job, it easily slipped off to other issues. It was February already, and he still hadn't proposed yet. He shook his head.

Unbelievable.

He'd put the ring back in his dad's safe that morning. Maybe they could manage to get away somewhere this winter. In March? On a beach? No. It would break Hattie's heart to not be close by. She was practically a mother to Gin, and who knows, Gin might want her—need her nearby, especially if she was unsure about marriage. She has strong opinions on religion, and they may carry over to marriage for all he knew. Better make it early-to-middle of the month, too, he decided, smiling as he remembered New Year's Eve.

He'd hoped to run his ideas about what Gabe was trying to do by his brother, but that hadn't worked out either. Case hadn't been able to see past his own misery the entire time he'd been home. He was lucky to have Ginny to talk to, and he'd loved having her working from home on and off over the past several weeks. They'd had lunch together, shared taking care of the kids, and a couple of times... He squirmed.

Mind on work, he reminded himself.

To be able to hold her every night, whispering whatever they wanted to talk about while touching each other, still learning what each of them... He stood up quickly and started to pace.

Work, dammit!

He picked up the mug and took it to the kitchen sink.

Mack came into the house, tossing his coat, shucking snow-covered boots, then rubbing his hands together, saying, "Let's get this demo started."

They went over Justin's plans, then started moving furniture, with Mack wanting an update on his potential tender purchase.

"I'm still balancing that against that private label idea, going direct to market," Justin replied. "Gabe had a good point on our last Zoom call. He said there's plenty of seiners and enough tenders—and to keep in mind that the canneries still call the shots with both. The real holdup, like when we get put on limits, is processing capacity."

"Huh," Mack grunted as they shoved the sofa against the far wall, after moving all the stuff that had lined it. Bookcases, recliner, and end tables were all going into the playroom for now; Justin had cleared space for them in there that morning. "So, you fishing this summer?"

"Looks like it. I don't think it's all going to come together before summer. Gabe's trying, though. His plans are good. Start small and grow, look for ways to partner with other businesses, stuff like that."

They moved the TV and its stand to Pete's bedroom, then took the dining table apart, stacking it and the chairs in the playroom. Moving the small kitchen table to the living room was a challenge. Angling it through the narrow doorway that everyone hated, they put it where the dining table had been, then added chairs around it.

Mack was peering into the arctic entryway. "Should we leave this for last? It's friggin' cold out there."

"Maybe. Let's get some of the clutter out." Justin pulled down coats that hadn't fit him, Case, or Robbie in years. He saved the smaller ones to see if they'd fit Mickey, then piled the rest. He'd wash them, then pack them away for the younger boys as they grew. Boots were examined for the same reason and tossed or relocated. A laundry basket was filled with hats, gloves, and anything else left in the small space.

Coming across a coat and scarf of his mother's had

Justin's throat swelling. He lay them carefully over one arm and quietly said, "I'll hang these up." Heading into his dad's bedroom, he slid the closet doors, expecting his mother's side to be empty. It was as full as if she were still there. He found hangers, hung the coat and jacket, and went back to the entry.

"Jeeze. Maybe all it really needed was a cleaning," Mack said. "Make a note to replace that shitty fixture."

"Already did."

"The whole door and frame needs replacing. This window doesn't do any good at all, either," Mack kept going, looking the small room over.

"Yeah, but Ginny mentioned that this might be good for cold storage. Potatoes, cabbage, stuff like that."

"She gonna start a garden? Women! They always want stuff like that. Hattie wants a friggin' greenhouse now, dammit."

Justin laughed. "It never ends."

"Keep laughing," he said sarcastically. "You're next. And what the hell's taking so long?"

"Ah, issues. Case made it pretty miserable over the holidays. Gin was tired. Shit happens. We'll get there. So, next, let's empty the cabinets on that kitchen wall, then take the hideous things down. Ginny started emptying them a week ago. Let's go see how far she got."

"I still like the tender idea," Mack said as they moved to the kitchen. "A tender-processor, maybe?"

Looking at light fixtures online that night, yet another notice popped up from the DNA service they'd used last year, and Justin hit delete. He'd jumped down that rabbit hole one day, finding people with a one percent connection. Ginny came into the bedroom with a load of laundry, and he asked, "Do you get all these DNA relative emails?"

"Nope, I opted out after I kept getting too many of them," she said, folding clothes. "I can't wait for the laundry room remodel," she teased.

"Yeah, work, work, work," he mumbled, hiding a smile, hoping she'd feel sorry for him.

She laughed. "Poor you. You're not the one doing the laundry."

He swung in his chair, ready to make another remark, then stopped. "Hey. What if there really are relatives? I mean, like, you might have family you don't even know about."

"Nope. I have everyone I need right here," she said, leaning down to kiss him before hanging a few of his shirts.

"But, wait, what if it's possible—"

"No. Seriously. I am absolutely not interested," she interrupted, then left the room.

He stood up and stretched, then looked at the laundry basket and piles of folded clothes on the bed. All his. Where were her things? He looked at the closet, knowing it held mostly his clothes, then the dresser, which had three drawers full of his clothes. They'd talked about buying another dresser, but she'd fit her things into the two drawers he'd cleared.

She needs more clothes.

He'd noticed how little she had last year, then forgot about it, until the roses had shown up. Case must have done it when he'd borrowed the truck. He'd gone to the bank, and must have bought the roses then. All the card had said was, "I love you", and Gin had assumed they were from Justin.

Justin had felt guilty ever since, thinking about how little he'd done to bring Gin into his arms and his life. He'd never even asked her out on a date. The only time they'd gone out to dinner was in Seattle, at the boat show. And now, looking around, he noticed that she barely had any clothes.

I should have taken her shopping in Seattle. Or even Anchorage, when we bought furniture. Maybe we should go for a weekend?

21

The pace of construction felt like a game of hurry up and wait. When Justin complained about it to Mack one frustrating morning, Mack had laughed until he'd had to sit down. Justin tried to order products needed and pick them up or have them delivered together, but it seemed that they were always missing some tool or component that brought their efforts to a halt. Then they'd shift focus, working in another area, waiting, leaving something half-done until the needed item arrived.

For Ginny, the weeks flew by. Al was in and out sporadically; his updates after each trip were exciting, and she and Pete often talked about them with Justin after work. She loved playing in the snow with the boys, offering to babysit, then taking them to the playground or the shore.

The house-sitting gigs were fewer now that the holidays were over. Pete settled into the routine of navigating a torn-up kitchen, perpetual sawdust on everything, and kids banging tools when they could get their hands on them during the rare times they came over to play and see the work being done. He particularly loved sharing the cooking, with Justin and Ginny taking turns whenever they were home.

Justin didn't plan anything for Valentine's Day, grateful to be at yet another short house-sitting gig—only a long weekend —so that his dad wouldn't be reminded of his single status. He bought Gin roses and daisies in what should have looked like an odd bouquet, but she loved it. She experimented with a recipe, making chocolate muffins that he swore made him gain five pounds by the end of the weekend. Then he'd squished her under him to prove how heavy he'd become.

"Muscles from building stuff," she'd laughed and wheezed, trying to push him off—completely unable to because she was giggling, and teasing him while she ran her hands over those muscles.

~

CHELSEA

I'm going to my dad's house in Lake Havasu, AZ for spring break. You & J want to come? Dad's gonna be gone on a business trip, mom's in Italy, house to ourselves. Case says he's staying at school, finishing up two projects.

Ginny read the text, then asked Hattie about Arizona on their lunchtime walk. They were experiencing a chinook, and the warm wind had melted all the snow downtown. It was hard to believe it was almost March.

Hattie told her about her trips to Arizona, her hesitation about using Mack's little camper and then how much fun they'd had and how relaxing it had been. She'd go back again in a second if she could, she finished. Ginny sent Chelsea a reply saying she'd ask Justin tonight, and Chelsea replied that if they wanted to go, to let her know before buying tickets.

. . .

She brought it up at dinner. "Chelsea sent me a text inviting us to Arizona over spring break. Her parents have a house in Havasu, she said, and they'll be gone traveling."

Justin stared off, thinking, then focused on her. "You wanna go? I was thinking about asking if you wanted to take a week and go somewhere warm."

"You should go," Pete interjected. "It's relaxing there, out in the desert. You can use my camper if you want to. It's parked at Mack's, about an hour's drive north of Havasu."

Ginny laughed. "Relaxing. That's what Hattie said. And Viv loves it there, too. I still think it looks like Mars."

"It's warm. After months of cold, snow, and ice, I'm all for it," Justin said, "but tickets are going to be outrageous over spring break. Lemme look after dinner."

"Okay. She said something about letting her know before we buy tickets. Maybe she wants us all on the same flight," she speculated, smiling at the thought.

Justin watched Ginny clear the table and take the dishes to the kitchen. He heard her loading the dishwasher, then putting away the leftovers. She has no idea, he thought, how much money Chelsea's family has, or that Chelsea would probably either buy the tickets or ask her dad to charter a private plane. He'd look at what main cabin rates were, then say yes to going, no matter what the price, and book them. "Ask her what flight she wants and tell her we'll book tonight," he called out over the noise of the dishwasher.

Ginny's face lit up, and she took off running for their bedroom and her laptop, where she could type messages easier.

"Guess that's a yes," Pete said, getting up from the table. "So, what do you need me to do here? You and Mack are sure making quick work of the demolition," Pete said, looking at the bare framing of his kitchen.

"We want to move appliances next and see how you like it. Now that it's more open, we're wondering if leaving the fridge where it is might be a bad idea."

"Let's go see. Where do you guys—do you even agree where it should go?"

"I'll show you what we both think," he answered, following Pete into the kitchen.

GINNY

Justin said yes. Tell us your flight info and we'll book. I'm sure I can get the time off work. I'm way ahead on my projects.

The reply came back almost instantly.

CHELSEA

Awesome. Tell J I've got the tickets handled. Be at the airport in Anch on March 14th, before 10 a.m. Earlier is better. See you then!

Ginny tracked Justin down in the kitchen, telling him what Chelsea had texted, then listened as Pete debated aloud about the location of the refrigerator and new pantry. He asked her opinion.

"I like it where it is," she said. "If you put it over in that corner, the door won't open all the way, and the fridge is the one thing everyone's into the most. I think it should be the easiest thing to get to, not at the back of the room."

Justin disagreed, saying it stuck out too far and took up too much floor space.

"It is big," Pete agreed. "Are we updating it? It's only about seven years old..."

"Not in the plans," Justin said, "but that could change, and the next one might be even bigger."

"No. Buy a smaller one," Ginny said. "You don't need a monstrosity—"

"But the boys will be getting bigger," Justin interrupted. "That's what lead to this one. My mom couldn't keep enough food in the fridge for us. She complained about having to go shopping almost every day," he finished, looking at Pete.

Pete remembered those nagging conversations quite well and changed the subject. "You guys are house-sitting this week, right?" He looked from a doubtful face to a stubborn one. "So, look at the place you're going to, and if you have photos of the places you've stayed, look at them, too. See how close the fridges are to doorways and corners, okay? Let's leave it for now. Can we do that?" he asked Justin.

"Yeah, I think we can pass on it for now. We'll work on moving the stove and then figuring out the cupboards around it next," Justin said.

"We're meeting the Taylors tomorrow afternoon to see their house and get the info on their pets," Ginny added. "We'll be back Sunday night. I think Justin has all the pics of the other places we've stayed, but I can make copies for you to look at."

Pete parked his shopping cart next to the apples, then looked for the vegetables on the list Ginny had made for him. He wanted to try making the jambalaya recipe she said she'd gotten from Viv. He loved it and had offered to make it when they came back from house-sitting Sunday night. Celery, onion, peppers—

"Pete! Long time, no see," Evie said, reaching in front of

him. He could smell her hair, and it instantly reminded him of their last time together.

He smiled. "It is. How are you? My kitchen is so torn up for remodeling, I'm lucky to be able to cook right now."

"Wow, how nice, though. A brand-new kitchen! I kinda miss cleaning up after you, especially after you cooked salmon," she said, holding a cucumber, brushing against him.

"Ah, that always makes such a mess," he said apologetically.

"Oh, it was worth it. Especially if there were any leftovers in the fridge. I confess, I had some once. It was divine," she said, smiling, moving a tiny bit closer.

"I never knew you liked it or I'd have cooked it more," he said, enjoying looking at her.

"Oh, I loved it," she gushed, and Pete suddenly wondered if they were still talking about his cooking.

"I, ah, would, I mean, I could cook it for you—"

"Oh my God, really? I have a night off. The kids are going to a slumber party on Thursday night. No school Friday."

"That could work," Pete said, his smile growing.

"Your kids?"

"Staying at Hattie's because of the construction mess. Justin and Gin are house-sitting through the weekend."

Evie ran her hand down Pete's arm, stopping at his hand on his cart. "Sounds like a date," she said, moving closer to him, whispering, "I can hardly wait." She backed away slowly, and Pete watched her take her cart and walk up the aisle.

"You made salmon!" Evie exclaimed as Pete opened the door. "Oh, my goodness, what a treat!" She kept going, peeling her coat off and toeing her boots off at the same time. "You're spoiling me," she whispered, wrapping an arm around him quickly, and he encircled her, kissing her thoroughly.

"Dinner's ready," he said, coming up for air.

"How about dessert? Is that ready, too?" Her eyes urged him to say yes, while one hand smoothed over his chest, the other reaching up into his hair. Pete groaned as the hand on his chest eased lower.

"Yes," he gasped, his mouth on hers again. She nudged him backward, and he pulled her waist, glad he'd cleared a path through the sawhorses and piles of cabinets.

"Oh, God," Evie exhaled, "I needed that," and then she laughed. Stroking Pete's arm absently, breathing deeply.

"If you keep that up, we'll be starting round two soon," Pete teased her, but her phone beeped before she could reply.

"Dammit!" She groped for it and knocked Pete's watch onto the floor. "Sorry. Why'd you take that off?" she asked, looking at her phone, tapping the unlock code.

"I, ah, don't want any surprises recorded. Hattie checks it sometimes, to see if I've had any heart events I might not have noticed," he said, sitting up and reaching to the floor. He felt his heart flutter a bit and hoped it would pass quickly. He lay back down slowly, on his right side, and saw the message she was reading.

CAROLE

Need you to pick up Evan and Erik asap.
Things are NOT going well

Evie put the phone on silent mode and put it back on the nightstand, leaning over Pete to do it, then slid her hand down his side.

"Maybe we should call it a night?" he suggested.

"Not a chance. Once was not enough. She can tough it out. It's a slumber party for goodness sake. There are bound to be little pissy fits." She lowered her head and kissed him, but Pete heard her phone vibrate with another incoming message.

Pete eased her away gently, then reached for the phone. The message popped up as he held it, but she leaned over him quickly, grabbing it from his hand. "I'll turn the damned thing off," she muttered.

"That sounds serious. I only saw part of it, but if they're threatening to call child services—"

"No-frigging-body is calling any frigging services," she gritted out, getting out of bed. "Good Lord, I can't get one damned night to myself," she ranted under her breath. She continued to vent as she tossed the phone on the bed and pulled her hastily discarded clothes on.

Pete watched her warily, waiting for her to use the bathroom before getting out of bed and dressing quickly.

22

The Taylor's house was an older one, not far from where Hattie had leased a house a couple of years ago—the one Ginny had moved into after her second season fishing with Mack.

Justin pushed away the memory of the issues he'd had with her living there, trying not to let that ruin his mood. They both loved having a place to themselves, and the Taylor's was close enough to the downtown area that Gin could walk to and from work if she wanted to.

Out of all the places they'd been house-sitting, it had the smallest kitchen he'd been in yet. A U shape, it fit one person only, and when the dishwasher or fridge door was opened, it practically hit the appliance opposite. Justin hated it and said so as he made spaghetti.

They sat on the sofa after dinner, the three cats circling the room haughtily, asserting their offense at being ignored by both Ginny and Justin. Looking through photos on their phone of other places they'd stayed, they were back to discussing kitchen layouts. Justin texted a photo of the Taylor kitchen to his dad, who replied that he didn't feel so bad about his own now.

"Gin, did you cook much, growing up?" Justin asked.

"Nope. Peeled potatoes and carrots, stuff like that, mostly."

"Soups?"

She looked up from her phone where she'd found a kitchen design she'd really liked. "Yeah, soups, stews. Look at this one." She handed him her phone, then stood up and picked up one of the strutting cats that had decided to strop itself on her leg.

"What do you like about this one?" he asked, noting again that any question about her past was instantly deflected. He couldn't decide if it was deliberate on her part or just not an interesting enough subject each time.

"The counter space around the stove." She put the cat down and sat next to him, leaning over, and he wrapped his arm around her.

"It is pretty good sized," he said.

"That's what your dad's kitchen needs. Like, when we have big dinners there, there's not enough space while you're cooking. The fridge is too close. But you guys are moving the stove to the outside wall, like Hattie's house. If you put the fridge in that back corner, you're just trading places. Might as well leave it as it is."

"Or only move the fridge?"

She pulled back and looked at him, then past him and into the kitchen, her lips pursed, eyebrows drawn together. "Can you—"

"Here, let me draw it out," he interrupted, easing her away, then standing, looking for his notebook. "Shit, I think I left the designs at my dad's."

"But the reason for moving the stove was the same as Hattie's—people walking behind you while you're cooking."

"It's not the same, though. Only the master's back there and the back hall. That hardly gets used. Not like Hattie's, where you have to go through the kitchen to get to the bathroom, the bedroom, or the garage."

"Oh, right."

Justin sat back down. "Can I ask you about that DNA stuff again?" Her mouth pursed—just as it had the last time he'd brought it up, and that stubborn look eased into her eyes before she looked away.

"Why?" she sat up straighter, looking at her hands in her lap.

"I think it's important. You might have sisters or something. Don't you want to know that?"

"No," she said emphatically. "Siblings are people you grow up with. I grew up with strangers. I wish I'd never taken that test."

"But—"

"No, dammit," her voice rose, and she stood up. "I mean it." She started pacing, and the cats scattered, jumping onto pillows and shelves among the clutter in the small living room. "It's not your choice. I'm not telling you what to do with other people, or people you call family."

She stopped, arms crossed, shot him a look he found hard to interpret, then she started circling the small room, mumbling, "Where's my freaking iPad?" After her second unproductive circuit of the room, she headed for the bedroom, and Justin wondered what the rest of the evening was going to be like. The Taylors didn't believe in TV or the internet, and their books and magazines were about off-grid life and homesteading. He picked up a random magazine and started flipping pages.

. . .

Justin cooked red salmon for dinner the next night, thawing a package from his dad's freezer, adding fried potatoes using Mack's recipe. Ginny's favorite meal. She walked home from work, up Dairy Hill to the house, running to the kitchen and nearly tripping over the circling cats when she opened the door and smelled fish cooking.

She loved watching him cook, especially if he didn't know she was there. But that wasn't possible in this tiny kitchen. He turned from the stove, watching her as she watched him, in a standoff of insecurity and tied tongues.

"Truce?" he asked.

"Babe—" she blew out, pulling her coat off, still trying not to step on or trip over a cat.

"I only have one—no, two—more things to say, please? Then we can accept that we don't agree, okay? I'm okay with what you said. You're right; it's your decision."

"Bribery," she accused, trying not to smile, her mouth watering. The long walk had done her a world of good, she'd decided.

"Absolutely. I'm not stupid."

She walked toward him slowly, her eyes admiring every-thing about him. "You're wonderful, and you know it."

"What did you eat for breakfast? And lunch? I'm making that every day from now on," he said, reaching out, and she wrapped her arms around him.

"Don't burn my fish," she said, squeezing him, then letting go as he turned back to the stove. "It was the walk. I needed it. I forgot how much I love walking."

"You walk at lunch every day practically," he said, flipping chunks of salmon over, then flipping the spicy potatoes.

"It's not the same as walking alone. That's what I miss. I used to walk everywhere—"

She stopped talking abruptly, backing out of the kitchen,

picking up one of the noisy cats, asking, "Did you give them any of the skin?"

"Yeah, and I think they might follow me home. Mighta been a big mistake," he admitted, watching her again as he leaned against the short counter between the fridge and the stove. He registered the immediate change in subject, as usual, and left it alone. He had one more shot at the DNA issue, and then he was going to call it quits. "Want to grab plates? I think it's done."

Waiting until they were both full, Justin opened with his best pitch and closed with his acceptance that they were both entitled to their opinions and, ultimately, it was her decision, and he'd respect that. He needed them to be able to talk about things, even if they didn't agree on them, he said carefully, quietly.

She listened to him, her mouth firmly set, eyes wary, until he finished. "Look, what you're not getting is that if there's some half-whatever," her voice rose, "they probably got thrown away too, growing up with who-knows-what issues, and I'm not responsible for that, and I don't want to deal with it. If they're looking for relatives, they want something. So, no. No fucking way. I don't owe anybody anything, and I'm not telling them what I have or where I am."

His jaw dropped, and he froze.

Thrown away?

He was completely unable to process what she'd said, and his reaction infuriated her more. She stood up faster than he could register, grabbing her coat, sliding into her boots before he could blink. The door slammed, setting the cats scrambling, one of them yowling up a storm. He guessed he deserved it.

Kids who were thrown away?

<h1 style="text-align:center">23</h1>

Squealing like five-year-olds, Ginny and Chelsea greeted each other near the baggage check-in area for Alaska Airlines. Chelsea handed them each printed boarding passes, then plowed them through security. Heading for the bar, the women didn't stop chatting. Justin ordered a beer, and Chelsea ordered wine seltzers for herself and Gin as they faced each other across the booth, talking non-stop until the final boarding call.

Chelsea answered Ginny's questions about school, Arizona, and Havasu and then asked Gin about her work, fascinated by the videos Gin was working on, asking to see one. Ginny pulled up the link to the one she'd shown Al, and Chelsea was impressed.

"Thanks. I'm kinda cross-eyed from working on it so much. A week away is going to be heaven."

"We might take off in my dad's camper for a couple of days," Justin said, trying to get a word in edgewise.

"That's cool. I've a friend I want to visit in Prescott. Wanna spend the last night in Vegas?" She looked at Ginny.

"Have you ever been there?" Ginny shook her head. "Ooooh, we better do that. I'll set it up. We'll stay at the Luxor and take the tram. Wait until you see the fountains at the Bellagio!"

"I've seen videos—" Ginny started.

"Nope, they don't do it justice. You have to be there." Chelsea turned her delighted face to Justin. "Hope you brought cash," she said and grinned.

Ginny's first clue that something was different was when the flight attendant greeted Chelsea by name. "Welcome back, Miss Westerly. I hope you're enjoying spring break. You and your guests are in five, six and seven. Your dad ordered champagne. Shall I open that now or wait until we're closer to Las Vegas?"

Behind Chelsea, Ginny's eyes widened as Chelsea replied. "Now's perfect, thanks, Carmen. These are my friends Ginny and Justin, and yeah, so far, break's great. How was your layover in Paris over Christmas? Everything you were hoping for?" Chelsea asked, following Carmen to their seats.

"He sure was," Carmen replied with a warm smile. "Be right back with your glasses."

"Aisle or window, Gin?" Chelsea asked, then seeing her stunned face, adding, "I prefer the aisle, but I'll scoot in if you want to sit next to Justin, or—"

"I'd love the window, thanks," Ginny gushed.

After five relaxing days in Lake Havasu, exploring lightly and sunning as much as possible, Justin drove them back to Las Vegas and turned in the rental car.

Checking in at the Luxor, the desk clerk told Chelsea that her father had made reservations for them for dinner in the steakhouse at six p.m., however, they'd be happy to change them if needed. "Can we up that to five?"

"Certainly, Miss Westerly."

"Thank you. And a booth? We aren't really dressed for a night out."

"Absolutely. Enjoy your stay, Miss Westerly."

Ginny took the tiniest steps walking through the suite, and Justin grabbed Chelsea's arm, tugging her back toward the door.

"Don't start," she warned him in her lowest voice, her back stiffening.

"Chelsea—"

"Look at me," she demanded, facing him. "When was the last time you've seen me this happy?" He stared back at her, his mouth a tight line. "Exactly." She tapped a finger on his chest. "Guess how many years it's been since I asked my father for anything? Anything at all?" She only paused to breathe. "Four. He almost cried when I said I wanted to ask him for a favor. Now," she tapped his chest one more time, barely pausing. "Let's do the math. Me, my dad, Ginny. That makes three people who are seriously happy right this very minute. How 'bout you join the party?"

She smiled at him, and her eyes softened. "I mean it. We're having fun, and most of it's watching her having fun. We all," she used the finger to draw a circle in the air, "may never do anything like this again. So I'm gonna make every minute count." She looked around cautiously, then bear-hugged him and let him go quickly. "C'mon, let's go see what Cinderella's up to."

Justin smiled, shaking his head, following Chelsea through the suite. They found Ginny in one of the three bathrooms, staring at a bubbling hot tub. "Look at this!" Ginny squeaked.

"Later," Chelsea said. "We have dinner reservations down-stairs at five, and it's a quarter till. Let's go; I'm starving."

Sticking to Chelsea's plan after dinner, they boarded the tram and stepped off near the Bellagio, then wandered the strip, taking photos of the bright lights, the passing crowds and each other, the two women talking a mile a minute with Justin watching them like a hawk.

It wasn't his first trip to Las Vegas, and it wasn't the first time he'd been treated to a trip by Chelsea's family. As a teenager, his father had told him to be gracious, accept what was offered, and offer to help if he saw a way that he could. The words rang in his head. The only way he could see to help was to watch out around them and let them do whatever Chelsea wanted, which seemed to make Ginny laugh more, which only made Chelsea bolder and happier.

"Damn, we have to wait. Let's get a good spot," Chelsea said, scanning the wide sidewalk. Ginny and Justin followed her as she picked a half-circle and leaned against the stonework, gazing at the water in front of them and the gorgeous hotel and casino beyond.

The surrounding lights dimmed, the speakers crackled with static, and Gene Kelly invited them to sing in the rain. Ginny watched the synchronized water show start, and Chelsea squealed, "Dance class!" She lifted her hand in invitation toward Justin, and Ginny watched as he did a slight bow while taking her fingertips in his hand. They moved together like they'd been made for it, swaying, separating, coming back together and then he twirled her, and she laughed, and Ginny clapped with complete abandon and glee.

"Cut in, Gin!" Chelsea called, but Ginny shook her head.

Justin swung Chelsea closer to where Ginny was standing, and Chelsea urged her again.

"I don't know how," Ginny said, quickly adding, "you dance," while waving her off with delight.

The song ended, and Justin bowed again, and Chelsea mimed a curtsey to him and then to the clapping crowd of bystanders who'd watched them, with the water show behind them.

"Oh, dammit! You missed the show!" Chelsea actually stomped one foot, then said, "Ow. Dammit, dammit!"

"It's okay," Ginny said. "That was so much fun watching you two."

"Dance class. We were partners. We used to practice together," she said, holding onto the stone wall with one hand and rubbing her foot with the other.

"Let's go inside, look at the lobby and come out and watch the next one, and no dancing next time," she ordered, laughing and leading the way like she was the queen of Las Vegas.

They'd woken, showered, and met in the kitchen area, wearing the plushest bathrobes and nothing else. Justin was first to arrive, and he'd made two cups of coffee by the time Chelsea walked into the room. She sat at the table, and he brought the mugs over while the third cup brewed.

"Cinderella in the shower?" she asked. He nodded, sipping.

"I want to take her shopping. She needs clothes."

"These hotel shops—the prices..." Justin said carefully. He'd never seen Ginny spend very much money on anything.

"Not the boutiques here. Let's hit the outlet mall. It's right around the corner from the airport. We'll do a little there, then maybe a bit more at the airport."

"I'd argue, but I'd lose against two women with credit cards, and you're right, she could use some clothes."

"My hero. Let's grab a quick breakfast at the steakhouse, then get a cab. I'll go get dressed."

It was the gown in the window of a smaller shop that drew the two tired women in, after buying slacks and shirts at a large retailer and underwear at a specialty shop. Chelsea had pulled dresses off racks, only to see Ginny shake her head and turn away. This time Chelsea stopped in her tracks, staring at the gown. She met Justin's eyes, then grabbed Ginny's hand. Justin was already carrying several large shopping bags, but he smiled, looking at the gown, and followed the two inside.

Chelsea didn't expect much in terms of service and was surprised to hear a clear voice say, "If it was the gown that brought you in, I'd be happy to show you the collection we have." Chess turned to see a petite woman with dark hair, very well dressed, wearing a tasteful quantity of expensive jewelry.

"Ballgowns, for the princess," she said, meeting the woman's eyes as they sized each other up.

"I'd be delighted to show you some. This way, ladies. Sir, there's a comfortable chair right here and bottled water or sodas in the cupboard next to it. Please make yourself comfortable."

"We only have an hour, Chess, and that includes getting to the airport," Justin warned, setting the bags down.

"I'll call a driver," Chelsea called, beelining it to the gowns, dragging Ginny.

"If you give me your name, we have a service we recommend. I'll make that call while you look. Does a ten sound right? Is there a color preference?"

"Ten's good. Not too tight, decent coverage, good swing, jewel tones," Chelsea said, pulling a card from her purse then handing it to the woman, who swung the gowns to the size tens, then stepped away. She came back within minutes with a gown in shades of green that took Ginny's breath away, especially when she looked at the price tag. The saleswoman hung the gown on the outside of the rack, and Chelsea selected another one, urging Ginny to try it on.

Returning from making the call, the saleswoman stood off to the side as Ginny came out in the gown and twirled, her face shining.

"Ladies, your car will be here in twenty-five minutes," she said, admiring the gown and checking the fit. "Like a glove, my dear," she admired. "You definitely have time to try another. I have one more you might like."

"I'd better get this one off," Ginny gasped, hurrying back to the dressing room. Chelsea sent a long look to Justin, who stood. "Get the tag on that one she just had on Chess, and don't let her know."

He turned to the saleswoman, taking out his wallet. "That one that she just had on and that green one you just showed us —if it will fit her as well as that first one?"

"I believe it will, sir. It's the bodice that matters most on these gowns. I believe Miss Westerly said that she has a seamstress for alterations, if needed, when I gave her card back."

"I want both gowns and wrap them up so that she doesn't know I bought them. It's a surprise." He held out his credit card and one of the shopping bags.

"Do you want to see the tag?" she asked, and Justin shook his head.

"No. She's fast, and she scares easily. I want them wrapped up before she goes into a panic."

"I understand. I'll include a few underthings. One sec..."

. . .

Chelsea slept the entire way back, and Ginny squeezed by her to sit next to Justin, because someone had decided to push their luck in Vegas, giving up their seat. They whispered for a while, then fell asleep, something Ginny was trying not to do. But the air below them was solid clouds, and she was exhausted.

24

"So, you're gonna need a skiffman?" Mack asked, as he and Justin rolled up the last of the old carpet in Pete's living room. They'd moved furniture for what felt like the hundredth time and were preparing to install flooring—finally.

Pete and Hattie had won that dispute, agreeing on a dark wood plank flooring that would cover the living room, dining area, kitchen, and hallway. The new kitchen wall was framed in, sheetrock up and taped but otherwise unfinished, and the countertop for the new breakfast bar was awaiting pick up.

"Yeah, I'm sure Case isn't coming back for that," Justin said.

"What's he gonna do all summer?"

"No idea. He's doing a double load. Says he's not going back, so I don't want to bother him. I guess we'll find out whatever he's planning when he comes home."

"Double load? He's graduating this year? Does Pete know that? Shit. Wait till I tell Hattie. We didn't plan on going up this year—"

"Don't plan on it. I'm pretty sure he'll leave the last day of classes and never look back."

"Huh. God, I hate carpet. Get your puller. Let's get the baseboard molding off. If we sand 'em, we can stain 'em to match, so try not to break any. I'll tell Wade to put the word out. He knows all the skiffmen."

"I was thinking about trying Ben. He said he was interested last year—"

"Nope. Not aggressive enough. Jesus, Viv would be better. Hey," he leaned back on his heels, holding his pry bar. "You taking Ginny finally? Do I need to hire someone?"

"I don't know about that either. I have no fucking clue what's gonna happen this summer." Justin shot Mack a look of total frustration and went back to easing the baseboard trim away from the wall.

"I better get ahold of Viv. Wade too. He should have booked his ticket back by now. Jeez, I wish the rain would let up. It'd be great to put these things outside instead of moving them constantly," he bitched, pulling off another piece of baseboard.

Pete and Ginny came home to a half-floored living room and had ten seconds to admire it before Mack interrupted their comments. "We need to talk about this summer. Did you know Case was doing a double load of classes? Graduating this year?" He sat at the kitchen table, rubbing his knees from kneeling most of the day.

Mack was tired and looked it, Pete thought, as he replied, "He told me he'd signed up for a lot of classes at the end of the season but wasn't sure he could pull it off." Pete eased into a chair at the small table, looking at Justin. "Is he staying in touch with you? Has he said if he's going to graduate?"

"Not a word. I'll text Chelsea. She'll know," Justin said, standing, stretching, arching his aching back. "I need to see if Ben and Greg are coming back, too."

"Is Case going to be skiffman?" Pete asked, surprised.

"Nope. He promised me one year, that's it, and I'm pretty sure he's gonna stick to it, and I have no idea what he plans on doing this summer." Justin dropped into a chair at the table and heard his neck pop.

"God, I wish I could fish again. If it was just this bay..." Pete said.

"How's that working?" Mack asked. "Last I heard, they were trying to separate us out." Pete shrugged and shook his head, and Ginny, taking the last seat, did the same. "Guess I gotta wait and see," Mack grumbled. "Okay, I'm outta here. See ya tomorrow."

"I'm giving notice for May first," Ginny said after Mack left.

"So, the private label thing is off the table for this year?" Pete asked.

"I think so. Gabe's still struggling with processing, and I'm not gonna take that battle on yet if he can't solve it."

"Damn. There goes my hope of being famous for Pete's Peppered Pinks," he said with a smile.

Justin gave his dad a half-smile. "Very funny," and shook his head.

"I'm not kidding. I peppered some up a few years ago? Remember us catching a few when we were fishing for silvers? No? Well, I kippered them with the silvers, but I sprinkled pepper on them. Ah, kinda, I don't know, playing around. They're great. I wonder..." He got up and went to the kitchen, opening cupboards.

Justin put his hand on Ginny's. "I never took anything out for dinner. Mack came in like a tornado, as usual, and I forgot."

"Mac and cheese it is," she said and laughed. She leaned

over, kissed him lightly, then stood. "Lemme look. You look beat. I'll figure out dinner." She went into the kitchen and backed up as Pete stood, balancing three small jars of salmon.

"Do we have any cream cheese?" he asked, carrying the jars to the table. "And can you bring some forks? Oh, and a can opener. That one stuck to the fridge is perfect."

She didn't find any cream cheese but brought three forks and a flat metal bottle opener, handing it to Pete. He popped the top of one jar, which gave a satisfying *thwack* as the vacuum released and the smoky-peppery kippered fish aroma burst out. Taking a fork, Pete scooped out a chunk of salmon and ate it, passing the jar to Ginny, who did the same and passed it on. Justin examined the contents, smelled it, then finally took a fork-full.

"Mmm, this is so good. Love the pepper," Ginny crooned, eyeing the jar Justin held.

"Get your own. I just found dinner," he said, forking more out and eating it. Pete laughed. Ginny went back to the kitchen, looking for something to cook that would go with the salmon. Maybe fried potatoes and onion, like Mack's. Or the breakfast concoction he called his specialty, which was great for breakfast or dinner and pretty flexible when it came to ingredients. She opened the fridge and started pulling out ingredients.

"Ginny, is there any chance you can do two more weeks? We have a project we just received funding for, and I think that, between you and Connor, we can pull it off fairly quickly," Al asked during what she thought would be her last Monday meeting in late April.

"I think so. The boats aren't even in the water yet, and we

shouldn't be fishing before the twenty-fifth, by my guess. What's the project?"

"Let's have you and Connor meet me in my office. We'll go over it."

The three settled comfortably, and Al began. "Connor's been working on updating contact information to our shareholders, and we're going to expand that using DNA services. Connor, you were the one who proposed this. Why don't you take the lead here?"

"Okay, well, in my village, some of us did that DNA test where you spit in the tube and mail it off. Anyway, the results came back with relatives we didn't know about. Now, you know that missing women and children are a big deal, and I thought, maybe we can track them down this way? I mean, what if they're out there, and they just need us to reach out to them?"

Before Al could open his mouth, Ginny jumped in. "But what if they don't want to be contacted?"

"Well, we'd like to let them know that the tribe's here for them. We really do have a lot to offer, starting with medical services," Al explained.

"Don't they have to be enrolled for that?"

"They have to be able to trace their lineage to an enrolled member, and that's already done because we're using the DNA tests of our enrolled members as the starting point," Al said.

"I don't believe in this," Ginny blurted out and then continued rapidly. "I did one of those tests, and I don't even know why. Then I kept getting messages, and I didn't want them. DNA people are not my family. I have my family—the people I grew up with, the people I know here. That's all I want. So, I don't really support this project at all. I think it's overreaching and intrusive. I'll help with the details, but I'm letting you know that I don't like it," she said, then stood up and left Al's office.

"Wow," Connor said, watching her go. "I never thought of it like that."

Al watched her settle back at her desk, rubbing his chin.

<h1 style="text-align:center">25</h1>

"Mine wasn't this good, Ginny. You're holding something back," Pete teased her with a huge smile on his face, his body completely relaxed. He was at the head of his dining room table, and his house was finally put back together in more ways than one. His new kitchen was installed, organized, a pleasure to cook in, and all of his sons were home. He radiated happiness. The younger boys were there for the weekend, and they were fed and playing in their playroom. His twins were at the table with him, and each had a companion sitting next to him, although the tension between Case and Chelsea was as hot as the spicy jambalaya Ginny had cooked for dinner, celebrating Case's graduation and return from Fairbanks.

"Yours was this good, believe me," Ginny assured him. Pete's smile was contagious, and Ginny had enjoyed hearing him humming as he fed the boys hamburgers in the kitchen while she pulled together her favorite spicy meal for the rest of them. Best of all, there was now room for both of them to cook, something Pete commented on regularly with surprise in his voice every single time.

"I'm making a small fire, and none of you," Justin scanned

everyone's faces, "better tell Mack." They all laughed. Mack's campfires were so large that they required a burn permit, so the fire department wouldn't come racing out each time he started one.

"Let's go," Case said. "I'll get the beer."

"I'll get the wine," Ginny chimed in.

"Glasses," Chelsea offered.

"Lighter," Justin added, and they laughed again.

"I'm gonna pass," Pete said, as their faces turned to him. "I promised to watch a short movie with the boys. They'll be out here demanding it any minute now. It's almost their bedtime. Leave your plates; I'll clear the table. I love my new dishwasher," Pete gushed.

Case went to get his jacket from his duffel. He'd be spending the night on the trundle bed in the playroom until the Calypso was launched, and Justin and Ginny moved aboard. They'd happily said he could have their room while they were gone and Pete had been deeply grateful to think he'd have one of this twins home with him through the summer.

Chelsea sat next to Ginny on the giant cottonwood rounds surrounding Mack's huge fire pit, while Case and Justin circled the fire, poking, adding small branches to it, adjusting the logs, and sipping beer.

"How's work going? Are you still editing videos?" Chelsea asked.

"No, we moved onto a new project, and I don't really like it. I can't wait to get back on the boat."

"Are you working with Justin this year, or staying with Mack?"

Ginny shrugged and looked away, and Chelsea decided to change the subject. "My dad is giving me a trip as a grad present." Ginny's head lifted, and her eyebrows went up.

"Europe."

"What! No way? How long? What cities? When do you leave? Oh, man, that's awesome!"

Chelsea laughed. "In a couple of days. I wish you could come along."

"Don't I wish. Dream trip. I'm gonna live it all through you. I want every single detail. Where—"

"A month each in Paris, London, and Rome. I'll be taking classes I really want in each place, while living there."

Ginny gasped, her hands flying to cover her mouth as she shook her head, unable to speak. Chelsea laughed again. They picked up their glasses and sipped, but Ginny shook her head again, still unable to process the idea of an entire summer abroad.

"I need to pick out the right clothes to take. Wanna help?"

"Oh yeah. Absolutely. When?"

"Now? Anything going on tonight?" They looked at Case and Justin, talking so intensely that they were finally ignoring the fire.

"Nope, let's go," Ginny said, picking up the wine bottle. "Bring this with us?"

"Yes. Leave the glasses. You can pick them up on the way back." Chelsea stood up. "Justin. We're going to my house."

He came jogging over. "I'll walk you over. At least as far as the creek."

Back at the fire, Justin stood across from Case. "She's still mad at you?"

"Oh, fuck yeah. I got to listen to that for the last hour of the deadly drive home. I don't know what love is; I don't know what friendship is; I wouldn't know a good woman if I met one; drinking my problems doesn't solve them; and a whole shitload more." Case poked the fire again, sending sparks flying, then looked at his brother, who shook with silent laughter, twisting away.

"I'll hit you so fucking hard—"

"You gonna skiff for me?" Justin interrupted, trying to wipe the smile off his face.

"No. I told you last year, I'm done seining. I'm taking flying lessons. I've been busting my ass at school, and I've had my balls busted by two women. I need a fucking break, and I want to have some fun."

"Okay, I wasn't expecting you to. Just had to ask. I may put Ben in the skiff."

"What happened to the tender idea, and that direct-to-market idea? And why don't I see a ring on Ginny's finger?"

Justin stiffened, gripping his beer. "Goddammit! Do you know how much I've needed to talk to you for the past *year*? You were supposed to come to the boat show with me and cancelled at the last minute. Why?"

Justin's eyes narrowed as he watched his brother cringe and turn away. "You blew me off for *her*? You knew how important that was to me!" He paced, staring at Case like he didn't even know him, his voice rising with every word, blowing out everything he'd been holding in for months, his blood boiling.

"And then at Christmas, I couldn't even talk to you. You were too wrapped up in your own misery over a woman who *never even loved you.* You shoulda celebrated being dumped by that lying slut." He stopped pacing, leaning over the fire, lowering his voice to a growl.

"And forget proposing. *You* were the center of attention. *As usual.* After that, I didn't want to bother you."

Justin took a deep breath and blew it out and Case held his breath. "You said you were pulling a double load, and I *wanted* you to pull it off. I wanted to talk to you about all of this stuff and I've been doing my best, all on my own, and it's fucking hard. Thanks for asking."

"Oh, fuck me running," Case mumbled, watching his brother stomp away through the alders back to their dad's house. Sitting down, his head in his hands, he continued to talk to himself. "Who the hell's gonna be next?" He cringed as Justin's words rang in his ears, joining Chelsea's biting tirade from the drive home a few hours ago.

～

"Thanks for helping me," Chelsea said, pouring the last of the wine into their two glasses. Facing each other on a soft loveseat in her bedroom, she and Ginny had been having the time of their lives.

Ginny thought Chelsea's closet was like a store with everything imaginable in it, and they'd gone through almost all of it.

"That was the most fun I've had since Vegas," Ginny said with a smile.

"Yes, and I don't often get help. You're a sweetheart, and I appreciate you being honest about what looks best. I hate shopping for clothes. So," Chelsea touched Ginny's hand lightly, "I have a question, but you don't have to answer if you don't want to."

"Okay."

"What, exactly, was this hellstorm named Nell like? Case said something about her fooling you and his aunt Hattie, too?"

"Oh, God. Yeah, she did." Ginny admitted, shaking her head, then noticed Chelsea waiting. "She's beautiful. I mean over-the-top beautiful. And she put these dots on her chin. Gorgeous. She did her hair like some of the women in the village wear. She wore beaded earrings and other traditional jewelry. She just looked the part, and we fell for it. And then, at the campfire..."

Chelsea waited, then prompted her as Ginny's face registered disgust. "What happened?"

"Oh, she made this birchbark basket. Right there while we were all hanging around, and we all were, I dunno, captivated by it. Amazed. And she acted like, *oh this little thing? I make them all the time*, and we just—argh. We fell for it. I think I was worse than Case!"

"Wow," Chelsea said, looking away, her eyebrows drawn tight together.

"You know the worst part?"

Chelsea looked at her again, curiously.

"There are videos on the internet teaching exactly how to make those baskets. I'm sure all she did was watch one and then tried it, and it became her trick. I mean, she fooled us all. Even Al, and he meets people from every tribe all over the country—even the world. Lying to us about her background, skills, everything—pffhhht," she blew out, her jaw clenched, hands tightened into fists.

"That's impressive."

"No, it's fucked up." Ginny heaved a huge sigh, her tone sad. "Poor Case. He didn't know what hit him. She singled him out. Probably because he's so handsome. And he's easy to talk to. He flirts with every female over the age of ten," she joked sadly. "But he didn't deserve that. I feel so bad for him. She deliberately used him, didn't care a bit about him. And then, from what Justin said, she was *vicious* when she dumped him. Like, that's just sick. Poor guy. Ahhh," she stood up and stretched. "I better get back."

"I'll walk you as far as the campfire. Those stones in the creek can be slippery."

"Okay. This was fun. Really. I've never really been into clothes, but you have such a great wardrobe. I want every detail, all summer long," she insisted, following Chess through the house. "Send me a thousand pics!"

Watching Ginny walk away from the campfire clearing, Chelsea turned toward the huge cottonwood rounds surrounding the last of the fire. She walked over to the ring and sat down, thinking about everything Ginny'd said.

"I'd sit next to you, but I'm pretty sure you'll push me into the fire," Case said, coming out of the woods.

"No, I won't. I need to apologize to you."

"No shit? Well then," he slid onto the round next to her, straddling it, and Chelsea twisted toward him. "Go right ahead," he encouraged.

"How much have you had to drink?"

"Fuck it, Chess," his voice rose. "You said apologize, not bust my balls some more." He backed away, his eyes narrowed, ready to get up and walk away.

"I just want to know if you're going to remember anything I say."

He leaned into her, scooting forward, almost nose to nose with her. "I remember a whole lot more than you think I do," he said very quietly.

She gazed at him warily, wondering what he was alluding to, trying to remember what she'd said when he'd been puking drunk and she'd been so furious.

"Ah, okay. The apology," she said, then hesitated.

"Aaaannnddd..." he drew out, sitting up stiffly, watching every twitch and movement she made.

"I need to find a way to say it that's not hurtful to you."

That surprised him. He relaxed slightly, his tone almost normal as he said, "Fine. Take your time. Two beers. That's all. I was thinking about reaching for number three when you two beauties wandered into my realm."

"Uh huh," she said, unimpressed. "I think I was too hard on you about, um…"

"Which thing—that you raked me raw for—were you too hard on me about?" he asked, curiously, as if it barely mattered anymore.

"Nell."

Case stiffened. "And why is it that you think that *now*?" he whispered, resentment surging through his voice again.

"Ginny said she targeted you. I assumed you were the one pursuing her," she admitted quietly. Chelsea looked down, then at the fire, then into his eyes briefly, which was always hard for her to do. Her eyes darted away. "I'm sorry. I'm sorry for what I said and for what she did to you. It's almost like—"

"Don't."

She closed her mouth and waited. "I'm sorry," she whispered, looking at her fingers twisting in her lap.

He put a finger under her chin, lightly guiding her face up until her eyes met his, peering deeply into hers and holding her gaze. "Yeah, I guess you are. Thanks for that." He held her chin for quite some time as they continued looking at each other.

"I'd better go," she finally said.

"I'll walk you home."

26

"Man, that bed's a lot more comfortable than I expected it to be," Case said, walking into the kitchen Monday morning, wearing baggy sweatpants and nothing else, going straight to the coffeepot, and filling a mug.

"It's brand new; dad wanted good ones in every bedroom. Put a shirt on," Justin said, sitting at the new breakfast bar with his own mug, watching his brother move around the new kitchen, looking at the changes.

"What's your problem now?" Case leaned back against the new pantry door, eyeing Justin suspiciously over his mug as he sipped.

"Gin loves chest hair and you have way more than me. Go put a shirt on."

"Ooohh," Case grinned. "Where is she? Your bedroom? God, that's perfect. Lemme go see what she thinks." He put the mug down and headed for the hallway.

"Don't make me hurt you," Justin warned, watching his brother's back. Case laughed as he headed down the hall, then turned into the new playroom, where he'd spent the night. He came back out a minute later with a T-shirt on, aiming for his mug.

"Alright, look, I'll help with the boat prep. If you absolutely can't get a skiffman, I'll do it, but you better ask everyone you know."

"Thanks. I've got the word out. So do Mack and Wade. Boat goes in the water the day after tomorrow at ten. I want to load the net the same day if the weather holds, and it's supposed to be decent. Mack's doing his tomorrow."

"What's the word on Viv?"

"Mack's trying to get ahold of her. If she doesn't reply soon, he's gonna hire someone else."

"Damn. She's the only reason I'd come back—"

"Hey guys. Case, you ready?" Pete came into the kitchen and poured coffee into a travel mug.

"Sure, let me get my shoes on."

Riding into Seward with Pete so he could borrow his car for the day, Case asked his dad how he'd been feeling. "No more episodes, and believe me, I'm grateful. I can't wait to start catching reds. We're gonna fill the smokehouse this year. It's been too long since we've had any strips. Have you made any plans yet, other than flying lessons?" Pete parked the car, and they both got out, Case coming around to take the keys.

"No. I told Justin that if he doesn't get a skiffman, I'd do it, but I'd rather not."

It was a gorgeous, sunny day with no wind yet, and they both admired the view down the street and out to the bay, each wrapped up in their own thoughts.

Pete's phone beeped with an incoming text. Pulling it out of his pocket, he thought he'd take a photo of the view after reading the message.

AL

If that's Case with you, would you ask if he
has time to come up?

Pete raised his phone to take a shot of the bay, then told Case to get in there too. Laughing, he stepped in front of the camera. Pete snapped a few shots, then pocketed his phone. "Al's asking if you have a minute to come up."

"Sure. I've never seen your office or his."

Pete led the way into the office, and Case stopped inside the door, looking around. Connor looked up, wearing his engaging smile. "Who ya got there, Pete? He looks like you, sorta."

"My son, Case," Pete said, standing a little taller, grinning as he put a hand on Case's shoulder. "Case, this is Connor. He keeps us all connected and informed." They shook hands as Al came out of his office in the far corner.

"That can't be Case. My God, Pete, how fast these kids grow. We're old men now." Holding out his hand, he shook Case's, looking up. "You must have grown a foot since I saw you last—when?" Al looked at Pete. "At the campfire, two years ago?"

Case and Pete shared a glance. That was the year Case had refused to fish with his dad, working instead with the enhancement organization at their weirs. Al caught their look and spoke quickly. "Pete, take your time. Show him everything. Case, when you're ready, I'm in the back there, and I'd love two minutes of your time."

They nodded, and Al returned to his office. Pete showed Case the interview room, where Ginny and Hattie had worked, telling him about the interviews, then pulled an extra chair up to his desk, and they both sat down.

"I do a lot of research and reports, mostly," Pete started, but Case, looking his desk over, pointed.

"Ah, the basket." Pete reached for it, handing it to him. Birchbark, with a whipped-on band. Nicely squared. Pete said quickly, "Ginny made that," and Case's head popped up. Connor brought his over, and Case examined it too, as Connor urged him to look closer at the differences between the two baskets. Pete explained that Gin had found a video and wanted to try making them. She'd made one for all of them, Connor added.

"A video," Case repeated, his voice flat.

"On the internet. Elder lady from up north in the interior. Good video. Gin makes great videos, too. You should see them," Connor said, walking back to his desk. "Pete can give you the link."

Case put the basket down gently. "I'll go say hi to Al. Thanks for letting me use the car. See you at five?"

"Sure," Pete said, looking at Case's closed-off face. He'd forgotten about the basket and would have hidden it if he'd known Case was coming in.

"Been a tough couple of years, yes?" Al waved to a chair at a small table in his office, taking the other.

"You're not kidding," Case agreed.

"I understand you won't be seining this summer? You have plans?"

"Only to get signed up for flying lessons, so far," Case said, grinning.

"Oh, that would be fun. The intern we just hired was supposed to do a lot of flying, but he quit this morning—before he even started." Case's eyebrows went up. "Exactly. I haven't even told Pete or Connor yet. I miss Ginny and Hattie already," Al sighed. "You were doing great work at the weirs, and I appreciate the fact that you sent information our way while doing so."

Case sat up straighter. "What happens with salmon matters to me."

"Yes. And what's your major? Third year, is that right?"

"I'm done. I did a double load last year. I stuck with the middle of the road, some business, some biology but settled on a BA in Fisheries. Pretty generic."

"Interesting. Has Pete told you about our Tessa?" Case shook his head, and Al spent more than his requested two minutes describing the work that Pete and Tessa were collaborating on, citing Tessa's experience and credentials.

"So, the endgame here is to make the local hatchery go away but also to establish a clear process that can be followed to close down other hatcheries within Alaska, possibly nationally," Al leaned forward. "The guy who bailed was our field guy. Funded for three months, including a leased car for travel, although some will be by small airplane. I have a list of places he was supposed to visit and the research he needed to do to help us shutter the local salmon hatchery."

Al sat back, encouraged by Case's rapt attention to his every word. "Would that list of places be of interest to you? Remote sites, weirs, hatcheries. Also, we are partnered with one stream-keeper organization, and we're looking to expand that. There's at least one conference out of state that would require attendance, although that's negotiable."

Case looked out Al's window at the gorgeous sunlit bay, its surface glittering as the wind pursed her lips and blew ever so slightly, roughing the surface only enough to create some texture and movement, sending continuous sparkling diamonds of light in every direction.

"I think this is one of those moments," Case said, his grinning gaze returning to Al, "where I say: you had me at *places to go*. The travel opportunities are exactly what I'm looking for.

Doing away with hatcheries is why my papers at school weren't all that popular. I didn't really get into the biology side that much, so your Tessa's credentials are intriguing. I'd love to see the list, and I look forward to meeting her. My only caveat is a promise to work for my brother if he can't find a skiffman."

"Let's stay in touch. I think you'd be a great asset to us and I'm willing to wait for the right candidate."

27

Sitting on the rail of the newly launched Calypso, Ginny checked her phone, looking for a text or email from Viv. After checking multiple times daily for the past two weeks, she didn't expect to see anything. She glanced up to see Case coming out of the cabin, with Justin behind him, locking the cabin door. Glancing back at her phone before pocketing it, there it was! "Wait one sec," she said as they crossed the deck to her. The message started with "Soon," and she scanned it quickly. "Viv finally emailed. I gotta tell Mack," she said, standing quickly, trying to remember if he was on his boat or not.

"He went back to the warehouse for more twine, brailer bags for his jitney, stuff like that," Justin said. "Text him while we head out there to get the net. She's coming back?"

"Yup." Ginny hopped up to the rail and jumped down to the dock, then spun around, smiling.

"Doesn't take much to make her happy," Case commented, walking next to his brother, following Ginny, who was bouncing up the ramp to the parking lot.

"Yeah. She misses Viv and now Chelsea, too."

"I must have pissed Chess off worse than ever," Case admitted. "She isn't even answering my texts anymore."

Justin stopped walking, staring at Case, who finally noticed and turned around, going back to him quickly, frowning at the shocked look on his brother's face.

"What? Is something wrong with Chess, and no one told me? What the fuck's going on?" he rushed out.

"She's in Europe. Jesus, man, she didn't tell you? She told Gin she was going for three months."

Case's face went from shock to a blank stare as his back stiffened and mouth tightened. He turned toward the ramp, heading to the parking lot where Ginny stood texting Mack.

GINNY

Viv's on her way!

"Hey, when you're done with the net, you gonna launch your skiff? Let's go get some reds for the smokehouse," Mack said, helping Justin back his truck up to hitch onto Mack's flatbed trailer, which was parked in the grass alongside his firepit.

"Yeah, I'm launching the skiff today, but I was thinking about taking the boat to Aialik for a few days."

"Okay. I was thinking about checking out Day Harbor." Mack bent over to lower the trailer tongue onto the ball hitch, then secure it for towing. "Go ahead, I'll catch up," Mack said, waving for Justin to take off. He pulled away, driving past the warehouse entrance, then backed the trailer inside, angling it toward his seine, until Case called out, "Stop."

Mack walked the long driveway back to the big warehouse, then watched the net as it was loaded, keeping it off the edge of the trailer. Case and Justin took turns pulling it off its pile, handing an armful at a time to Ginny, who stacked it, walking back and forth across the front of the long trailer.

"How many days are you gonna spend in Aialik? If we each bring back twenty reds, we can load the smokehouse. That'll make your dad happy," Mack said, continuing the conversation.

"I was thinking maybe three or four days."

"Dammit! I wanna go," Case complained.

"You wanted that job over being skiffman. Working stiff. Nine to five," Mack gloated.

"I'm really gonna miss fishing with you," Case countered sarcastically, and Mack laughed. "I'll be flyin' over your sweaty, slimy, stinking, bug-covered asses, having the time of my life."

"It does sound like the perfect job for you," Justin said. "And I'm sure I'll get a skiffman hired soon."

"How many places are you really going to?" Ginny asked between breaths. Hauling and stacking bundles of the net, from corks to leadline, was a strenuous workout, and she was enjoying every second of it.

"As many weirs and hatcheries as possible," Case said, walking past her to start the truck and pull it forward, so she could load the rest of the net on the back half of the trailer.

"Let's do that," Justin agreed, replying to Mack and pausing to catch his breath. "I'll get at least twenty and run the RSW. I need to test it anyway," Justin offered, while the truck and trailer pulled forward with Ginny sitting on the piled net, catching her breath.

"Right. I'm only going for one or two days after Viv hits town, but if you want to leave sooner, go for it."

"Okay, so boat grocery run to Costco next Monday with both trucks and pick up Wade, then Tuesday I'm taking off," Justin said, hauling more net.

"Sounds good. I'll tell Pete to get everything ready for

stripping and hanging next Saturday morning," Mack said, walking out of the warehouse toward Pete's house.

~

Justin left Ginny and Case on the boat after loading the net, towing Mack's empty trailer back to the property, braking the instant he saw Hattie's car in the driveway. She often let the kids run around out there, and he had no idea whether they were inside or out. Leaving the truck running, he walked toward the clearing, saw her sitting on a cottonwood round, and called out, "Hey."

She spun and waved him over.

"The kids hiding here somewhere? I gotta put the trailer back..."

She pointed to Mack's huge gravel pile. They were on the other side of it, playing with trucks, covered in grey glacial silt, and they hadn't seen or heard him. "I'll make sure they stay there while you park it." She looked over his shoulder. "You're alone?" He nodded. "You're headed for Aialik with Ginny for a few days next week?" she asked, watching his face.

He sat down next to her, looking at the ashes of the last campfire. "I'm not gonna ask her out there."

"Why not? It sounds perfect."

"I thought I should do it when she has someone around to talk to." He finally met his aunt's eyes. "You would probably be best. In case she—"

"Honey, she's going to say yes."

He shook his head. "She's... I dunno. The way she grew up. She doesn't think family's important. She might not want to get married."

"What? Bullshit. She loves everyone in this family. She practically *is* family already. And she knows we believe in marriage."

"She has DNA relatives she doesn't want to know about or meet. Like, she gets mad even talking about it."

"Strangers," Hattie emphasized.

"Family," he countered. "Anyway, I want her to be able to talk to you in case she needs to. We're just gonna go have some fun in Aialik. She'll love the glacier."

"Are you still going to ask her, or have you changed your mind?" she asked quietly, then quickly said, "Never mind, that's none of my business. I shouldn't have asked. You do what's right for you." She scooted sideways, wrapping an arm around him and hugged. He returned her quick squeeze and stood up, looking away, heading back to his truck.

"You have all the clothes you want on the boat now?" Justin asked Ginny that evening as they cleaned up their bedroom. Case's things were piled on the floor by the closet, waiting for them to move out, so he could take over the room.

"Yeah, I'm good here. I want a new rain jacket, but I can get that anytime." She finished tidying the quilt and looked around the room.

"Charging cords, curling iron for your hair..."

"Very funny," she said, poking him, and he wrapped his arms around her.

"I'm gonna love being on the boat, just you and me, for four days." He rocked her gently. "You'll love Aialik."

"I'll be happy just living on the boat again. Being on the water."

"If we don't have to be in the harbor when we get back, I'll anchor out in the bay. It'll be just the two of us until the bay opens."

28

Coming back into Res Bay early in the morning, Justin stood at the helm on the flying bridge of the Calypso, steering with his right hand, his left arm around Ginny, who'd been smiling so much for the past few days that her face muscles ached.

The glacier had been impressive, the weather perfect, the fishing easy, the nights on the beach with a small campfire so cozy, and sleeping on the gently rocking boat, wrapped around Justin, had been the best of it all. She must have taken a thousand photos. And so many videos.

Justin had taken them in the skiff to several streams where she'd taken video of all the salmon returning. Far more than she'd ever seen in Res Bay.

Tying up behind the Stormy C, Viv came out of the cabin and walked along the dock, waiting as Ginny finished tying up the Calypso. They hugged and exclaimed how good each other looked.

"Hey, Mack wants to talk to you as soon as possible," Viv said. "He wants those videos. Jesus, if the SAT thingy had let him, he'd have texted videos to the fish and game guy. He's at his house now. Fair warning," she finished.

167

She and Justin greeted each other warmly. He'd heard what she'd said to Ginny and knew it was coming. He and Mack had used their satellite devices to stay in touch, and Mack said the reds were flooding into Day Harbor, too.

Both Justin and Mack already had their twenty fish cleaned, the fillets in coolers, waiting to be stripped, brined, and hung for smoking. As soon as that was accomplished, Mack wanted video footage in a format he could share with people, and Ginny said she'd do it. While everyone else was hanging strips, she went into Pete's house and pulled out her laptop.

Inside the cramped smokehouse, Wade repeatedly reached into the cooler, selected a strip and opened the sopping string loop, then handed the opened loop to Viv, who milked the strip, then held it up. Mack and Pete took turns taking the strips from her and hanging the string ends on protruding nails above their heads.

Justin sat on an upturned bucket next to the cold wood-stove, listening to voicemails from potential crewmen on his phone, with the speaker mode on so everyone could listen. When he did a final tally, he had deleted five from parents trying to send a drug-addicted teen away from friends for the summer; three from guys who'd been fired from other boats; eighteen people from out of state; and one guy Wade said was always a problem on every boat he worked on. He was left with five potential deckhands—not one of them claiming to be a skiffman.

Justin returned each of those calls, also on speaker. They discussed each one after the call ended. Justin immediately said, "Nope," after talking to Jess. The sex of the recorded voice had been ambiguous, but during the call it was easy to tell that she was female.

"No, because she's female?" Viv asked, and Mack jumped in quickly.

"Nope. That season in the Sound means she's out."

"I wasn't asking you," she shot back.

"What he said," Justin answered. "I've had to work with deckhands who've worked Prince William Sound. It's a whole different style of seining, and they don't get it. The ones I worked with wouldn't listen or learn. I'm not hiring one." He tapped to call the next guy.

"Hey, Pete, I brought you a king. Forgot to tell you," Mack said as Justin's call rang.

"Oh, nice, thanks! Guess I know what's for dinner now. You guys are all invited to stay and eat if you want."

"Justin, you catch any kings out there?" Mack asked.

"One nice one. We ate it. Took two days." The number rang on and on, and Justin left a brief message.

The next guy on the short list was obviously stoned and still smoking. Justin ended the call quickly. "Two left." He tapped to call, and someone answered by asking, "Who's this?"

"I'm returning a call from a guy wanting to work on a seiner," Justin answered.

"A boat? What boat? Where?"

"In Seward, working the lower Cook Inlet area. You the guy?"

"Nah, well, nah, but I need a job, man. Seward? Can you get me a ride there? I'm in Palmer."

"No, I can't. But if you get to Seward, you can give me a call." Justin ended the call before the guy could reply.

"Why not that guy?"

"He's not the one who called, and my guess is that he just got out of the Palmer correctional center," Justin said, and Mack agreed.

"Jesus Christ. Cream of the crop here, huh?" Viv said.

"Some years are like that," Pete said.

The last call was to a local landline, and the woman who answered, probably the caller's mother, said she'd take a message. Justin asked the guy's age, and she laughed and said fifteen. He confirmed the name, thanked her, and ended the call. "Too young. I'll put up a card at the Harbormaster's and check the online sites again," Justin said, standing and stretching, then taking over for Wade, who stood up achingly, saying he needed to walk, groaning as he stepped out of the small building.

Done hanging strips, Mack and Pete went into the house to wash up. Viv headed for Wade's temporary apartment in the warehouse to do the same thing. Justin sat on the smokehouse step, texting Case.

JUSTIN

No announcement yet. Still looking for crew. Where are you?

CASE

Homer. Meeting. TTYL

Justin stood, stretched again, and headed for the house to see how Gin was doing. Walking up behind her at the dining table, he stood beside Mack, who was leaning over Gin's shoulder and watching the screen. Pete called from the kitchen to ask if they wanted to eat now or later.

"Now," Ginny piped up. "One vote for now," she repeated, looking up eagerly, smiling and raising her eyebrows.

"Okay, sure, now it is," Pete agreed happily.

"This is great," Mack said, looking up at Justin quickly, then back to the screen. "Using polarized sunglasses as a filter was brilliant. Man, that underwater shot..."

"I know. I wish I'd had a drone."

"Oh, my God! A drone! We need to get one," Mack said. They continued to watch her edit clips and save them, talking to each other as Mack reminisced about fishing there many years ago. Then Ginny downloaded Mack's videos from Day Harbor.

Justin had been amazed at the number of salmon returning in Aialik. Far more than he'd ever seen in Res Bay. When he'd texted that to Mack, the message he'd received was: because there's no "enhancement" program fucking things up out here. Thank God! Enhancement = run ruined.

"Send me those links when they're uploaded, right? I'm goin' home. I have fish to cook, too," Mack said.

"Almost done here," she told Justin, as he pulled out the chair next to her.

"Take your time, then I'll tell you about the calls."

She stopped working, looking at him. "Got someone?"

He shook his head, and she went back to uploading files, filling out descriptions of the video, adding the latitude and longitude for each one, then copying the links. Compiling the video links into an email, she sent them to Mack and Al, then cleared her stuff off the table as Pete brought out a platter loaded with fried king salmon.

Thanking Pete, saying they needed to walk off their early dinner, Viv and Wade left to go back to the boat and walk the docks, then check in with Russell to see if he was having any luck at the gold mine.

Pete settled into his recliner with a sparkling water. Ginny sat cross-legged on the sofa with her laptop and a sparkling water nearby, and Justin sat on the other end of the sofa with a lemonade soda in one hand, the TV remote in the other. He was playing Ginny's videos for Pete to watch, and now Pete was reminiscing about the last time he had fished Aialik commercially.

Case walked into the house, going straight to the pile of fried salmon on the table, picking up a piece, and biting into it while he pulled out a chair and straddled it. "Hey, the gang's all here," he said.

"I thought you were in Homer," Justin said, pressing pause on the video.

"Meeting was over, and I didn't feel like spending the night there, so I drove back. Gotta be in Anchorage by tomorrow night, though."

"What are you driving?"

"Leased car. Nice one. Want a ride?"

"I want the keys—"

Case laughed. "Not a chance. Who caught the king? When're the strips coming out of the smokehouse?"

"Mack's king. The strips just went up, so five days or so, maybe six. Depends on whether it rains or not," Pete said.

"God, this is good. Damn, I'm gonna miss the strips. What're you guys watching?"

"Videos from Aialik and Day Harbor. Shitload of fish." Justin said. "Mack wants to send the vids to the Fish and Game guy. See if he'll fly and open it."

"Good luck with that," Pete murmured.

"He's always trying. Better than doing nothing. Hey, beautiful. Are those your video talents?" Case asked, turning to reach for another piece of fish.

Ginny grinned at him. "Yup. I'm stitching stuff together fast. No finesse, but you get the point. What have you been up to?" She shut her laptop and looked at him. "You're looking pretty satisfied."

"I pulled some interesting people together today, and it was a blast. Is there any ice cream here?"

"You ate the last of it. I went to get some last night and zip," Pete said.

"Oh, sorry. I'll get more. Promise."

"What people?" Justin asked.

"A guy from the Kenai Water Protectors group, two guys from the Park Service, and two guys from Ducks Unlimited, up sport fishing for halibut. And Tessa."

"Jesus. You didn't unleash her on those unsuspecting men, did you?" Pete sat up straight in the recliner and spun to face his son.

"Yup. Sure did. They loved her."

"No way," Pete whispered. "That woman's a tornado."

Case laughed. "God, I know it. I love her. That energy! It's you she steamrolls. Everyone else she talks to like they're in first grade, which is usually their comprehension level, anyway. These guys actually steamrolled *her*. I think three or four of them are biologists, like her, and just as passionate as she is about salmon and their habitat. They went to town, talking non-stop. I had a hard time following some of it, but they want to get together again. That's what we were doing when your text came in," he said, looking at Justin. "Looking at our schedules. Turns out we'll all be in or near Fairbanks in two weeks, and Seattle in about six weeks. Or eight. I can't remember, but I'll be there. I can't wait. Neither can Tessa. Beer, anyone?" He stood up, grabbed another piece of fish, and headed for the kitchen.

Pete's mouth was still hanging open. Justin turned down the beer, saying he and Gin were headed back to the boat.

Walking down the ramp, Justin and Ginny saw someone sitting on the dock railing alongside the Calypso. A lanky guy with shoulder-length, dirty-blonde hair, wearing worn work clothes and well-used deck boots. Approaching closer, they could see huge loops in his earlobes and plenty of tattoos. The guy stood up and said, "Hey," and Justin replied likewise. "I'm looking for work. You work on this boat?" he asked, looking from Justin to Ginny.

"My boat," Justin said, watching the stranger's face, noting clear eyes and a steady gaze. He looked to be in his late twenties and showed surprise at Justin's reply.

"Wow, good for you, man. Need a deckhand?"

"I'm short one guy, but what I really need is a skiffman."

"Ah. I did a season but only on corks."

"Where?"

"Here. That boat over there," he pointed to the Stormy C. "Four or five years ago."

"That's my uncle's boat."

"Mack's your uncle? Oh wow. I was gonna ask him for a job, but I don't have his number anymore."

"He's set for crew this season," Justin said, although he and Ginny talked almost daily about her coming to work on the Calypso. If she did, Mack would need a deckhand, or Justin would have to give up Ben or Greg in trade.

"I'm Finn. From New Jersey. Maybe he'll remember me. I'll give you my number if you want, or I can come back tomorrow..."

"Let me get your number," Justin said, pulling out his phone. "I worked this boat with my dad back then. I think I remember you."

"New Jersey's the armpit of America," Ginny said, watching Finn, who looked surprised but not as surprised as Justin. "Congratulations on getting out alive."

"You sound like a snotty Vermonter," Finn countered. "You working this boat?" he asked, looking at her, then Justin.

Ginny opened her mouth, but Justin was faster, his voice hard. "When she's on this boat, she's deckboss. If she says jump, don't even ask how high. If you can't handle that, say so now." Finn's smile grew as Justin spoke.

"Nah, man. Just givin' her shit. I hear New England in there somewhere. Did I guess right, ya tree-hugger?"

Ginny laughed and shoved Finn's arm. "I love trees. Burlington."

"Figures. Girls," he rolled his eyes. "I got three older sisters, man. Don't worry. I won't argue with her. Just looking for work. Your uncle was a good cook. I remember that specialty thing he made for breakfast. God, was that good."

29

Ginny walked along the dock with Finn, asking where he was staying, not surprised to hear that he was camping in a tent. As she stepped back aboard the boat, she could hear Justin talking, probably on the phone with Mack, she guessed, as she went into the cabin.

She settled herself and her laptop at the dinette while he stood next to the captain's chair. He usually either sat at the helm or touched the captain's chair in some way whenever he talked about running the boat, she thought, smiling and looking down at the table.

"You're happy with the videos?" he asked.

"Oh, yeah. But when you said drone, I wanted one. I need to learn how they work." She waited, knowing that was just a lead-in question.

"What did you think about Finn? Any impressions?" Justin leaned back against the well-padded chair. His dad had followed Mack's example and bought a vehicle bucket seat, installing it after tearing out the miserably uncomfortable captain's chair that had originally come with the boat.

Ginny looked down at her hands. "No, not really."

"Those tattoos or those ear things bother you?"

She shook her head. "Nope. Did you just talk to Mack about him?"

"Yeah. The guy did a season with him but left before putting the nets away. Said some family thing came up. But," he pursed his lips, then continued, "he admitted to being a heavy user. That's why he was in Alaska, to get away from all the people he knew who kept him in that cycle."

Familiar enough with the catch-22 of users who don't want to see each other dead but still shot up together, Ginny didn't even nod. There wasn't much she hadn't been exposed to in seventeen years of foster care.

"Then, according to Mack, he fell right back into it."

"And now he's here again..."

Justin raised his eyebrows and shook his head. "I don't mind givin' the guy a chance, but that track record... Mack said he was a good worker, though."

"What about those last messages?"

"Last possible guy got a job in the Sound. And I'm not taking a fifteen-year-old."

Ginny looked around the boat, remembering that Justin had taken it over mid-season last year. "You've never hired anyone before..." He shook his head. "Maybe, ah, have Mack talk to Finn, too? See what he thinks?"

"Yeah. He goes one hundred percent by his gut. I'll see what he's up to. See if he has time to meet Finn this week."

Justin sent a text to Mack, asking what his plans were, and quickly got one back.

MACK

canning reds until something opens. Sure you can help

"Mack's going for more reds, for canning and maybe freezing," Justin said, watching the smile grow on Ginny's face. "He said we can help—"

"Yes! Oh, God, yes. Then we get some, right?" She was practically floating, and he laughed.

"Yeah, we'd get some. I bet my dad would love some, too. Eating peppered pinks. Yuk. He's never gonna live that down."

"I liked the peppered pinks. Can we pepper some reds? Have you done that?"

"We never did. Not that I remember. I dunno what he was thinking, doing that pink. You can ask Hattie, though. Mack used to talk about putting jalapeños in his."

Ginny laughed. "He'll put jalapeños in anything—no, everything, if he can get away with it."

He texted Mack back, saying they'd both go fishing, then help with the canning or freezing.

"You tired? Ready for bed? I'm thinking about taking the skiff out. I want to see the creeks. Just a couple, not far..."

"Oh, let's go." Picking up her laptop, she put it in her bunk, then swapped shoes for boots, while he did the same.

"Gin, sort the fillets when you're done rinsing 'em. Anything with a snag mark or scar, anything like that, goes in that cooler," Mack said, pointing to his little blue cooler on the dock next to the cleaning station. "Nice ones in the red one. We'll freeze the good ones, kipper the rest."

Ginny scrambled to keep up with pulling whole cold salmon from the coolers and lining them up on the large cutting tables for both men, then rinsing and sorting the bloody fillets they slid toward her. Seagulls lined and strutted the gut barge, hoping for a miss as the two fishermen flung carcasses after slicing fillets from the sockeyes. Ginny barely had a second to glance across the sparking, still water of the harbor as boat after boat putted by, aiming for the breakwater, their occupants eager to catch their limit of bright red salmon. It was barely ten in the morning, and Mack and Justin had already caught their limit and were back in the harbor cleaning their catch.

Done filleting, Mack cleaned his table, then dumped the cooler of imperfect fillets back onto the cutting table. He cut them into chunks, removing punctures and bruises in the meat, tossing the good chunks into his cooler, counting them as he flung them in.

"Forty pieces per batch," he said. "If we have extras, we'll eat 'em. Maybe give Pete some."

"Sounds good," Justin agreed, still filleting his pile.

Mack was a machine when it came to filleting salmon; no one could keep up with him. Justin didn't even try. He focused on getting the best slice he could—with the most meat—from each fish, and he didn't care how long it took.

"There's three left," Mack said, washing his lethal weapon of a fillet knife. "Give 'em to Pete? We've been eating fish for a week." He laughed and glanced at the pile still in front of Justin. "Want help there?"

"Naw, I've got it. I'll get mine cut up and bring 'em over. "Yeah, we've been living on salmon, too. I'll give my extras to my dad, too. He can freeze them—"

"Okay, I'm gonna get these brining. See ya," he said, holstering his knife, then hefted his coolers, walking along the dock to the ramp and parking lot.

"Man, somebody needs to dial him down," Ginny mumbled, and Justin laughed.

"He's always been that way. You should be used to him by now," he said, pausing his cutting, rinsing his bloodied hands and knife while Ginny sprayed the blood and slime off the table in front of him.

"I am on the boat. But right now? This isn't life or death; it's just canning fish."

"Doesn't matter. He moves at one speed—faster than the next guy. Always has."

"I like your speed," she said, and he leaned over to kiss her quickly, then went back to work.

Empty wide mouth pint jars covered every available inch of Hattie's kitchen counters. The newly washed canning jars, sitting on towels, were ready to be filled, and Ginny said, "Wow," as she walked into the kitchen. "Where are the kids?"

"Summer camp, thank God," she said, rinsing more jars.

"Looks like you're ready. Anything I can do?"

"Once we get into canning mode, it doesn't stop. Ah, no, not yet, thanks."

The vacuum sealer sat on the dining table, ready for use. Mack and Justin were outside, taking the first forty chunks out of their brine and putting them on smoker racks. Ginny stepped aside quickly as Mack came in, heading straight for the stove, setting the timer to one hour. Justin followed him in with a cooler and put it on the floor. "Ack, that thing's filthy," Ginny blurted out, looking at Hattie, who was drying her hands. Justin started picking it up again, and Hattie motioned for him to put it down.

"That's why I chose this flooring and these counters. They're practically industrial. One step up from concrete and stainless steel," she smiled. "Don't worry about the floor or the counters."

Ginny looked unconvinced, then noticed that they all still had their deck boots on, and Hattie caught her look. "See. I need it. And I don't want to worry about the floor. There are far more important things in life than a spotless floor."

Mack was cutting vacuum sealer bags, and Justin asked, "Want me to rinse these again?"

"No, but get 'em on a cutting board. I like to cut 'em in half, then layer, skin side out. That's been working really good for the past few years."

Hattie pulled a fitted cutting board away from the sink, holding it. "Dump them in here. Then I can rinse them one more time, and he can cut them however he wants," she said. Justin lifted the cooler and emptied the fillets into the sink, then took the cooler outside to rinse it with the hose.

Ginny stood back and surveyed the kitchen. She remembered helping Mack in the old kitchen and wondered if the process would be smoother now with the new kitchen layout. She glanced at Hattie. "How..." she started, waving her hand, her brows drawn together.

"Stuff jars here," Hattie pointed to one open spot. "Wipe, then canner," she finished, pointing to the stove.

"But, standing?"

"Sitting was killing my back," she said. "Table was too high, the counters too low. The buffet is the perfect height. That's why I wanted it where it is and the height it is."

Ginny laughed, surprised and impressed. "You designed your kitchen for canning fish?"

"Yes. It's a lot of work, and I can't take being uncomfortable while doing it anymore. For the rest of the year, the kitchen works just fine; the heights of things aren't critical. But right now is when it's going to be perfect. And that's what I wanted."

Ginny couldn't wait to see it in action.

30

Wiping the last of the jars, then sliding it to Hattie for a lid and band, Ginny said, "These floor mats make all the difference."

"Don't they?" Hattie agreed. She'd bought two of the best mats she could find for standing on as they worked on the kitchen side of her new extended counter top, the area she called her buffet. Mack and Justin sat opposite them, working over salmon-specked cutting boards with empty, half-pint, wide-mouth canning jars surrounding them.

"The chairs are comfortable, too," Justin said, leaning back, stretching. The timer on the stove went off, and Mack got up, washed his hands, then went out to change the chips in the smokers.

"I'm really glad it's working so well. I've wanted something like this for as long as we've lived in this house," Hattie said, picking up the cutting boards and taking them to the oversized sink.

Justin followed her and washed his knife and his hands, drying both with one of the many small towels lying around the kitchen. "What's the plan for the rest of the day?" he asked as Mack came back in and reset the timer to one hour.

"Run two batches through the canner, start over tomorrow. Still waiting on an announcement." He pulled his phone out of his pocket and scanned his emails. "Nothing yet, but hmmm. Al loves the videos," he said, glancing at Ginny, his brows together.

"I thought he might like to see them, too," she explained.

"You have time to meet that old crewman of yours? Finn? I'd like to know your impression before I hire him," Justin asked Mack.

"Sure. Let me know when."

"Okay, thanks. Have you heard from Wade? Are they getting any gold up at Russell's place?"

"Hahahaha, wait till you see this. He sent a picture of the wing-dam they built. It's huge. He said Viv's threatening to drown them both, and she refuses to lift one more rock. But yeah, they found some nice nuggets. Here, check this out..." He pulled up some photos and sat next to Justin, swiping through them, and Ginny went around the counter to look over his shoulder.

"I wonder if this is what it might be like to start a small processing business," Justin said Tuesday morning, his fingers stuffing another jar with partially smoked red salmon. "Gabe's trying so hard. He sent me some pics of a place he's looking at leasing."

"How's he's doing?" Hattie asked, going back to peeling skins off smoked salmon chunks.

"Still working on it, I guess, trying to pull it all together. Direct to market. Catching, processing, selling."

"Lotta work," Mack said, stuffing jars with the fish Hattie

set on his cutting board, as she peeled skins off the smoked chunks piled next to her.

"Lotta payoff," Hattie countered. "Have you priced a jar of kippered fish lately?" Mack shrugged as he continued stuffing, but it was Justin who answered.

"Fifteen bucks or more for the short jars." Mack choked loudly. "We get paid about, oh, ten cents or less for the amount of fish that's in these jars. Less if it was pinks," Justin added.

"But you'd have to sell at least," Mack did the math quickly, "thousands of jars, to make what we make. And that's not including the cost of processing or shipping."

"Storing, payroll, marketing, leasing space. All those too," Hattie added, then asked, "Are you seriously thinking about doing that? I thought you were just helping Gabe."

Justin shrugged, continuing to pack and pass jars to Ginny, who wiped the tops clean, then put on lids and bands. "Just thinking," he finally replied.

"Pete's Peppered Pinks," Ginny said, and grinned at their surprised looks.

"Right," Justin said. "Have you ever peppered any? My dad did. A pink of all things. Tasted pretty good though."

"We did that once, didn't we?" Mack asked his wife. "That year Dylan was here? You two were doing everything imaginable to those poor fish. And to me, too. Made me fish eggs," he grimaced, and Ginny laughed loudly, covering her mouth.

"Caviar," Hattie corrected him. "Yeah. We should try it. Gin, grind some pepper into a couple of the small jars, while Justin's packing. Let's try it again."

"Okay, sure," she agreed eagerly.

The long-awaited announcement was released Wednesday morning, anticipating an opening the following Monday.

They all discussed it while canning more sockeyes. There were three advisory announcements issued for the area their permits covered, an area that was approximately two hundred miles from east to west and was roughly the size of the state of West Virginia. But it was the opening of two sub-districts he hadn't been able to fish in for years that took Mack's breath away.

June 12

Advisory Announcement for Eastern District, Lower Cook Inlet Salmon

ADF&G anticipates opening Resurrection Bay, Day Harbor, and Aialik Bay for Common Property Commercial Seine Fishing on June 17 dependent upon achieving desired escapement goals.

Mack hadn't fished Aialik commercially for over ten years, and he loved it there. He spent the entire morning stuffing jars and telling stories about fishing in both Aialik and Day Harbor, all of which had happened before Justin started crewing on his dad's boat. Since he wasn't familiar with either bay, Justin said he was planning on staying in Res Bay for the first opener.

The peppered jars, processed Tuesday afternoon, then cracked open Wednesday morning as a celebration to the new announcement, were an instant hit. Before they started filling jars for the next batch, Hattie poured peppercorns into a small grinder, pulverizing them. Ginny sprinkled the coarsely ground pepper into small jars as Justin packed them, eventually seasoning three dozen small jars.

. . .

Mack and Justin met Finn on the docks that afternoon, and on Mack's nod, Justin hired him. Justin said he'd start him in the skiff, with either himself, Wade, or Case showing him the ropes.

After reviewing and signing a contract, he let Finn bring some of his things aboard, showing him his bunk and checking his gear over, then took him to buy good raingear. He still had his brown deck boots, which were practically indestructible. Finn picked out gloves he liked, and Justin paid for it all, saying it would come from Finn's check at the end of the season, then paid cash for Finn's commercial fishing license. He dropped his new skiffman off at the campground he was tenting in, saying it might be a few days or a week before they actually started fishing—the newest announcement was only an advisory notice.

Justin brought up his most difficult conversation while walking the docks with Ginny after dinner. "I need you to do what's right for you," he said, for the third time, admitting he was unwilling to influence her.

Ginny dragged her feet while walking the docks as much as she dragged her thoughts back and forth. She wanted to be near him, she said, but was scared of being overwhelmed and overtired, which she left unsaid.

In the end, Justin summed up the issue. "If you aren't jumping at the chance to change boats, then it's probably not the right thing to do." They stood at the end of a dock, looking at the seiners across the flat water of the harbor. She thought about it and reluctantly agreed, then hugged him, and he felt her shivering.

"I'd rather lose you as crew than lose you completely," he whispered, tightening his hold on her. "We'll still be together, right?" He tipped her chin up, searching her eyes, finally seeing peace in them.

"Yes. I can work anywhere, but I..." she buried her face in his neck. He stroked her mass of curls, tipping his head down enough to kiss her forehead.

"Okay. That's done. Let Mack know, okay?" She nodded her head against him, still holding tight. "If we change our minds, he'll swap crew," Justin said, more to himself than to her, and she nodded. They walked back to the Calypso, and she texted Mack and Viv with her decision.

The fishing and canning routine continued for the rest of the week, and by Friday, Ginny was sure she loved Hattie's kitchen, with only one exception—it was too small for four people, she said.

Hattie agreed. "I never thought of anyone but us doing this," she laughed, swerving around Ginny as they almost bumped into each other for the umpteenth time. "But I'm not complaining. It's as nice to have help as it is to finally have a dishwasher."

Mack refused to sport fish after Friday morning. The crowds of weekend fishermen were something he didn't want to deal with. He went into full season-prep mode the minute the official announcement came out on Friday afternoon.

They'd be fishing the local bays on Monday, and he could barely believe it. He texted Wade and Viv, then started listing, aloud and repeatedly, everything he needed to do to be ready. Justin finished packing the last of the fish on his cutting board, washed his hands, and texted Ben and Greg to be in the harbor by 8 p.m. Sunday night, ready to work Monday, reminding them to bring all their raingear and have their commercial fishing licenses on them.

Putting the last of the packed jars in the fridge for

processing tomorrow, Hattie waved Justin and Ginny out the door, saying she'd clean up. They headed for the Calypso.

"Our last two nights alone out here," Justin said, holding Gin as they sat on the flying bridge anchored across the bay, watching boats traveling in and out of the harbor. Wade said he'd spend Sunday helping train Finn in the skiff, and Ginny would move back to Mack's boat Sunday night, giving up the other top bunk to the new skiffman.

Bringing the boys out to Pete's on Friday night, Hattie cycled them through the shower while sitting on the sofa with Pete, chatting between trips into the bathroom to supervise them.

"You have no idea how much watching them launch the boats and load the nets was killing me," Pete said. "Now Aialik's open..." He shook his head. Everything they'd been working toward lately—finally happening—and he was stuck at home.

She'd felt the same, after crewing for Mack for a few years. Watching him leave the harbor with a new crew, leaving her behind, had cut her heart out. She still felt the pain, even though it had been fifteen years ago. For a guy like Pete, who'd seined his whole life, well, maybe she didn't quite know how bad that felt, but she could still empathize.

"You know you could take the boat out on weekends or something," she tried. The look he gave her had her changing the subject quickly. It was the work he missed, not the boat itself, and one weekend wasn't going to change that. It might even make things more painful.

"Do you want Evie to start cleaning again, now that

Ginny's gone? I mean, with only you and Case staying here this summer..."

"Evie. Um," he twisted uncomfortably. "No. Case and I can handle it. But I was thinking about letting her boys come over maybe for—"

"Don't."

Pete turned, looking at Hattie in surprise. "The kids don't get along like they used to—" she started to say, but he interrupted.

"But you meet them..."

"Sure. At the playground. With other kids around. She's there watching them like a hawk. But when she's not around, things change, and they don't listen to me." Her voice was cold. "I'm not putting up with that. You know me. I know how to handle kids, but these two... Nope. Not anymore. And our two started picking up some of their bad behavior."

Pete sat up straighter. "Okay. I'm with you. We don't need that kind of problem."

"I, ah, was getting the impression that there might be something between you and Evie?" Hattie hinted, watching his reaction.

Pete gave nothing away as he shook his head. "No. I don't want another family, and I don't need another relationship. I'm not sure what her status is, and I don't want to know."

31

Pete loved the process of smoking salmon strips almost as much as he loved eating them. From cutting the thick, red salmon fillets into long strips, to hanging the brined strips, then finessing the week-long smoking of the strips—it was a week's worth of slow-building anticipation. His mouth watered every time he went into the cramped hut to check the temperature, adjust the air flow, or add wood to the wood-stove, following the same process his mother had used and her parents before her.

Friday night, seven days after hanging them, he took the strips down and started trimming and packaging them. Checking the seal on the last bundle from the vacuum sealer, he gazed at his dining table. Piles of sealed packages and another pile that smelled so tempting: the trimmed ends of each strip. The salty delicacy that everyone devoured first.

He'd begun nibbling as he sorted packages. Half to Mack because he'd caught half the fish. Justin had said to split his half the way Pete had always done, in thirds, but Pete wouldn't eat as much as he used to. He made large piles for Justin and

Case, taking a handful for himself as he continued to snack on the trimmed bits.

Returning the vacuum sealer to its spot in the cupboard, Pete stood looking at his sofa, wondering what to watch on TV, when his phone rang. Crossing the room to the dining table, where he'd left his reports, phone, and keys when walking in from work, he saw Evie's name and answered it quickly.

"Evie, hi."

"Pete, hi, oh God, I'm in such a bind. I didn't know who to call. I just don't know what to do here," her voice quavered, sounding out of breath, and there was a lot of noise in the background, men yelling instructions to each other over loud engine noises.

Pete pulled out a chair, sitting down quickly. "What? What's wrong? Are you safe? Tell me—"

"I'm okay. The kids are okay. Did you hear all the sirens out here? There's like, four fire trucks—"

"Jesus! No, I didn't. What? Your house?" He could feel his heart starting to race and took deep breaths.

"Apartment. Not mine. I'm on the lower floor. The one above me. It's burnt out completely. They say—" her voice caught, and she coughed. "They say I can't stay here. We can't stay here. They have to go inside with me while I grab some clothes, that's it."

"Holy shit, come here. Can you drive? Want me to come get you? I'll be right there—"

"No, Pete, ah, I've got the kids in my car, but we have to go somewhere, and I don't know where. Can I come there for a while until I figure this out?"

"Yes, come here."

"Oh, God, thanks. You're a lifesaver. We're on our way." She ended the call.

Pete called Hattie, letting her know, knowing that his heart app would notify her of his racing beats, totally out of rhythm. Standing, he paced the room, waiting for her to answer.

"Pete, sorry, I couldn't find my phone. What's up? Change your mind about us all coming out tomorrow?" she laughed.

"Evie called. Her apartment building had a fire. She can't stay there. I told her to come here, but well, um, my heart started racing. My watch is buzzing now. I'm walking in the house. Pacing. I'll follow all of our steps if it gets worse. It just—, ah, I was scared for her and the kids, and then you said—"

"Okay, Pete," she said slowly, keeping her voice calm and even. "You did the right thing. Deep breaths too, remember? Are you going to be good? Want me to come out there? You can send her here. I can double the boys up..."

"No. No, that's okay. They, ah, can have the kid's room, and she can have mine or the sofa. Oh, right, we even have that pull-out now..." He took another deep breath, then saw car headlights through the window. "She's here. I'll talk to you later."

"Okay, deep breaths. Bye for now."

Pete stood at the open door, then went to help her unload kids and suitcases. Everything smelled of filthy garbage smoke, so unlike campfire smoke. They piled inside and settled in the living room, Evie taking the sofa, with a boy under each arm. Pete sat in the recliner and turned to them. "You guys must have been scared a little, huh? The fire alarms going off, all those firetrucks coming?"

They nodded, eyes still wide, blinking a lot, and he guessed it was probably from the smoke.

"Evie, baths? I, ah, can get some laundry started? Please,

please feel at home here," he spread his hands out. She probably was as familiar with the house as he was.

She sagged and sighed. "Thanks. I'm sure we stink. Baths would be great—"

"Aw, mom, you said we could have a treat for doing everything you said," Erik whined.

"I have ice cream bars. Case just stocked the freezer. You guys go with your mom into the tub, and I'll bring you an ice cream. You can eat them in the tub," he offered, smiling as they laughed. They jumped up, heading for the bathroom, peeling off their shirts, talking about how weird it would be to eat ice cream in the bathtub.

"If you'll toss their PJs in a pile, I'll get them washed, or they can wear an old shirt of mine or Justin's to bed," he offered, standing. "You must be exhausted. There's a pull-out under one of the twin beds and another one in the playroom. You'll probably want to be near them tonight. Want me to supervise bath time? I have plenty of experience."

"Thanks, that's sweet. I've got this, but you know what? I'd love an ice cream, too."

"Sure. Be right in." He headed for the kitchen, and she followed the clothing trail to the bathroom, picking things up as she went.

Pete unwrapped the ice creams, handing one to each boy. Evie took hers and tipped it toward the hallway, giving the kids another assessing look before following Pete out and closing the bathroom door.

"It's Evan's birthday tomorrow," she whispered, her eyes tearing. "I left his presents—"

"You stay here, I'll go," Pete insisted. "Let me have your keys. What's the address?"

Evie, drooping, mumbled, "Thanks," and went back to the living room, getting her keys from her purse, giving him directions.

"Okay, I'll hide everything. Now go get some rest, please."

Pete parked across the street from the burnt apartment building and crossed the tape barricade that had been put up, looking at the fire trucks that still remained on site, their crews replacing gear.

"Hey! No-go there, guy," a fireman called to him from one of the florescent yellow trucks parked off to the side.

"Hi, ah, I'm here to get Evie's kid's birthday presents out of one bedroom. She didn't have time. Downstairs apartment, number three."

"Oh, hey, Pete. How are ya? What a mess here, huh? You know Evie?"

"She cleans the house for me, and her kids play with mine. She's dead beat. I said I'd come and do this for her."

"Hey, sure. Can't have kids havin' a birthday with no presents, right? I gotta escort you, though…"

"Sure. Is that Steve? I can hardly see you under all that gear."

"Yeah, Steve-O. How's it going? Heard you got out of fishing." They walked inside and down the short flight of stairs. Pete pulled out Evie's keys, and Steve flicked a flashlight on so he could see what he was doing as he searched for the right key, then unlocked and opened the door.

"I sold my boat, but I do miss it," Pete said, then started coughing. The waft of smoke was like a wall hitting them as it escaped the apartment.

"Don't stay long. This smoke'll do you in," Steve urged. Pete found the master bedroom, with the help of Steve's flashlight, then looked for the packages. There weren't many and between the two of them, they carried them up and loaded them into the trunk of the car. Pete remembered to grab the party decorations from the top shelf of her closet, as Evie'd asked.

Pete opened the driver's door and stood next to it. "Thanks man. You guys are the best. You saved the day yet again."

"Sure thing, Pete, but ah, I gotta tell ya something. Just between us, right? It's not official…"

"Okay. What's up?"

"Um, this fire. We thought it was the upstairs guy. You know, smoker, older guy, but naw, chief says it looks like it was set outside his front door."

"Set?"

"Yeah. Somebody did it. Amateur. In fact, you might say —if you knew what you were dealing with, and I do 'cause my kid was in Evan's class last year—that it was set by a juvenile."

Pete gripped his car door. "Jesus, Steve. Seriously?"

The big fireman nodded, his bulky hat bobbing.

"Holy shit. I, I let her and the kids come stay at my house. They're there right now."

"Might wanna think on that. And, again, this is not official, but if we get prints, that kid's going away somewhere. Juvie lockup, probably."

"Christ. He's only—"

"I know. My kid's about his age too. And he's not allowed to go anywhere near that troublemaker. They start young sometimes. The bad ones, anyways."

"Thanks. And I mean it, man. You may have just saved me from—" he waved one hand, the other still had a death-grip on the open car door. He didn't even think about his heart anymore, hammering away from adrenaline. Steve nodded, putting his big fire-protective glove over Pete's hand for a moment, then walked away.

• • •

Steve knew that Pete had lost his wife recently to cancer and felt bad for him. He had no idea what to say to Pete about his loss, but he sure as hell could help him avoid more tragedy. Pete had a young son to protect, a boy who wasn't much younger than Steve's.

32

Hattie stared at her phone, wondering what in the hell was going on.

She'd assumed, from the interactions she'd seen and questions Evie had asked at the playground, that the small family might just settle in with Pete. But there was also a sort of awkwardness between the two of them. Hattie'd sensed it before, wondering if it was just her. Now, it seemed it was real.

Carrying her coffee to the living room, she sat on her new sofa and stared off into space, wondering where they could put the family in this tourist-packed town in late June. It would be completely impossible to find long-term housing, she knew immediately. Every available space booked up months in advance; homes turned into B&Bs; apartments turned into weekly rentals. She went back to her kitchen counter, where Mack and the boys were eating cereal.

"Small change today, guys. Um, Evie's apartment building

had a fire. But," she hurried, "she's fine and Evan and Erik are too. They're gonna stay at Pete's for a bit, so you'll be here this weekend."

"Evan likes fire," Robbie said, and Hattie felt the blood drain from her face as her throat swelled shut, staring at the boy.

"Yeah, he has lighters and matches and cans of stuff. He wanted to start one in the playroom, but we said no," Mickey added, examining his superhero figurine.

"Tell dad not to let him burn our playroom or our toys, okay?" Robbie asked, looking at her as he started gathering his toys around him, his lower lip trembling.

Hattie's eyes bulged, and her hands covered her mouth as Mack's mouth hung open. She shot him a warning look as she eased over to hug Robbie, assuring him that Pete would not let that happen, saying that she was going to call him now and let him know to be on alert.

Grabbing her phone quickly, she headed into the garage, with Mack right behind her. He shut the door, turning to her as she tapped to call Pete.

"Pete, you probably can't talk, but are you in a spot where you can listen, privately?" she put the call on speaker so Mack could hear.

"Sure thing, Hat, one sec, let me check the fridge." Pete jumped up from the edge of the recliner, where he'd been watching Evan open his presents. Evie had made 'birthday' waffles, and they'd all sung Happy Birthday to him and then enjoyed breakfast.

She was on the sofa now and probably couldn't hear the conversation on his phone, but Pete stood and walked through the kitchen, down the hallway, into his bedroom, and shut the door. "In my bedroom, they're in the living room."

"Pete, Robbie just said that Evan wanted to start a fire in the playroom. Do you think it's possible—"

"Yeah. It is," he interrupted, speaking rapidly, panting as if he'd just run an uphill race. "I went to get the kid's birthday presents from the apartment last night, and one of the firemen —you can't repeat this—said that it looked like a juvenile started the fire."

And there goes my heart. Even worse.

She couldn't reply, managing only a low-throated growl.

"Yeah, that left me choking, too. I didn't sleep at all last night. God, I kept smelling smoke, and everything they own is saturated with it. Um, I was thinking. Those cabins. Where Nell was renting. Remember, she told us about them once in a meeting? Any idea who owns or manages them? I can't leave the house for fuck's sake, and I can't make calls either. I wanted to spend time with *my* kids this weekend," his voice cracked.

"Pete. Hang in there. I'll get on it. Mack, too. We'll have something as fast as we can. Soon. Promise me you'll take deep breaths."

"I promise," he sighed.

"God, this is all my fault for ever—" Hattie blew out.

"No. No, don't. You were helping me. Let's just—"

"Right. Solve it first. Starting now. Okay, bye for now." She ended the call.

"I'm calling everyone I know," Mack said, then went inside and grabbed his phone and keys. Coming back into the garage, he gave Hattie a brief kiss, then went out to his truck and started calling people, explaining he was helping a fire victim and needed housing for three.

After three hours of calling and no luck whatsoever, Hattie's protective instincts took over. Recognizing her mother-bear mode, Mack merely listened, nodded, and started gathering what he needed. Hattie texted Evie first.

HATTIE

Playground?

EVIE

YES. I need a break. They need to run. On our way

She messaged Pete next:

HATTIE

She's coming here, and I'll deal with her. This will be over soon—today. Deep breaths. Mack is coming to you now.

PETE

Will do. TY

Her last text went to Ginny.

HATTIE

Big favor. Can you come up and stay with the kids for a while right now?

GINNY

Sure. On my way. Bringing a load of laundry :)

Zigzagging her way downhill along residential streets filled with old houses and large yards, Hattie crossed the last boulevard and headed for her favorite bench at the playground, planning what to say, choosing her words carefully. Several minutes later, she heard car doors slam and boys yipping as they ran to the play area. Evie plopped down beside her, and Hattie could smell the stench of trash-smoke on her clothes.

"My God. I can't believe this. That asshole upstairs is gonna buy me an' the kids new clothes, that's for sure," she blew out. "Where are the boys? Hiding?"

"No, I left them home. I need to talk to you about something they said," Hattie started, and Evie's back stiffened.

"Like what?"

"When I told them about the fire, and that you were all okay, they said that Evan likes to start fires. He has lighters and matches..."

"That's bullshit!" She stiffened and turned away, watching her sons. "Evan's a good kid. Your kids are just jealous because he's older. It's probably something they watched on TV or in a movie."

"No, I don't think so, Evie. And I don't think they were lying. I don't think they'd lie about something like this. They weren't telling on him—"

"Oh, right. I know. *Your* kids are perfect. This is bullshit. And I don't need it. I see what you're up to. You're trying to get us out of Pete's house. Well, he *likes* me. *That's* what this is all about. The fact that he likes me, and he likes my kids. You better get used to it." She sat back, crossing her arms, her mouth turned down and tight.

"Evie, he has a heart condition, and the kind of stress that a situation like this—"

"There *is* no *situation*. He has room for us, and he asked us to move in. He said we can stay as long as we need to. It's none of your business—"

Hattie'd had more than enough and cut her off as her hand went up. "Stop talking. He needs peace in his life, and that's our priority here. No, don't interrupt me again. Shut up and listen," she growled, the bear taking over completely, claws coming out. "We will give you some money, but you'll be leaving Pete's house. We tried to find housing for you, but it's impossible in the middle of tourist season. I suggest you take the cash and head to Anchorage, where you can find work and housing."

"I'm not fucking going anywhere," Evie gritted, standing

up, giving Hattie a look so filled with hate that she actually felt a stab of pain in her spine. Evie spun and stomped to the edge of the playground.

"Let's go, boys! Uncle Pete's waiting for us. He wants us back home now. You can play pirate-treasure there," she yelled. "C'mon, c'mon. Yes, I mean now and no arguing or no ice cream." Evie turned one last smug look at Hattie, then straightened her back and strutted off, grabbing Erik's hand and dragging him to the car.

Hattie twisted on the bench and continued watching as Evie loaded the kids and herself, started the car and then pulled out in front of an oncoming car, its brakes squealing while Evie's tires threw gravel, spinning out of the unpaved parking lot.

"Jesus, Mack. You didn't have to get the police involved," Pete said, looking out the window for the twentieth time and seeing a patrol car roll slowly down Thunder Bay Avenue, past his driveway.

"Sit down, Pete," Mack said, for probably the tenth time. "And I didn't. If they're here, I don't know why. Hattie asked me to come out here and bring that old lockset of ours and change your locks if they needed to be changed. And from what she said on the phone, I'm thinkin' they do. What the heck? They parked by the warehouse. What the fuck's going on here?" He reached for his phone to call Hattie.

"She's here," Pete said breathlessly, still at the window.

Mack pocketed his phone without calling, walked into the entryway, telling his brother to stand back, using the tone he reserved for ordering around green deckhands on his boat.

Evie pulled into the driveway, and Pete's heart immediately went into double-beats. His neck tightened, and he saw stars as he gripped the window frame for balance. Mack stared at his brother, who'd turned as white as a sheet. Getting right in Pete's face, Mack said, "Go sit down, right fucking now."

"I'm okay, I'm okay," Pete blurted. "I gotta see this through."

The locked doorknob rattled as Evie turned it, and she immediately yelled, "Pete! Are you okay?"

Mack put an arm out, refusing to let Pete step forward, but Pete was at his brother's side as Mack swung the door open and quickly stepped forward, blocking the doorway, his hands on the frame.

"Mack! Pete! Jesus, you're so pale. We need to get you into bed," she said, stepping forward, bumping into Mack, and taking a half-step back.

"Nope. You're not coming in. Turn your car around and open the back hatch, and I'll load your stuff. Stay in the car while I do it."

Evie stiffened, her mouth tightening. "No, I won't. This isn't *your* house. Move," she ordered, trying to shoulder him aside. "*Pete* is letting us stay here."

"I'm sorry, Evie, but I can't. I just can't. We're going to give you money for a motel or something, but this isn't—"

"Peter," her eyes filled, and her lip trembled. "We need a safe place—"

"Save it," Mack said as he shifted his bulk sideways in front of his brother. "Back in the car or leave without your stuff." Mack saw the officer standing in the alders, between the warehouse and the driveway, watching. "Now."

"Who is she?" Evie spat, twisting and reaching for Pete, her face distorted, twisted with hate.

"Back up," Mack growled, and she shoved him. Or tried to —he was as immoveable as the house itself. But the moment her hand touched him, the officer started walking forward.

"Step away from the door, ma'am, and keep your hands to yourself."

Evie spun and gasped, seeing the cop, and then saw Hattie's car pull in and park on the far side of the driveway. Her eyes darted from the officer, to her own car, to Hattie, getting out of her car. "Awful lot to go through, just to dump a woman. I already knew. Didn't you think I'd see those dresses? I actually thought they were for me!" she rambled, walking toward her car.

"Stop right there, ma'am. We have some questions to ask you and your son."

Evie's eyes popped, and she ran for her car, but the officer wasn't far behind her. He beat her to the car, pressing a hand against the driver's side door as she reached for the handle. "You do this the hard way, it's not going to go well," he warned.

Hattie passed by on the other side of Evie's car, anxious to get to Pete, who looked like he was ready to collapse. She didn't spare a glance for Evie, who hissed, "Fucking bitch."

"Shut it," the officer ordered. Hattie made it to the doorway and grabbed one of Pete's arms. Mack saw his brother slump and grabbed his other arm, kicking the door shut with his foot.

33

"Recliner," Hattie directed, and Mack aimed for it. They eased Pete in, then raised his feet. "Get me ice," she said, not taking her eyes off Pete. She felt his pulse, then looked at his health-watch, then scanned the room quickly for his phone. She needed to see those heart app readings.

Where the hell is it?

"Pete," she whispered. "Deep breaths. Breathe with me," she put his hand on her chest, taking deep breaths, and put her hand on his. "Nice... and... slow." He sighed. "Thanks. Find his phone please, hon," she said to Mack, taking the plastic bag of ice and putting it on Pete's throat. He jerked, coughed, took a huge breath, his eyes flying open in surprise as he sat forward.

"Jesus. I think that fixed it."

He stretched an arm, like he was going to get up and she sent him her *I'll hurt you* look, saying, "Stay there." He relaxed slowly, watching her face warily. "Where's your goddamned phone?" she growled, frustrated.

"I turned it off," he whispered, staring into her eyes with regret and more than a hint of fear.

205

Hattie looked at Pete as if he'd completely lost his mind, then realized why he'd done it. "You and I, Mister Nichols, are going to have a *discussion* when you're feeling better," she said quietly. Pete rolled sideways and pulled the phone out of his back pocket, handing it to her as he swallowed. She turned it and several health app alerts popped up.

Hattie went out to her car to get what she considered to be her 'Pete's emergency' box. Coconut water, electrolyte powders, and vitamins crowded the small box, along with printouts she'd taken from medical websites about A-Fib.

She made a concoction for him to drink, asked what he'd eaten, asked about his sleep, then looked at his health app to see what else it had to tell her. Very little sleep, broken by many stretches of being awake. She continued to check everything it monitored as Mack leaned against the new countertop, watching her.

"I'm taking my half of the strings. Damn, I forgot how salty these things are. God, this is good," he said, a strip hanging from his mouth as he chewed on it.

Hattie's head flew up from scrolling on Pete's phone, and she stared at Mack, licking his fingers, then reaching into the bag of cut-off strings—the tips of the strips they'd hung that held a morsel of skin and salmon meat. She knew exactly how salty those tips were, and her head rotated to look at Pete.

"Salt! You've been eating nothing but salted strips? Do you know the damage that does to your heart?" Her eyes widened as she stared at Pete, who refused to meet her gaze. "Drink the rest of that. I'm making another one. Oy, Pete..."

"I feel better already, Hat. Honest. I just need some sleep."

"Yes, I see that. I'll save my bitching for later, but oh, you're gonna get it."

"Did you change those locks?" she asked Mack.

"Workin' on it," he said, wrapping the bag of strips back

up. He went for the box of tools and the lock sets he'd brought.

"I'm going home. You," she looked at Pete, "are going to bed." She stood up and walked to Mack, kissing him on the cheek. "Thanks, man. Remember to stop and get keys made. Case and Justin both need new keys now."

"Right. Will do."

"Ginny too," Pete said, easing up from the chair. Hattie followed him to his bedroom. "Hey, wait. Open that closet," Pete said, pulling his T-shirt off over his head.

Pete's side of the closet was open. She slid the doors to see Linda's clothes and felt a wave of regret and loss. Her sister-in-law, confidante, friend. Gone forever.

"Pete. I'm sorry. I should have—"

"No. I wanted them there. But Evie said something about clothes. Did she take any? Or put something in there?" Hattie reached in, pushing hangers, then saw the garment bag at the back of the closet. *Linda's wedding dress?* No way. She wouldn't have kept it hanging for twenty years. Hattie unzipped it and saw the most gorgeous ballgown she'd ever seen in her life. Sparkling bodice, chiffon that floated like a dreamy cloud, with what looked like shantung silk beneath it, all in the most gorgeous shades of green.

Pete stood behind her, and she twisted to meet his puzzled eyes. She touched the gown gently, looking for a tag, then saw an envelope at the bottom of the protective bag. She bent to pick it up, then opened it. Price tags, a business card for a dress shop with a handwritten phone number on the back, and a receipt. She gasped at the prices, and the blood left her face at the total bill. She closed the envelope, put it back, zipped the garment bag, saw the padded hangers behind it, but didn't look at the clothes, her mind going in circles.

Who—what?

Stepping back, she closed the closet door.

"What, exactly, did Evie say about this?" she asked him.

Pete sat on the bed, taking his shoes off. "She just said something like, 'Who's clothes are those?' I don't know. I hardly remember. Maybe it was, 'Who is she?' and that she'd seen the clothes."

Mack walked into the room. "Jeez, I thought maybe you two were having an affair or something." His eyes went from one dazed face to the other. "What the hell's the problem now?"

Hattie circled her hand to Pete, motioning for him to get into bed.

"Locks are changed," Mack said, staring at Hattie, brows tight together as he scowled.

"We'll have extra keys made. Keep that watch on and hang onto your phone, too. Call me later, when you're up. You're safe now. Sleep," Hattie urged.

Heading for the door, she said, "I'll tell you later. Let's go, man. We need to get Evie's stuff out of here. I'll back my car up to the door, and we can drop it off at the police station. They can deal with her."

"So, we're done here? You think this is over now? Did you call the cops?" Mack asked, as they loaded Evie's things from the house entryway into the back of Mack's truck.

"I called and said we might have an issue and asked if they might do a civil standby. I heard a whole lot of 'no-can-do' until I said Evie's name, then it turned into 'we'd be happy to assist,' so I'm guessing they were already looking for her."

"I doubt she'll try to come back," Mack said, walking to his driver's door.

"Maybe we should get some cameras up out here, anyway," Hattie contemplated, waiting for him to start the engine and pull out.

"I'll go drop this stuff off, then I'm going to the boat. I need to check the fuel, make sure I have plenty of gas for the skiff, stuff like that."

"Okay, see you later." She watched him pull away, then walked back to Pete's and made sure his house door was locked, swearing to herself that she'd make damned sure he spent all day tomorrow in bed, if she had to stay there and babysit him to make sure he did.

34

Pete left home early every morning, driving to the far side of the bay and parking on the bluff. He'd watch his boat and his son as they cruised the bay making sets. He had to stop himself from doing the same thing when he left work each day. He'd never known love could be so painful.

He loved his son and loved the boat, wanting the best for both, but it hurt to his core to watch them both on the water, where he longed to be. He missed Justin and Ginny and hated going home to an empty house, hoping each night that Case might be there.

Mack loved reporting in with how much he was catching and delivering from Aialik, often sending photos of his sets and videos of the bay, which all came through to Pete when the Stormy C came into Res Bay to deliver, when Mack's phone finally found a cell signal. He never said so, but Pete knew his brother missed their private competition and still hoped to see Pete on a boat again.

· · ·

Calling Hattie on Friday afternoon, arranging to have the kids for the weekend, Pete asked if Mack was coming home for the weekend or staying out in the bay. Hattie said no, he was going to set some shrimp pots and check out some of the other creeks in Aialik. He'd deliver that afternoon, get fuel, then head straight back out.

Pete drove across the bay and saw the Calypso anchored, the strong afternoon wind keeping her bow pointed south. Several sailboats were out, taking advantage of the strong breeze and sunny day. As he watched, someone went onto the bow of the boat and started the anchor winch. Finn, easily recognizable by his blondish hair, was watching Justin secure the skiff with a safety line. They're moving? When the anchor was up, Justin turned off the hydraulics and went into the cabin. Moments later, the boat headed out of the bay. Pete's phone pinged with a text:

> JUSTIN
>
> Going to Aialik, Mack wants to show me where he's fishing. Maybe steal some shrimp from him

Pete smiled, watching the boat leave, his soul emptying the farther away it traveled. He swallowed, wiped his eyes, texted *good luck, hope you catch lots* to Justin, then started his car and headed home.

Justin tried to pretend he cared about learning where Mack fished in Aialik and that he wanted shrimp, but all he thought about was seeing Gin. Even if they couldn't be together—and he instantly remembered his skiff. He could pick her up, and they'd go walk on a beach somewhere. He'd bring a blanket, maybe some cooked salmon? Oh, God no, no salmon on a beach. *Bears.* No food, just the two of them. He left the helm and raced up to the flying bridge, grinning in anticipation.

Mack dragged Justin from creek to creek in his skiff, showing him the best places to make sets, and they videoed the runs again. On the big seiners, the crew gathered stuff for s'mores and Wade's newspapers for fire-starter, then took Justin's skiff to the beach.

Returning to the boats, which were rafted and anchored together in a small protected cove, Mack said he was tired, hungry, and hoped his crew had left him something for dinner. Justin went into his cabin, saw a plate of food on the table, and ate it quickly, then grabbed a blanket from his bunk. He took off for the beach in Mack's skiff, tying it up alongside his own on the beach.

In Mack's cabin, Wade reached for the binoculars, getting comfortable on the dinette bench. He proceeded to report every movement Justin and Ginny made, like a sports announcer giving play-by-play coverage of the Super Bowl during the fourth quarter of a tied game, with Viv and Mack adding their own crude comments about touchdowns and field goals, which made them all laugh louder and longer.

"We staying here?" Viv asked Mack, blowing her nose and wiping her eyes as Wade ended his report when the young couple disappeared around a corner of the cove carrying a blanket.

"I'm thinking about going to Day Harbor sometime. I want to make at least one set there," Mack said, finally cleaning his plate. He'd almost knocked it over, laughing so hard.

"Just because?"

"Yup. They opened it; I'm fishing it. And if no one else is there, the catch won't be reported."

"What's that mean?" Viv asked, turning back to look at him, but it was Wade who answered.

"If less than three boats fish an area, the catch isn't made public."

"Ohhhhh. So the competition doesn't know. Hmmmm. Interesting," she said to herself, twisting again, watching the beach and the campfire.

She missed beach campfires, but not enough to expose herself to the no-see-ums that seemed to be plaguing this cove. She already had one vicious bite on her forehead, and she was sure the mark would last for the rest of her life. She'd opted to stay aboard and read a book when Gin had urged her to get into the skiff and go ashore with them.

Al's text in late June, asking to meet with the skippers next time they were in the harbor, took both Mack and Justin by surprise, along with his request for Ginny to come along if possible. After delivering their catches, they tied their boats to the dock and walked up to the parking lot, taking Mack's truck to the pavilion, where they'd agreed to meet Al.

Pete and Al were standing outside of the building, looking at the sunlit bay, their hair ruffled in the breeze. Two sailboats and a yacht in the bay, along with a smattering of small pleasure boats, made the late afternoon scene post-card perfect. They met under the pavilion roof, and Al thanked them for coming, getting straight to the point.

"The videos you took in Aialik and Day Harbor have started a chain reaction that I didn't foresee," he said, looking at Justin and Mack across the table. "We moved some of our stream watchers to both places. The fact that our people are so well trained—I don't know if you remember Tessa, the former Fish and Game biologist, but she handled their training, and it's excellent. The clear video footage they're now taking is giving us and Fish and Game a much better assessment of what's out there in real time. Fish and Game is using the footage, accepting it as if they'd taken the video themselves."

"I hear a *but* coming," Mack said, and Al nodded.

"It's good and not so good," Al admitted. "The escapement—and Pete has the historical data—is not what *we'd* like it to be. I want to ask you if you'd be willing to voluntarily either stop fishing, say for a few days, or maybe be slightly less successful at it?" He buffered the request with a smile.

Justin returned his smile, then looked at his dad, who spoke up quickly. "They're not that low, but in order to build up for the future, I'd rather see escapement on the high side. Fish and Game isn't as picky. You know that they open with a minimum escapement. They won't close the area, so it's up to us. I can give you the numbers—"

"Nope," Justin interrupted. "If you say stop, I'm stopping. We've had several good days, and I'm happy with that. I'm close to covering expenses, and I want to be able to keep fishing—right here."

Mack took his time replying, looking from his brother to Al. "I've always said that they needed to get higher numbers here, so I guess I have to choose, and I choose escapement over catching. We're not making that much here, anyway, and I'd rather keep fishing here in the future than have to run to K Bay. So, I'm in. But," he looked at Pete, then Al, "you'll tell us when we can fish again, right?"

"Sure. And if you want to do every-other day, that's—"

Mack was shaking his head already. "No. That just drags things out and then, what if you don't get the numbers? Nope, full stop, and it's a damned good thing it's only us, right?" He nudged Justin.

Justin nodded his agreement, echoing Mack. "Full stop, right now, and yeah, I am glad it's only us working these bays."

"Okay, I thank you guys. I know this is your livelihood—"

"Meh," Mack muttered. "We get good-money fish in the Outer District, too. And it's almost time to get out of here, anyway. So," he turned to Justin, "mend nets?"

"Yeah."

"Any word from Case?" Justin asked, looking from Pete to Al.

"Ah," Al stood up, "I'll let your dad update you on Case. Ginny, I wonder if I could have a minute?"

"Sure," she stood and stepped away from the bench she'd sat on, watching and listening to the fishing conversation, then followed Al out into the sun.

"I really want to thank you for sending me the videos of the fish," Al started, and Ginny only tipped her head. She didn't think this conversation was going to be about fish.

"Video. Who would have thought we could do so much with it? The clips you and Hattie worked on are doing more than you may have anticipated. They've certainly gone farther than I ever expected."

He stopped walking and looked at her. "The elders are contacting each other as they watch each other's clips. New conversations are happening, old connections being renewed. It's like," his hands spread out with fingers spread wide, "a wave, and now the ripples are overlapping."

She watched him, waiting, and Al looked out at the bay.

"I need to respect your personal boundaries, but I really feel like you're a catalyst here." He met her eyes, his heart in his words. "Connor's taken a very personal interest in these connections, and I know it's the opposite of your views, but now some of the elders are bringing it up, too."

"Bringing up what, exactly?"

"How to use video to connect with our missing members

—respectfully." He steepled his fingers and tipped them toward her. "Respectful of anyone who feels as you do. That they don't want to be contacted." He watched carefully for her reaction, then asked, "I'd like to know what kind of video we could create, and you don't need to answer this now, or ever," he emphasized. "But if you had any thoughts to share..."

"Did you ask Hattie?"

"I did, but she said the very best ideas came from you. She would, she said, be happy to talk to you, but she didn't want to put you on the spot. And yes, I do feel like I'm putting some pressure on you, but for what it might accomplish for us, I felt I needed to make the effort." He wore his very best I'm-sorta-sorry-but-sorta-not look, with a hint of a smile on his face and in his deeply caring eyes.

"What, though, really, what does it accomplish? I guess I don't get what the big deal is."

"We have an obligation and a mission to offer services to *every* member. We may be able to help them financially, with medical care, things they may be struggling with. And," he looked at the bay again, then back at Ginny, "and we need them. We need their numbers, their voices. The tribe needs their lost members, and if they are now elders, well, we owe them even more. You won't hear Pete or Mack talk about it, but the damage done to their ancestors—children removed from their homes, families, friends, towns, everything they knew. There's lasting damage there. Generational damage, we are now learning."

He spread his hands wide, his face reflecting regret for issues he hadn't caused but desperately wanted to fix.

"So say that," Ginny offered. Al tipped his head quizzically. "Say that's what you're doing and why. Maybe make a lead-in with that. Then, if you really do have personal stories, get people to tell them. Do they know who's missing? Connor sounded like he actually knew someone. Have him talk to the camera. What's the message he wants that exact person to hear? We miss you? Have *him* say that."

Al looked at her, looked away for several moments, then turned his unfocused gaze back to Ginny.

"A personal plea? Please come home? Could it be that simple?" he said, more to himself than to her.

"Sure. Add a little bit about," she waved a hand toward the panoramic bay, "here's what you've missed," then she paused. "Maybe, um, edit in some photos that might, I don't know, be important to that person. You know, of other family members, maybe? With updates on them? Show them how they'd fit in. What their place would be in the community? I," she hesitated, looking out over the bay. "Well, I kinda loved the concept that the whole village is your family when I first heard it. Anyway, you could make a short vid for each person you're trying to find. Or, well, at least start with that, maybe? It might have meaning for more than one person, too. Or make them wonder about what's happening in their own family, or their own village. Maybe enough to take some action—reach out, maybe? Put ways to contact people at the end."

"My brain is exploding," he said happily. "I can see that. I get it. You've nailed it. Thank you so much," he reached out for her hand, holding it. "You are the best. I miss you. I hope you are enjoying working on the boat," he smiled at her, and she returned it.

"Oh, I miss you guys, too," she said as he squeezed her fingers gently, then let go. "But being covered in jellyfish and salmon slime, smelling the salt air, and being on the water is really what I love. And the fish."

"I'm happy for you. I hope it's a good, safe season for everyone, and I look forward to seeing you in September." He smiled warmly, and they walked back to the pavilion side by side.

35

"Case comes and goes so much, I can't keep up," Pete confessed, shaking his head.

"He seemed like he was pretty happy the last time I saw him," Justin offered, keeping an eye on Ginny and Al, who were wandering across the grass surrounding the pavilion, having what looked to be a serious discussion.

"He is. He loves the travel, and he's excited about bringing people together. It was his idea to move some of the people out to Aialik and Day Harbor and get them to take their own video, then send it to Fish and Game. He has a talent for getting people to work together, I guess."

"And you?"

"I, ah, had a bit of an issue with Evie. Her older son, it seems, likes to start fires, and there was a fire at her apartment building. I, um, tried to help, but things didn't go well."

Justin looked at his father closely as Pete gazed across the grassy strip toward the bay. "Anyway, we had to change the locks on the house." He stood up and pulled out a keyring. "Mack didn't say anything?"

"Only that he changed the locks, and I needed to get another key."

Pete handed him two keys and continued watching Al. "Looks like Al's ready to go. Thanks for taking a break on fishing. Sorry we had to ask you to," he said, meeting Justin's eyes.

"I want to be part of making things better, too. Now I get to do my share. We'll mend nets, then I think I'm going to head out to Nuka and see what things look like there. Probably be gone in a couple of days. I'll let you know before I leave."

"Okay. I'm watching the announcements. As soon as anything else opens, I'll text you."

"Thanks," Justin said, watching Al take Ginny's hand. It looked like they were almost done talking.

Justin stood at the helm on the flying bridge of the Calypso, watching the Stormy C navigate the harbor's entrance as the crew waved to Hattie and Pete, standing on the breakwater. Hattie had texted him a goodbye message, saying that the boys were at camp, but she'd be watching as they left for the season, wishing him luck and safe travels.

He wished he'd thought of keeping Gin aboard for the trip out to Nuka and was definitely going to do it on the return trip. She stood next to Mack on his flying bridge, waving to Hattie. Mack waved to his wife, then had to watch out for other boats coming into the harbor. He turned out of the flow of boat traffic and slowed, preparing to release his jitney on its towline.

Justin swallowed hard, taking one last look back at his dad and aunt, both trying so hard to keep smiles on their faces. He couldn't bring himself to go below into the cabin, to steer. The wave of loneliness was too much, and he didn't want his crew to see it or sense it. He had no idea where his twin was and missed him, and now he missed his dad and Ginny, too.

The winter he'd spent looking into other options suddenly felt like an overwhelming waste of time, completely unproductive. He wondered if he'd taken on the remodel project as a way of avoiding everything, just like staying at his dad's house avoided independence. They should have gotten their own place. That's going to happen this fall—before winter.

And why hadn't he proposed yet?

It's not that hard. One question, for God's sake.

I wish Case was here. He'd laugh at me, then probably offer to propose for me—

Justin choked back a laugh and shook his head, coming back to reality as he saw Ginny climb down from the flying bridge behind Mack, who went into his cabin. She walked to the back of the boat, holding onto the ropes that secured the power block, smiled, then blew him a kiss, and he stood up, doing the same.

Case decided that a beer, maybe two, might help him wind down after spending an entire day with Tessa. Tessa the Tornado, his dad called her, and it often fit. She could be a whirlwind, talking without stopping, jumping from one relevant bit of data to full conclusions, but today she'd accomplished something no one else could have done in such a short time: she'd succeeded in getting the biggest wetlands-focused group in the *world* to commit to working with the stream protectors on the Kenai Peninsula, focusing on salmon habitat.

Once they started, they promised to look at other areas of the state as well. They were calling it a cooperative effort at this point, and Case was the connection between them. Case assured everyone that although he was on a three-month contract, he'd still be part of it all—that he was thoroughly committed.

Today's meeting had been a follow-up to a conversation started at an impromptu get-together he'd orchestrated a short time ago. Because they were now all in Seattle, far more people had attended.

At Case's urging, the organization had invited fishery biologists from the Pacific Northwest, stream-keepers, and other groups interested in stopping hatcheries and fish farming, as well as a good number of their own staff and some of their most dedicated supporters and donors—people who *cared*.

Tessa had almost levitated during her talk, emitting pure energy as she spoke. You could have heard a pin drop, he'd observed from the back of the room. Best of all, her presentation had been clear and focused, her replies to questions had been laser sharp, the numbers she quoted were specific and overwhelming, and she named each study they'd come from, often citing multiple resources. They'd loved her. Case, who'd helped her prepare, was thrilled and utterly exhausted.

Relaxed after a steaming hot shower, he dried off, then dressed in casual clothes. Pocketing his room card and wallet, he took the elevator downstairs to the hotel bar, which was surprisingly empty.

The announcements opening specific small areas of the Lower Cook Inlet district seemed to be calculated to gradually bring the seiners to work while keeping them as far apart as possible. On the west side, Kamishak and K Bay opened on the same date that Day Harbor, Res Bay, and Aialik had opened on the east side, the two areas at the opposite ends of the district.

The next announcement, a few weeks later, opened

Chugach Bay to the west and Nuka Island, east of Gore Point, which were slightly closer but still hundreds of miles apart.

The timing was perfect. With Finn fully trained in the skiff, Mack and Justin arrived on Nuka Island and swung into fishing eagerly, their crews quickly falling back into the rhythm of making set after set, bringing in the net, delivering to the tenders, eating and sleeping when they could.

Weeks later, the last weekend of July, an announcement opened up Windy Bay, Rocky Bay, and Port Dick in the center of the huge fishing district, and the debate between the Seward skippers began.

Mack stayed in touch with Gabe and Joe as they worked their way east, but Justin had him at a standstill—he didn't want to go around Gore Point. He was happy, he said, with how well they were doing in Petrof, and when they were done there, he wanted to go back to Nuka Island and anywhere else Fish and Game opened—east of Gore Point.

Mack wanted to go around Gore and hit Taylor Bay. He always did well there, he insisted, and even though he'd lost his jitney going around Gore last year, he wouldn't hesitate to round the dangerous point again. He'd been making that crossing for over twenty years, he asserted confidently.

Mack thought Justin was making too big a deal of a fluke situation, and eventually, Justin pulled out last year's tide book. He pointed out Mack's mistake, misreading the tides, saying it was his own fault, too, for not checking the book. His point, he said, was that it wasn't a fluke at all, and that had nothing to do with his decision.

Working for his dad and then running his own boat, Justin had watched Mack bounce from bay to bay for years and had eventually decided that Mack had a bad case of *the grass is always greener—and the fish are probably thicker—in the next bay over.* It was a waste of fuel, he said over the dinette in Mack's cabin.

"I'm going," Mack insisted.

"Okay. Good luck. I'm staying here, heading down to the tip of the island. I liked that bay, and it paid off really well last year."

"These fish are a two-year cycle, you know," Mack reminded him.

"Yes, I know. I remember you saying you did great here two years ago." Justin smiled easily, looking out the cabin window.

"Well, I'm just sayin'. We should stick together as much as possible."

Justin sighed. "Okay, Taylor it is, but I'm not going into West Arm."

"Taylor, Takoma, Sunday Harbor. Clean up, then back here," Mack clarified, smiling, sliding out of the dinette.

"Alright. Let's look at the tide book."

36

While the seiners were working their way toward Taylor Bay, Case was cruising high over Kachemak Bay on a small commuter plane out of Homer, headed for the village of Kicarwik. Watching the pilot and enjoying the sights made Case eagerly anticipate the flying lessons he'd signed up for. He'd already started studying.

He was looking forward to seeing the stream he used to work at, grateful for the clear day. He wanted to walk it, making sure it wasn't blocked again, and visit the small camp at the lake where he'd monitored salmon two years ago. It felt like coming home, he thought, smiling. He'd taken the earliest possible flight, just to be able to go for that hike before meeting with the village council, Unca, and Al.

Walking away from the landing strip, he slung his back-pack onto his back as he strode off quickly, aiming for the trail to the creek.

Sitting on a salt-stained log on the beach, he pulled his boots out of his pack, then his water bottle and a holstered revolver. Boots on, tucking his shoes into the pack, he stood and belted on the weapon, checked the safety. He slung his pack over his shoulders, then picked up his water bottle, taking a long swig. Tucking it into a side pocket of his pack, he started walking up the creek, feeling happier with every step, listening carefully, his senses tuned for bear, his eyes on the water.

Watching each step carefully, crisscrossing when he needed to, Case took care not to bump any salmon as he walked in the low water. Satisfied that there seemed to be plenty of fish and that they were getting upstream fine, he reached the small plateau and kept going, looking for a technician or anyone monitoring the return. A woman, bending over the creek, stood and flung her long, black hair over her shoulder.

Oh Christ, not her again.

He didn't even know her name, only that she supported the enhancement program's efforts, and she hated his guts. And she was gorgeous. She spun as he stepped onto the moss, breaking a twig. He moved toward the tiny pond she stood next to.

"What you doing here?" she growled at him, and Case's eyes narrowed. She'd added another line to her chin, and just seeing them stiffened his back.

"Looking at the stream and the run," he answered quietly.

"You got no business up here anymore," she pointed back to the trail.

"Yes, I do. I'm working with the tribe—"

"Bullshit. Hit the road. Don't need you here," she squinted at him, taking an aggressive step forward, but she spun around as several fish swished in the pool, splashing water everywhere. She bent over, looking at them carefully, grabbing a clipboard and making a note, then opened the spillway barrier and waited patiently as the fish funneled through it, swimming on their own.

"You're not even touching them," Case said in amazement, standing behind her. "That's wonderful."

She stood up rigidly, her back to him. "Argh. Told you to leave."

"I want to see the sheet." He held out his hand for the clipboard.

"No. Not your job. Fuck off," she said, her back still to him. She was now clutching the clipboard to her chest, and Case gave up. He turned around and headed for the path around her small camp and back downhill toward the village.

Case settled into a chair in the corner of the community center, watching as residents came in, greeted each other happily, chatted with whoever was inside, then wandered back outside. He made some notes to himself on his phone, which he was shocked to see had one bar of service.

Tower's up and working—it's a miracle, he thought, then smiled.

Al sat down next to him, asking how he'd liked the flight over, but Unca walked into the room before Case could reply.

Followed by a long string of people who all took seats at the mishmash assortment of portable tables and stacking chairs, Unca remained standing, and people began to settle down. Watching people seat themselves, Case stayed against the wall. This wasn't his show. He was only there in case Al needed him for something.

Unca called the meeting to order and stated the reason they were gathering. The contract for the long-planned hatchery was on the table in front of him and after years of delays, the enhancement program wanted the final amendments approved and signed. Unca wanted it cancelled and an unofficial tally had the village divided. Some saw it as a necessary evil, some as a source of jobs. Very few thought it would do any good for the salmon.

Al was asked to speak, and he kept it brief, quoting recent studies published in scientific journals that reported overwhelmingly negative impacts of hatcheries, particularly on local wild stocks found in fragile streams. He reminded them of the way pink salmon feed—increasing their weight by 500% in the last few months of their lives, eating voraciously—and the damage that did to other species, including wildfowl, that dependent on the same resources. He quoted Alaskan studies of salmon run destruction due to hypoxia, the lack of oxygen in the water caused by an overabundance of hatchery salmon. Al closed with a short summary on the financial burden the organization held, showing an inability to ever make a project feasibly return even a portion of the money invested in it, and the fact that they were millions of dollars in debt.

He pointed to a poster he'd hung on a wall, saying it showed the overwhelming mortality rates from their hatchery projects. He listed the names and locations of hatcheries that had needed to be closed due to multiple failures and showed that the debt carried by those closed hatcheries was now an issue, also. He urged the tribe to be sure they would not be liable for anything they didn't expect if they did proceed with the contract, then sat down.

Unca then called Tana, and Case groaned as the gorgeous woman from the weir stood proudly, her long hair swinging as she gazed around the room before speaking. She spoke of the fish and their traditional importance to the village. How industrial overfishing had decimated stocks and the need for repleting those stocks. She closed with the fact that this year she was seeing a tremendous return, but that couldn't be relied upon. That's why they needed the hatchery.

Case tapped Unca, whispering a request to speak as she finished, promising to keep it short. Unca nodded, stood, thanked Tana, and introduced Case as the former weir technician, a local seiner, and a member of the tribe in Seward.

Case stood and thanked everyone, saying he'd be brief and that they'd sat through enough, receiving some of the smiles he was looking for. He spoke of his love for salmon, fish that were both food and income to him, then he talked about them as if they were babies.

"They're so delicate," he said, speaking about their quality when caught and how the canneries graded them for payment and processing. There was a lot of head nodding. These were people who knew how salmon were graded at canneries.

Then he spoke, and had to pause to swallow hard, describing what he'd seen while traveling the state. Mishandling of live fish, lifted by the tail and thrown by careless workers who were never taught to respect the fish or handle them properly. "They can't spawn when they are that mistreated," he choked out, then paused. "You don't see that at first glance. You see a lake full of fish. You have to watch them closely before you understand that they're dying, and they can't even spawn." He had no closing; he hadn't expected to speak. He lifted his hands, unable to finish, rubbing a hand over his face.

Al stood quickly and spoke to the silent room. "Case, didn't you work the weir here two years ago?" Case nodded. Al surveyed the room. "And of course, you never mishandled the fish—no, don't be offended. I can see that it upsets you, and I know you'd never have done that. But," he scanned the faces around the room, "that clearly explains the increase this year. He cared for our salmon two years ago and now they are returning to us. That's all it takes, my friends—my family. Care for our cherished resource." He paused, looking at Case again.

"Didn't your family come here, bringing their chainsaws, to help clear the creek for the salmon?" Case nodded again.

"And what were your instructions from the enhancement program, when you told them that the streams were blocked with downed trees and the fish were unable to reach the lake to spawn?"

"They said to stay at the weir, that the stream was not my problem, and to stop bothering them about it." Al motioned for Case to sit beside him.

"My friend Tessa has followed this issue her entire life, and her personal theory is that the organization deliberately tried to destroy the natural run in order to justify their hatchery operations. When our salmon are protected and treated with the respect they deserve, they return to us in abundance. I am so very grateful," he closed, sitting down.

Two days later, Pete looked up to see Al coming into the office early in the afternoon. "Hey, I didn't think you'd be back until tomorrow," he said, relieved to have him back. The number of callers asking for Al had tripled that week, as he'd traveled to another important salmon conference out of state. The callers all wanted details on where he was, what he was doing, and what the status was on specific projects they'd talked to Al about. Pete took detailed messages without revealing any specifics, eager to learn the answers himself, especially on the proposed new hatchery they were trying to scuttle.

"Good news. Things wrapped up smoother and sooner than I anticipated. I'm so grateful to Case. He had a big hand in these results."

Pete's jaw dropped, and Al motioned him into his office as he went in and started unpacking his attaché.

"Has he never talked to you about his work?"

"Not really. I mean, he's told me where he was going and,

a few times, mentioned the people he was meeting with. The wetlands organization was a major coup, I think…"

"That was a miracle. But amazingly, it wasn't the only outstanding connection he's managed to make. He has a talent, and I'm looking for a way to keep him. I hope he hasn't taken a position elsewhere?"

"No, no, he's just focused on getting his flying certifications as far as I know."

"Excellent. Can you ask Connor to set up a time for him to come in? Unless you want to set it up? I want us all in on writing up this summary."

"Sure. I'll do it," Pete said quickly.

"Thanks. Aha, plenty of messages. Thanks for that, Pete. As soon as possible for Case," he murmured, scanning a message.

Pete went back to his own desk, looking forward to Al's next project update meeting as he contacted his son, explaining what Al wanted.

"We'll need Tessa there. She talked to as many people as I did," Case replied. "Let me see when she can make it. I'll call you back."

Case texted her and within minutes realized she could be there tomorrow. "Tomorrow it is," Pete replied to Case's returned call.

"I think we need a review," Al said, opening the next morning's meeting, moving to the whiteboard on the wall, and uncapping a marker, "starting with our efforts to remove the weir here and ending with our goal of shuttering the old hatchery. And now, we're waiting on the vote to cancel the new hatchery. I think we'll get it. This is a process that worked for us and hopefully it can work for others. Let's all document what we've done."

37

Following up on his heart issues after Evie's fire, Pete sat patiently in the clinic, waiting to be called. He missed going up to the bluff to watch the seiners, and he missed Justin and Ginny. The house seemed so empty without them, even with all their coming and going. They'll be back by the end of this month, maybe sooner, he reassured himself. We used to quit the third or fourth week of August, he mused, looking out the window at the bay. Three weeks—

"Peter Nichols?" the aide called out. Pete stood up and followed her into the sterile looking room, wondering who the hell he'd be dealing with today. He took the customary seat on the paper-covered exam table and pulled his T-shirt off, seeing a technician tugging her ECG machine toward him.

Leeches attached, she took a reading. Tearing off the printout, she turned the machine off, then peeled the sticky electronic tabs off his body, apologizing for the hair she yanked.

"Doctor be right in," she mumbled, leaving the room. Pete pulled his shirt back on and slumped.

"Awww, it's not that bad, is it?" a voice asked after tapping the door and entering.

He sat up straighter. "I'm alive," he replied, trying to be funny, and it fell flat.

"You sure are, and you're in rhythm. That's good news. I'm Doctor Susan. So, tell me about this last episode."

Pete relayed some bare facts, involving stress, anxiety, lack of sleep, too much salt, little to no food, and the barest amounts of water, and how his heart had felt. He held out his phone to show her the readings from that date.

"Oh, email me these, okay? I'll get the email address to you before you go. Hmmmm," she scanned, tapped, "right, right, oh, right there. And then, hmmm. Aha, back in sinus, all good. And how did that happen? Meds?"

"Coconut water, magnesium, a protein smoothie, and nine hours of sleep after a personal problem was dealt with."

"Sounds like you had that all planned, Pete—okay if I call you Pete?" She continued at his nod. "That's exactly what I want to hear. You felt safe, you hydrated, you slept. Excellent control." She made a few notes on the chart she held. "So, anything else we want to talk about today?"

"No. That's it? I mean, that's it."

She laughed. "It's perfect. Proactive. You were back in rhythm within hours. You get a gold star."

"Okay, well, they said to come in if it happened again, so here I am."

"Doing the right thing. Good for you. I'll be cycling through the state. I think I'm due back here in, ah, looks like October. I'll see you then, okay? And here," she tore off a scrap of paper and clicked a pen to write, "is my email. Send me those PDFs. If it happens again, you contact me immediately, okay? I want to know, and I want to see the readings."

"Okay. Thanks."

. . .

Pete was surprised to see Case's car in the driveway when he went home after work. Entering the house, he smelled something delicious and could see Case in the kitchen, at the stove. "My God, I'm starving all of a sudden. What are you up to? What's cooking?"

"Corn on the cob and stuffed chops. Straight from the butcher in Anchorage."

"Oh, I don't believe it. You're my favorite son. Don't tell Justin I said that. Do you know how long it's been since I've had those?" Pete put his hand on Case's back as he poked the corn, rolling in the boiling water.

"These'll be done in two, chops in," he looked at the timer on the stove, "twelve. I even found the cob holders," he said, pointing to the counter. Little tiny pool balls with sharp prongs.

Pete laughed. "I forgot all about those. Good find. I'm going to put on some sweats."

Pete dropped one more wedge of spruce on the small campfire and leaned back in his dad's old camp chair, staring into the flames. It wasn't even dusky, but it felt good to be outside, full from dinner but not stuffed. He'd eaten half the chop, saying he'd have the other half for lunch or dinner tomorrow, and wanted a beer by a small fire.

"Are you home for a while now?" he asked after Case had recounted his recent trips.

"We'll see. Al's doing all he can to swing that village vote. It's a big deal to him. Shuttering this local hatchery, which I think he has sewn up, and stopping that new one. If he needs me to go anywhere, I'll do it. Otherwise, nothing big. I'll be done in two weeks and then back to my flying lessons," he pumped his fist, happily. "Any word from the boats?"

"Justin texts when they move, so I know where he is.

Hattie texts me too, if Mack moves. Sounds like they're both together, and they both say it's a tremendous return. They headed to Taylor; Mack insisted, but Justin says he won't go into West Arm. He's going back to Nuka Island when they're done in Taylor. Crew's all good. Decent tenders."

"Good for them," Case said, raising and tipping a beer in his own salute, before drinking a good bit of it.

"You don't miss it at all? I'm dying to get back on a boat," Pete murmured.

"Nope, not one bit. Being on the water? Yes. The bugs, the work, the noise, the months of being stuck with three other rotten-smelling guys, nope."

"The bays..."

"I can get to them in a float plane."

Pete twisted to look at his son, sitting in a matching camp chair. "Is that what you want? To fly out to bays?"

"Maybe. I miss walking the streams, checking the runs, the health of the fish. I tried to do it in the village, but..." he waved a hand.

"But what?"

"Ah, this *female*. She hates me. Told me to fuck off—"

Pete spit his beer out as he laughed, gasping, trying not to choke, hoping it didn't set off another heart episode.

Case shot Pete a dirty look. "Thanks for your sympathy. It means so much to me."

"She said that to you? No way. What the hell did you do to her?"

"Nothing. She hates outsiders, and I couldn't be bothered telling her that my family's from out the chain. Prejudiced c—"

"Ack. Don't use that word."

"I hate women," he said calmly. "All of them. Except Chessy. And Ginny. And Viv. The rest of them are miserable, back-stabbing, worthless, mindless—"

"Argh, son—"

"Oh, and Tessa. I might be in love with her."

Pete, tipping his beer for another sip, choked again. He put the bottle down, deciding that it was not his night for beer.

"Seriously. Don't joke about that. About her. She's off the rails."

"No. She makes sense. You just have to listen long enough. I thought she was ditzy when I first met her, but now... I think she knows more than all of us put together. And she's got a silly sense of humor. Like a little kid." Case laughed, remembering their last meeting. "She ran off this hooker I was talking to in Seattle. Told her she looked old enough to be my mother and to go find another corner to work," Case continued, laughing, remembering the looks on both women's faces as he talked. Pete stared at his son, his jaw hanging open. When Case finally noticed, he laughed even harder.

"A hooker? You—"

"I was only chatting with her. Offered to buy her a meal."

"On a corner?"

"Nooooo. In a bar. She was sitting at the hotel bar, and yes, I knew she was working, but there was no one else there. She had just told me, not so politely, to piss off when Tessa came charging in." He laughed lightly and felt the tension—some of it anyway, ease away.

He leaned forward, grabbing Mack's fire-poking staff, and reamed the logs, sending a swirling vortex of sparks up in the air, flickering into bits of ash as they rose on the thin columns of heat.

"Then she lectured me. It was all I could do to not kiss her."

"She's old enough to be your mother," Pete blew out, sitting up straight, staring at his son.

Case leaned back and looked at Pete with his usual teasing

grin. "I like 'em older. So much more exciting," he drawled, and Pete shivered violently.

"Oh, my God. Why on earth..." Pete left that hanging, shaking his head, and Case smiled, closing his eyes, melting into the chair.

38

The two trips around Gore Point, going to Taylor Bay, fishing, then back to Nuka Island, went smoothly, and fishing in Taylor Bay was perfect. Like last year, there were only two other boats working the bay, which was wide enough for the seiners to keep their distance easily while still filling their nets.

Back on Nuka Island, the seiners worked together in the larger bays and split up to fish the smaller ones, with the area now open seven days a week. The middle of August saw the strongest surge of natural pink salmon, and that meant they worked from the 6 a.m. opening until the mandatory stop at 10 p.m. every day unless a storm blew in.

Delivering to the Lady Luck, Justin chatted with the skipper, who took the time to show him the entire bridge when he mentioned going to the Expo and checking out another tender.

"I get this year, maybe next year too, but that's it," Elliot had said. Gary, his deckboss, took Justin through the crew quarters and engine room, happily showing off as much as he could. Sending him back to his seiner with two gallons of chocolate ice cream, they wished him luck, saying they hoped to see him again, as Elliot gave Justin another business card, with his personal number written on the back.

His crew quickly devoured the ice cream, even though it was 10:30 at night, while admiring the big tender as its crew pulled the pump hoses back, and the big boat used its bow thrusters to push off.

With his boat anchored for the night, Justin curled up in his bunk and had two minutes to think before falling asleep. He missed Ginny more than Case or his dad now. His arms ached, not from the repetitive work but from his need to hold her. To him, the work was almost mindless, which made his loneliness worse.

He was glad Finn was working out. Eager, quick to learn, intuitive about maneuvering the skiff, he was already a good skiffman. If I'm still at this next year, he's got a job if he wants it, Justin thought, nearly asleep. *I'm keeping Gin with me next year, too, dammit.* He slept.

"Comin' in from Kodiak means it's gonna hit here," Wade said. Justin sat at Mack's dinette, next to Ginny and across from Wade and Viv. Mack sat at the helm, turning the marine radio off. He'd texted Justin to come over after the wind started howling. He'd called it a day after delivering. It was only 6 p.m., but they could all use a break, Mack had said on the radio. Justin looked more wrung out than any of them, and Viv mixed him an electrolyte drink, urging him to drink it all and take the powder back to his boat.

"So, you think it's gonna hit here when?" Justin asked.

"Let's listen tomorrow, then make the call. My loads are getting lower every day. I'm ready to be done. No silvers this year. Glad we filled up the freezers at home with reds," Mack said.

Justin chugged the drink, nodded, and eased out of the

dinette, thinking how grateful he'd be for a few extra hours of sleep. Ginny followed him on deck, watching as he untied the skiff and held the rope. She hugged him, and he kissed her briefly, then handed her the rope while he climbed down and started the outboard. She tossed the tie-up line into the skiff, watching as he headed back to the Calypso anchored on the other side of the cove.

❧

Extending his car lease for a week, then arranging to stay a week in a hotel near the airport, Case reported for flying lessons eagerly, grateful for good weather in the latter half of August, where it could easily have been storming, grounding him. He'd knocked out the written portion over the three months he'd been working and was excited to be so close to obtaining his license.

His nights in the room were spent getting caught up on emails from Tessa, Al, his dad, and the numerous people he'd connected with during his time working for the tribe. He still had a final report to do, but Al had said to take his time, especially because he was still helping Tessa.

Falling asleep to the sound of airplanes taking off and landing, the only thing he longed for was the chance to talk to Chelsea —to tell her about his summer and ask about hers. He spent every night pushing away the question of why she'd stopped talking to him, deciding that once he was home, he'd walk over to her house and keep checking until she came back. He refused to acknowledge or even consider that she may not come back or, worse, would come back but still keep her distance. Hoping she'd contact him when she finally came home, Case texted, offering to take her to dinner when she landed in Anchorage.

If she says yes, I'll buy her roses, he thought, falling asleep.

Checking his messages and emails the morning of his last day, still hoping to hear from Chess and talk her into flying with him, he was stunned when her reply popped up.

CHELSEA

I'm in Anchorage for a couple of days.
Dinner would be nice

He quickly typed back a time and restaurant name, then made reservations. He couldn't wait to hear about Europe. Finally! She's back! God, it's been too long.

Wait till I get my license. She'll fly with me; I know she will.
Jesus, it'll be good to see her again.
I need to order that bouquet.

He looked up a florist and made the call, wondering if he should add chocolates to the order, then decided to give her some as soon as they were both back in Seward.

39

Arriving an hour early, Case sat in the car, staring at the expensive roses he'd just picked up. One in every color. They'd added just the right accents to make it work. Made to his specifications, it was a one-of-a-kind bouquet.

Just like Chess.

He still had no idea what he'd done to tick her off so badly that she hadn't even told him she was leaving for the summer, but he intended to find out and then make up for it. Whatever it took.

Goddammit, Chess. I need you more than ever now.

He stared at the bouquet, then at the restaurant's sign on the building, and froze in place for several minutes.

Shaking his head, blinking rapidly, then taking several deep breaths, he opened the car door, picked up the flowers, closed and locked the car, then walked through the parking garage, using the elevator to go up to the restaurant. He was still early, despite the time he'd lost sitting in the car.

Case wanted to be inside, watching her enter the restaurant. He'd see her first and surprise her with the bouquet, then tell her how much he'd missed her before she could say a word.

He swapped the bouquet from hand to hand, reaching into his pockets to wipe the sweat off each palm, then forced himself to stop, afraid he was damaging the flowers.

The maître d' wasn't at the entrance, and neither was anyone else. Case stepped inside, scanning the room for the right place to position himself, his nerves on edge, hear pounding. He hated the unusual feeling of anxious anticipation. He was never nervous, especially not around Chess. The uncomfortable knot in his throat grew, and he wondered what the hell was wrong with him.

The entrance won't work, dammit. Not enough privacy.

Maybe the bar, then? Text her to meet him there? Then they'd get their table.

Good plan.

Still scanning the room then looking at the bar, he walked toward it hesitantly. People were scattered around it, but there were still plenty of open seats between them. There, several empty chairs near that woman with the deep tan and gorgeous hair. Taking his time, he aimed for the open seats near her, his anticipation now a knot in his gut as well as his throat. As he neared the chairs, he slowed, and she turned toward him.

"Are those for me?" she asked, her voice low and soft, her eyes playful, her poise confident as she smiled warmly at him. Case melted like butter in a hot skillet, relief flooding through him, his stiff shoulders releasing some of their tension. He swallowed easily, his voice instantly finding its most sensual tone in response to her playful query.

"Darling," he said, with a smile that went from his mouth to his teasing eyes, his deep voice low and intimate. "I want to say yes with all my heart, but I'm meeting someone special, and I need to see her beautiful face when I give her these," he said, with regret so deep it sounded like he was breaking the news that the world was ending in four minutes.

Her sensual laugh surprised him, and he stole a quick

glimpse, taking in her generous lips, which twitched under his gaze. He looked away quickly.

Goddammit! Not again. I can't let Chess see me flirting with this beauty.

"Is she all that special to you?" she asked with a gentle, deep-throated voice.

Case desperately wanted to lean closer and put his arm around her, letting her whisper in his ear to feel her lips on his skin. She'd touch his neck with her fingertips; he'd turn his head slightly... He felt a familiar surge and the inner vibrations of instant connection. Waving a hand at the seat next to her, focusing on it and missing the way her head tilted slightly, he asked, "Is this taken?"

She shook her head, looking at him curiously as he sat down facing the door, glancing toward her briefly, not meeting her eyes.

"Yes. She means everything to me. And..." he looked at the restaurant entrance: no one there.

And I need her more than I need a new lover.

"And?" she prompted.

"And," he sighed, gazing down at the bouquet. "She's mad at me," he admitted quietly.

"Oh, dear."

"Oh, it's way past *oh dear*," he said. "We're deep into *I'm fucked* territory."

"Oh, no. What did you do?"

Case swore he heard teasing amusement in her voice at his miserable predicament. It ran down his spine like a lover's finger. He stole another quick glance at her, then went back to watching the doorway.

"I wish to hell I knew. I have no clue why she stopped talking to me." He forced himself to sit up straighter and stiffen his shoulders. "Please don't take offense, my dear, but the minute I see her, I have to get up and give her these. If she sees me with a gorgeous woman, I'm a dead man."

The woman hesitated, looking flustered, he saw from the corner of his eye. "She's... the jealous type—"

"No," he interrupted, back to watching the entrance. "No, she absolutely isn't. She's the best, but, I, ah, I made a big mistake with a... a kind of good-looking woman. I can't let her think I'm doing it again. I was a total jerk. To her and to my brother. I love her, and now, I'm scared to death that she hates me," he confessed, and could not understand why he was sharing such a personal struggle with a total stranger. He never talked about himself to anyone except Chelsea, and he never talked about Chelsea to anyone, ever.

Why am I even chatting with her?

How was she drawing his most intimate struggle from him? Why did he want to whisper in her ear?

"And what do you want from her?" she asked quietly, as if the answer held the key to a question in her life, too.

He swallowed hard, staring at the door, wondering where the hell Chelsea was. Talking to the gorgeous woman was keeping him from panicking. Her voice was soft, warm, deeply caring, and she was easy to talk to. So easy. And she was enticingly lovely. He adored the way the lights at the bar caught the many colors in her hair.

What do you call that mix of colors? I love it.

Why did she have to be so attractive, so alluring?

Why do I want to run my fingers through that magnificent hair and mess it up?

Her boyfriend, or whoever was meeting her, was a lucky man.

Case had no idea why he was telling her everything in his heart, but he was grateful to her for asking and for listening. "I don't want her to hate me," he whispered. "I need my friend back."

Leaving Alaska in mid-May, Chelsea spent four weeks each in Rome, Paris, and then London. During her first two weeks in Italy, she lost seven pounds and felt better than she had in seven years. She hadn't even been trying. The Mediterranean foods agreed with her metabolism, and she walked everywhere. Plus, she was happy. She left her past behind and immersed herself in—*the past*.

The history and architecture lifted her spirits; the crowds and people accepted her; the sun adored her; the food agreed with her, and the classes she took excited her.

She bought a health-watch and started tracking her steps. By the time she left for Paris, she was down fourteen pounds and needed new clothes.

Staying with the foods she'd eaten in Rome, she walked even more in Paris and said goodbye to another eight pounds. Determined to continue the trend, she changed her reservations in London and found the best places to eat the healthy foods she was now accustomed to.

Arriving back in Alaska, she needed to downsize again and buy clothes for the coming fall and winter. She stayed at the family condo in Anchorage and started a shopping list. Turning her phone on for the first time in three months, she left it to update, heading for an outdoor clothing store, looking for warm slacks, sweaters, and jackets. It wasn't cool at night yet, but it would be soon.

Returning home to the condo with a Greek salad and a case of protein drinks, she checked her phone and saw new messages. The few people she'd wanted to hear from through summer had been given her temporary contact info—a phone she'd picked up just for her travels. She'd kept up with emails on it. The only messages on her primary phone should be from spammers or...

Case.

He'd sent several messages—the first ones demanding to know why she wasn't replying. Then a short one:

CASE

Heard you are in Europe. I hope it's the best time of your life. I miss you, C

Her eyes teared instantly, her throat constricted, and her heart ached, but her mind hardened and her back stiffened. She'd spent as little time as possible thinking about him in the past three months. In fact, her agreement with herself was that once the plane landed in Rome, she wasn't going to think about him again. She surprised herself by sticking to it. The rare times he'd crossed her mind, she wondered if the reason she was having such a good time was because she refused to think about him. She'd been thinking about him since she'd been thirteen.

E-fucking-nough already.

His last message had her wavering. She wished she could talk to Ginny. But the seiners would still be fishing in the middle of August, and worse, they would be in the Outer District, where the only communication was via SAT phone or GPS texting device. She didn't even have the boat's contact info for that.

She'd have to wait until the boat was back in Seward to have someone to confide in. But she'd never confided in anyone about her feelings for Case, and she wasn't sure she could do so with Ginny, either.

He wanted to meet. He was close to the end of his summer job, had started his flying lessons, and had even flown once. He wanted to see her as soon as she landed in Alaska, and if they met in Anchorage, where he was taking his flying lessons, he'd like to take her to dinner.

Oh, he'll see me alright.

From across the room, she thought.

Her cute, plump face had gone from girl to woman. A makeup artist in Paris had shown her how to emphasize her assets, then passed her to a personal shopper for clothes in colors and styles that worked best for her. They'd finished with her hair, which she'd finally stopped coloring. The natural auburn looked good with her tan, and the summer sun had added interesting highlights. But it was the cut that made it work, tying the look together. She barely recognized herself.

Agonizing most of the night, losing sleep, she cried into her pillow, finally accepting that she couldn't avoid him forever and didn't want to. Being brutally honest with herself, she accepted her deep need to see him again. To be near him. To hear his voice. To tease and laugh like they'd always done.

Taking a hot shower and mentally preparing herself, convincing herself that she was strong enough to meet him as a friend, she finally slept, texting him over her coffee the next morning, smiling at his quick reply.

Arriving very early, then watching the restaurant entrance in the bar mirror, Chelsea saw Case walk in, then pause as he scanned the room. Weaving between tables, he headed straight for her with the most gorgeous bouquet of roses she'd ever seen. Her heart raced in anticipation while love flooded her entire body at the sight of him, drowning her the closer he came, setting every single nerve she had zinging, constricting her throat, and taking her breath away.

Oh, for fuck's sake. Absolutely nothing's changed. If anything, it's worse!

She cried inside. She wanted so much to be done loving this man. Done with the stinging pain of seeing him with other women. Done longing for his attention, his touch, a kiss.

Keep your poise and your distance, she reminded herself,

refusing to let him see her love or her pain. Turning to face him, he slowed, his handsome face looking at the empty seats next to her. He hesitated, looking lost and unsure of himself, the same look she'd been comforting for many years.

She desperately wanted to reassure him that everything would be fine, then give him anything he wanted or needed. Instead, she asked if the roses were for her, and he flirted with her!

What a nice change. She loved it.

Prompting him, soothing him with her warmest voice, speaking softly, the throatiness of her own voice surprised her as her hormones surged. And now she knew how all his other women had felt.

Special. Noticed. Flattered. Attracted to his magnetic smile and outstanding body.

He'd flirted with every female he met.

Except her.

They chatted more. She was coy, enjoying the banter, listening to him pour his heart out. The tingling within her sparked sensations throughout her body that she'd never felt before, making her breath catch. Her eyes filled with delight; her smile genuine—until it hit her.

He has no idea it's me.

40

"They're coming in. Great season, everybody's fine. They'll be here tomorrow night, running ahead of a front hovering over Kodiak. Only stopping in Nuka to pick up the jitney," Pete said, looking at his phone as he sat in his recliner.

Stretched out on the sofa, Case looked up from scrolling through planes for sale on his phone. "Justin."

Pete looked at him curiously. "What?"

"He'll want his room back. I need to figure out what I'm doing. Fuck me." He stared at his hands, his phone sliding sideways, landing on the sofa cushion as he sat up, swinging his feet to the floor, his head hanging.

"You can have the kids' room for as long as you want. There's no hurry. It'll be nice to have you both here—"

Case shot his dad a sad look. "No. Seriously, no. I need to get my shit together. Christ, what a fucking mess."

"What's up with you? You've been dragging ever since you got back. Did flight school not go as well as you wanted? You said you passed. Change your mind about the whole thing?"

"No." He ran his hand through his thick hair, grown long and curling around his neck. He'd worn the same sweats every day and hadn't left the house in the five days he'd been back. Unshaven, wearing a torn T-shirt, he looked like a vagabond as he sat slumped on the edge of the couch.

"Case. What's wrong?" Pete leaned his chair up to sitting and locked it in place, then leaned forward, wondering if he should go sit next to his son. "I'll do anything I can to help you, but I need a clue."

"Women. Fucking women," he groaned.

"Oh, God. Which one?"

"All of 'em."

Pete laughed, but quickly apologized at Case's dirty look. He went to get two beers out of the fridge, sitting next to his son and handing him one. Case drank half of it in one gulp, then held it with both hands between his legs, slumped over again, staring at the floor.

"What happened?"

"I finally heard from Chelsea."

Pete waited, but Case just kept staring down. "Is she back from Europe now? Justin said she spent the summer there."

He also said she left without telling you.

"I talked her into meeting me. In Anchorage. As soon as she was back. I was still taking the flight classes. I couldn't wait to tell her about them. To take her flying. To hear all about Europe. Everything she's been doing. I ordered roses. One in every color, arranged just for her. I got there early. Fuck, I've never been so nervous." He ran a hand over his face like he was trying to erase the memory and his face at the same time.

Justin had told Pete that Chelsea was pissed off at Case about Nell and that it might even be the end of their friendship, but Pete had seen far more than friendship in Chelsea's eyes over the years. He hoped his son hadn't hurt her.

People thought that Case had it easy because of his good looks. But he'd also been singled out by the worst users for that very reason. Girls who couldn't care less about him, only concerned with how they looked standing next to him, were constantly attracted to him. They couldn't have cared less about Case's twin, either, which always rubbed Pete the wrong way. Chelsea had never been one of those girls. Pete couldn't believe she'd put up with all the girls who claimed Case was their boyfriend.

"She stood you up?"

"Oh, no. I wish she had. Nope, she was there and even earlier than me."

Pete tried to envision what could have gone wrong and gave up. "So, what happened?"

"I didn't recognize her."

Pete sat up, stunned. Chelsea was adorably cute, growing plump in the past few years. But after the tragedy that had struck her family several years ago, no one blamed her. Linda had carefully talked to both boys about the need to be kind to her, their friend, when she needed it most. Pete remembered it well because it had been one of the last times that he'd felt respect for his late wife.

"So… what? You… You walked right by her?"

"Oh, fuck no. I walked straight up to her and started chatting while I was watching the door. Telling her I was meeting a friend. And she fucking let me do it!" He stood up, yelling, "She knew who I was. Could she squeak out a little *how do you like my new look?* Fuck no!"

He was on a tirade now, and Pete watched with relief as Case waved his arms and paced, yelling louder. "She let me ramble on, then called me an asshole and said she never wanted to see me again!"

He sat back on the sofa in a deeper slump. "And she fucking means it," he finished quietly.

Pete leaned back, looking at Case, wondering if it was really possible that he'd pushed her that far or if she was merely pissed off at being unacknowledged. She'd had a crush on him for years. And now he'd hurt her feelings—again.

Christ, what do I say to him? How can I help?

"Son, if I knew anything about women, I'd try to help you. But I married way too young, and the last two women I've touched have proven that I should join a monastery."

Case blew a sorry laugh. "Well, fuck. That Candi was a rising star from all I heard. Who else?"

"Evie. Her son's an arsonist, and she knows it."

Case jerked up. "What?"

"It's a long story."

"I'm getting another beer, then I want to hear it. All of it all. Did you actually have sex with her?" he looked at his dad, narrowing his eyes.

Pete's head hung down.

"Fucking women," Case mumbled on his way to the kitchen.

Pete told Case how he'd met Candi. In telling the story, he could finally see that he'd been both manipulated and marked as an easy target. Then they'd laughed. The story about Evie coming in to clean on a different day—the one day that Pete had slept in, had Case making crude jokes.

"So, it was only a couple of times, but according to Hattie, she planned on living here. She actually told her kids to call me Uncle Pete, for God's sake. Can you believe that?"

Case looked at his dad, realizing he was probably more naïve than Justin, then decided to keep that to himself. "No more women until I've met them," he decreed, shaking his head.

"So, back to your issue. What can you do? Any ideas?" Pete asked, watching Case finish off the dregs of his second beer.

His head hung, and he shook it. He was done talking about Chelsea. "I take it Justin hasn't asked the big question yet."

"Not that I've been told. Out on the boats, I don't know. I don't know why she doesn't swap boats. I mean, Hattie and Mack worked together—" he stopped suddenly.

Case laughed. The beer had finally relaxed him.

Maybe now I can get some sleep.

"I can imagine that, and so can Justin. I think that's why they stay apart. Last year, we worked non-stop. I don't think he wants to push her like that, either. Mack said he was taking it easy, and he actually did. Did Justin ever tell you about the bear attack?"

Pete's eyebrows bolted up, and Case told him the story, all the way to the end, when he and Justin realized how good they'd had it growing up.

41

Hattie hoped to enjoy the last few days that the kids were in summer camp, but the call from the fire chief put her on edge. He wanted to talk to her boys, and she refused to give permission. He asked if he could stop by and talk to her first, and she said she'd think about it and call him back. She immediately called Pete, asking his advice.

"Why don't I come over? He can talk to both of us, then we'll decide if he talks to the kids or not. And no matter what, he's not doing it without us being there. Agreed?"

"Yes," she said, feeling better. "When?"

"As soon as Connor's back from his lunch, I'll be down. Let's say one-thirty. What time are the kids out of camp?"

"Three."

"Good, see you in a bit."

"Oh, Pete," she sighed. "I hate bringing this back up again for you—"

"No, it's okay. I'm good, and I'm glad you're including me. Really."

"Thank you. See you soon."

She called the chief back, giving her address, saying he could stop by at one-thirty.

The fire chief explained that he, personally, needed to hear the kids say that Evan had the supplies for starting a fire and had proposed starting one in the playroom. He was polite but firm.

"But what good is that going to do for your investigation?" Pete asked.

"I need direct testimony—it's called probable cause—to get a warrant, and that's only to get his fingerprints."

Pete twitched, sat up straighter, and looked at Hattie cautiously, but the captain caught the look.

"What is it? Did he do something in your house? This is triggering something for you..."

"I, ah, forgot—"

"Seriously, Pete, we need help here; otherwise, the kid's gonna do it again, and next time, he may kill someone. We can't even keep tabs on her if we don't get something soon, and I think she's gonna run. We have prints from the apartment fire, but they don't match anything on file."

Hattie nodded encouragingly at Pete, and he took a deep breath. "When Hattie called me to tell me what the kids had said, she was scared to death, and it scared me. I, um, I forgot I did this, but I gave the kids some sticky candy, then said they should have a glass of water to wash it all down. I gave them little glasses, not their usual plastic cups. Evie was doing laundry... Anyway, I kept the glasses. I didn't touch them—"

"No shit? You have their prints? Just the boys, right?"

"No. I took the one she'd been drinking from, too. I swapped glasses when she wasn't looking. She'd have put it straight into the dishwasher and I don't know why, but I poured her iced tea into a clean glass and kept the one she'd been using, too."

"Whoa. You may have saved the day. Where are they?"

"My house, out by Bear Lake."

"Okay if I follow you out there?"

"Um, well, I'm on lunch now, but—"

"In and out, I promise. I'm gonna bag them, then process them. I'd really, really like to do that as soon as possible," the chief said, rising from the sofa.

"Okay, sure, let's go."

Pete opened the cupboard and pointed as the chief looked. "Do you know which kid's is which?"

"The one with green is Erik's; the orange one, for fire, is Evan's."

The inspector pulled out three plastic bags, wrote on them with a marker, then bagged each glass, reiterating his thanks and leaving immediately, saying he'd contact him later if he still needed to talk to his boys.

Pete stopped at Hattie's after work, and they walked to the playground with the kids. Leaning on the perimeter fence, watching them race around with other kids, their conversation returned to Evie.

"I honestly thought that she was on the run from some abusive relationship," Hattie confessed.

"I never got that kind of vibe. She—"

"She what?" Hattie looked at Pete, who quickly looked away, looking completely embarrassed.

"You didn't..."

"Oh, God," Pete moaned, his head hanging.

"Pete," she put her hand on his back, then rubbed. "Please don't tell me she played you, too."

His head shot up. "What? No, she showed up on an off day. It was a fluke..." He watched Hattie shake her head.

"I'm kinda doubting that. I think she saw a place she could

be safe, where her kids would be welcome, or at least not be rejected, and she decided to use it."

"I told Case about her, and he said I'm not allowed to date anyone until he meets the woman." He didn't clarify that Case's exact terms were: no sex without my consent. He smiled, remembering that conversation and the bit of male bonding he'd enjoyed with his son.

"I agree. Put me on the interview panel," she said, smiling.

Taking their final walk on the beach while Wade helped Mack fetch his jitney, Justin held hands with Ginny, asking, "Want to travel home on the boat with me?"

She stopped walking, unable to believe she hadn't thought of it herself. She almost bounced, turning to him happily. "Yes! Before we leave in the morning? Wade can drop me off."

He bent over and kissed her, holding her gently. "No trip to Chena this year, unless you want to go? I was thinking about another trip to Aialik?"

Her slow grin was all the answer he needed.

Viv stood on deck as Mack, on the flying bridge, steered the boat through the islands protecting Resurrection Bay.

So close to the water, two steps away, and she'd be in it. She felt a surge of love for the ocean and the islands that called it home. The sound of the splash, even over the constant drumming of the diesel engine, was a sound she would never tire of. I'll be glad to not hear that engine for another year though, she thought, smiling.

The boat turned again, as Mack aimed for the middle of the bay, letting the racing charter boats and sport fishermen have the straight shot to the harbor.

I can feel the cold air coming off Bear Glacier!

Her skin had goosebumps under her outer thermal top, and she moved into the sunlight and out of the breeze as a twang of excitement zinged through her body like an electric shock.

Again?

I need to pack up, she thought, and in her soul, she felt the deep rumble of a whispered word: *yes*.

They had hours before they'd be in the harbor. She looked around at the choppy water, the far shore, and its mountains, then followed Mack into the cabin, watching him as he climbed into his captain's chair. She started in the galley, heating water for doing the morning's dishes, tidying up the cupboards, washing down the counters, and scrubbing the two-burner propane stove.

"Who ticked you off?" Wade asked, dropping the corner of his newspaper as she cleared the table, then wiped it down, tossing away his old newspapers and other useless things that had piled up over the season.

"If I do it now, I won't have to do it later," she said, in her mind-your-own-business tone.

"Right," he agreed, shooting a look at Mack, who was setting the autopilot.

Viv cleaned up the bench behind the captain's chair and Mack, who was now reaching for his novel, turned to look at her suspiciously. When she crawled into her bunk and pulled all of her things out, dumping everything on the wide bench behind him, Mack glanced at the dinette and met Wade's eyes again. They both shrugged, sharing a wary look.

"Cabin fever," Wade mumbled, lifting his newspaper again.

Mack went back to reading, grinning behind his book, and Viv ignored them both. She went back to the galley, pouring the now boiling water into the sink, adding cold, and washed every mug, dish, pot, skillet, and all the silverware.

Finished drying and putting away everything in the galley, including Wade's old coffee percolator, she went back to the bench behind Mack and started sorting her clothes, folding, rolling, fitting everything into her backpack. She wondered about her raingear, then decided to pile it on deck. As soon as she left the cabin, headed for the outside locker, Wade asked, "What crawled up her ass?"

"Dunno and don't care. I just want to make it home alive, and I don't want to hear another one of her end-of-the-season tirades."

Wade laughed and raised his paper again as Viv came back into the cabin. She heard his laughter, a deep rumble, as she walked by, then bent over to check her bunk for anything she might have missed. She sat down and pulled her deck boots off, putting her sneakers on.

She walked back out on deck, thoroughly overheated from the work and the warm cabin. Pulling her fleece shirt off, standing there, looking around again, she wore only her light camisole and thin leggings.

"Jesus, she looks like she's getting ready to jump in," Mack mumbled, twisting to look out the door. "Stripping down to almost nothing,"

"Lemme know when she's naked," Wade said from behind his paper, and Mack laughed.

42

Hattie received a regular text from Mack, sent from his phone, not the satellite GPS unit, and she replied quickly.

MACK

ETA 3:30

HATTIE

Dinner at 5 invite Wade & Viv

She texted Pete the same info, with Mack's ETA, saying she'd be on the breakwater with the boys by 3 p.m. because he was always earlier than he said he'd be. Pete replied that he and Case would be there too, and that Case would drive Wade's truck to the harbor, so he'd have a ride.

Not only did it set Hattie's world right to see the seiners coming home, but Robbie and Mickey went into a frenzy, seeing Justin steering the big boat, unshaven for the season, with Ginny next to him on the flying bridge.

Finn, Ben, and Greg were on deck, and Wade and Viv were on Mack's deck. They all waved to the boys, and the kids flung themselves as high as they could, waving and shouting. It was a

260

challenge for Hattie to get them back into the car, so they could drive around to the north harbor where the boats docked. Pete said he'd take Justin and Ginny back to his house for showers before coming back into town for dinner.

Case followed Pete and Hattie down the ramp and onto the big floating dock. The boys had raced ahead and were waiting as the crew came off the boats, carrying their duffels and backpacks.

He skirted the noisy group, aiming for the edge of the dock, watching all the happy greetings as Ben and Greg's families came to get them, too.

"Who died?" Viv asked, walking toward Case, her backpack slung over one shoulder, boots clamped in one hand. She smelled from weeks of dried sweat, old sun-baked seaweed, bug spray, and a hint of something she used in her hair.

"I think I did," Case said, looking from the group to her. "Have you ever felt like you're not really here? Invisible? Or looking in from the outside of a bubble?"

"Every day."

He stared into her clear eyes, seeing the same connection they'd had since they'd met. She could see right into his soul.

What's her issue? I'm not the only one lost in this happy crowd?

"What do we do?" he whispered.

"Try to get the message. You have a chance to see things differently; maybe learn a lesson if you can see it. Not everybody gets that. Respect it," she said quietly. "Or you can keep repeating the same stupid mistakes. May not get another outside view again, though."

Behind them, in a voice so deep it felt like a vibration going through him—and he saw Viv react to it too—came one word.

"Vivien."

Case looked beyond Viv, to a man who could be him in

fifteen years. Tall, exactly Case's height, dark hair grown too long and laced with stands of grey, face stubbled with a beard thicker than Case's, wearing the clothes of a man who lived on a boat: worn, salt stained, sun faded.

The man from Chena.

Viv tensed.

If she doesn't want him—

Case stepped closer to her, and she immediately put a hand on his chest, stopping him. Raising her eyes to meet his, not even acknowledging the man behind her, she said, "Tell Gin I'm gonna miss her."

The man turned away, walking toward the far end of the dock. Viv followed him, and Case stood there watching them both as they stepped aboard a world class sailboat tied up at the end of the dock.

Everyone else had scattered by the time Case turned around. He walked up the ramp, turning to watch as Justin talked to his crewman.

"You're in charge, Finn," Justin said, handing him cash for the hamburger he'd been craving.

"I got this, man. As soon as I'm done stuffing myself, I'm settling back with one of Wade's books he loaned me."

"Okay, see you later."

Hattie had her buffet counter set with huge amounts of food, leaving space for a platter of roast beef, which she was carving. Mack, fresh out of the shower, in clean sweats and a T-shirt, was in the living room letting the boys pull on his beard, telling them about fishing, listening to their stories of swim lessons and learning how to tie flies and cast.

"Letting them hang around Henry, huh?"

"He is so patient. I hear a car—"

"Justin's here! Dad's here!" Robbie yelled, and Mickey added Ginny to the list as they ran for the door.

"Come in and grab a plate," Hattie called as Pete gathered the boys and led the way inside. Justin hugged Hattie, and she touched his sparsely bearded face, smiling at him. Case came in carrying a bundle of roses, handing them to his aunt, then he started rooting around in cupboards for something to put them in.

"Oh, I haven't seen roses like this since... New Year's Eve," she said, looking at him curiously. He winked and went to the cupboard she pointed to, reaching in back for a tall vase.

"Justin got me roses then, too!" Ginny exclaimed, admiring the bundle.

"Did he?" Case drawled, trying to hold back a laugh. Ginny looked from Case to Justin, who looked guilty, and back to Case, who was doing his best to keep a straight face.

"He... you didn't?" she squeaked. Justin reached for her, but she backed up quickly, right into Case's waiting arms.

"Aha, the better man wins in the end," Case gloated, wrapping his arms around her and holding her tight.

"You let me think you got those roses!" she accused Justin, trying not to laugh.

He merely watched them both and smiled. "He left. I got the reward. He owed me, anyway," he said, stepping closer and peeling his brother's hands off her.

"Fill up your plates," Hattie said. "Wade just pulled in. You'll be holding up the line."

Justin and Ginny did as ordered, then found places at the dining table that had been extended to take over the living room. Case finished adding water to the vase, leaving it next to the sink, then touched Hattie's arm, leaning into her, whispering, "Viv may not be coming. Long story."

"Alright, thanks."

"You must have cleaned out the floral section of the store," Mack said, continuing the conversation as they ate. "Two dozen! The clerk probably thought you were in hot water," he said and laughed.

"Three dozen. And I told him I had three girlfriends, and I'd pissed 'em all off," Case clarified, with his best drawl, and everyone laughed.

Ginny looked at him, guessing that the last dozen must have gone to Chelsea, who'd driven him home and then back to school in Fairbanks. She'd gotten a text from Chelsea when she'd powered up her phone on the way into the bay, asking if Ginny could talk and then another one saying never mind, she must still be out fishing. They'd both probably been sent weeks ago.

Ginny watched Case while she ate, wondering if either text had anything to do with him. She'd asked Justin, on one of their beach walks on Nuka Island, what the story was with Case and Chelsea, and he had only said enough to make her even more curious, while assuring her he'd shared everything he knew.

He told her that they'd all been friends since grade school, but Chelsea had been closer to Case than to him through high school and at college. Then he told her about Chelsea's older brother's death as a teenager.

"Oh, but there's more," Case added, pausing until he had the floor. "We decorated your car in Anchorage last year. Didn't you wonder? We laughed like idiots. Did people write on the poster?"

"You did that?"

"Me and Chess. We were on our way home and she thought it would be fun. We bought the poster board and pen, and she found a piece of string. Then we got the balloons."

"I loved it. It was so sweet. Lots of people wrote messages," Hattie replied, leaning forward to Case, who sat diagonally across from her. "I should have thought to include her today, and I'm sorry I didn't. Call her now. Invite her for dinner or desert," she suggested.

"I can't. She's had enough of me," he said quietly, looking down at his barely eaten dinner.

43

Dominating the dinner discussion, Mack gave Hattie a recap of how great the fishing had been, how few seiners they'd had to hassle with, how great the tender service had been, and that brought him back to Justin.

"I was surprised to see the Lady Luck again. You still thinking about buying a tender?"

"Yeah, Elliot was sure happy to be back. Gary too, his deckboss. He says he might be able to pull one more season. I've pretty much put the whole thing on hold for now."

Mack remembered that the long-awaited marriage proposal hadn't happened either, and he started wondering if maybe they weren't getting along as well anymore. He'd been shocked when Gin came back to his boat this year. He'd already put out the word that he might need a new crewman for the season and had three guys interested when she said she'd be on his boat for her third season.

"Ah, bummer," Mack said. "But yeah, he was happy to be back. Sweet boat. They're good guys."

Justin looked around the table. At one end, Mack and

Hattie were paying attention to the boys. Ginny was watching them too, listening to the kids talk about hooking a fish. Across the table, Wade put his refilled plate down, sitting between Mack and Case. Case looked rough and was hardly eating the small amount of food on his plate. Justin stared at him, but his brother never looked up. They used to get each other's attention that way, and he wondered when they'd lost it.

He felt Mack's gaze on him and returned it.

"What about that direct-selling idea? That still on the table?" Mack asked.

"I'm going to keep researching it," Justin said. "The big hurdle is a place to process—"

"Hattie's kitchen," Ginny interrupted.

Justin laughed while Hattie quickly said, "No way."

"Awwww. It's perfect. Look at how many cases we did. Hey, Case, did you ever get to try our peppered batch?" Ginny looked from Case to Pete to Hattie.

"Ah, no, I never pulled that out while you guys were gone. We'll do that. Maybe at the campfire?" Hattie said.

"Gotta pull nets, get the boats up—" Mack started.

"Yeah, yeah. I know the routine. When all that's done, we'll have our big fire. Anybody look at the weather lately? Are the nets dry enough to put away?" Hattie asked over the voices of the boys, who were instantly excited about a campfire.

Phones were pulled out, weather checked, and plans made for putting things away. Some plates were filled a second time as appreciation for the wonderful meal was expressed.

Justin leaned back in his chair, watching Ginny and Hattie leave with the boys, taking them to the playground for a few minutes, to run off their energy before bed. They'd relaxed over the meal for nearly two hours, and he was starting to get sleepy.

"So, what are your plans now?" he asked, looking at Case, who seemed reluctant to meet his eyes. With his elbows on the table, head balanced on his hands, Case glanced at Justin, then went back to looking out the window, merely shrugging.

"I'm thinking about putting bunkbeds in the boy's room and letting Case have the playroom," Pete offered, looking from one twin to the other.

"No, don't do that. I'm pretty sure things will settle themselves out easily enough. Case can stay where he is," Justin said.

"And you?" Case asked, raising an eyebrow? "If your boat comes out..."

"I'm storing the net, but I'm not taking the boat out yet. I'm paid up until the end of September in the harbor. I'm thinking about taking it out somewhere for a while. We'll see. I'm good living on it, but I may come back for a shower—"

"Of course. You and Ginny. Anytime," Pete said, his eyes full of questions, his mouth firmly sealed.

"Did you love the flying lessons? Gonna buy a plane?" Justin went back to Case, hoping for a little insight into his mood. He seemed to be off in his own unhappy world.

"I did, and I might," Case said, finally looking at his brother. "They're pricy though. And only good for the few months of summer. Expensive to store. Still," he paused, "I'm tempted. Could have a fun year, then sell it," he grinned.

"So, what happened with Viv?" Wade asked Case, twisting to look at him. "She was talkin' to you, then, pffhhht," he said, waving a hand through the air.

"You didn't see the guy behind her?" Case asked, and Wade shook his head.

"Same guy that was at Chena," he said, looking at his brother. Justin perked up, his brows drawing together. "Came up behind us, said 'Vivien', and she said to tell Gin she's gonna miss her, then got on a sailboat with the guy."

"Oh, for fuck's sake. Not again!" Justin picked up his phone, scanned his contacts, then called Viv's number. No answer. He texted her.

JUSTIN

Where are you?

VIV

Leaving the bay now, sailing around the world. Hope to be back next year. Sorry about not helping post-season. Tell Gin I'll miss her. Won't have cell service.

JUSTIN

Goddammit, get a GPS and text us. We want to know if you're okay

Please. I'll give you mine. I'll run it out in the skiff right now

VIV

He has one. I'll miss you too. Thanks for everything

"Fuck me running. Ginny's gonna bawl her eyes out," Justin blew out, banging his phone down on the table as Case held out his hand, picking up his brother's phone and reading the messages.

"Why?" Case asked.

"She hates people leaving suddenly. Dammit! Here they come." The noise of the kids in the garage was easy to hear. "I think it's from the life of foster homes. She hates it. And Viv did the same fucking thing last year, saying she was staying at Chena the morning we were leaving. Don't say anything about Viv yet, please," he blurted out as the house door opened.

∼

"Why aren't you surprised about Viv?" Justin asked, standing on the breakwater, looking at the harbor full of boats, holding Ginny's hand. They were walking back to the Calypso after dinner, and he sighed with relief that she wasn't upset at the news.

"She seemed different this year and didn't really want to talk much. I figured she'd take off again. It seems to be what she does. I hope she sends us a message sometime. Around the *world*?"

"Sailing. Jesus. I'd rather swim," he said as they walked through the harbor, and Ginny laughed. "Let's check on Finn, get our stuff, then I'm coming over to Mack's boat for the night," he said as they walked down the harbor ramp.

"Hey, how's it going? How was that burger? Everything you've been dreaming of?" Justin asked Finn, who was sitting on the hatch covers.

"Oh, God, yeah, man. So, um," he stood up nervously, "like, my friends, they really need me to come home. Ah, one of 'em is in the hospital. They think if I go in, it might help him," he finished, wiping his hands on his jeans.

Justin drew a breath, but Ginny stepped in front of him before he could utter a word, her voice urgent. "Don't do it. Don't go. You said you were starting over here. These are the same users, right?"

Finn froze, staring at her, his face a mask of fear.

"Finn. You said so. They're sucking you back in. Don't do it."

"Nah, they, ah, they won't do that. I have to go. I have to help my friend," he said, as if he were repeating someone else's words.

Justin jumped in, copying Mack's, I'm-the-skipper voice, "Nope. You don't. There's post season work to do. Remember the contract. You only get the bonus if you finish out the season. It'll be a week, maybe two, before we're done putting everything away."

"Yeah, so, that's okay, um, but I told them I'd be back, like, I said I'd leave tonight. Thumb a ride."

"No," Gin insisted. "That's not safe. Plus, you don't even know how much you'd be giving up. You should stay and finish the season. That was your goal when you started. You said so," she insisted, walking across the deck to stand face to face with him, her words getting firmer with every step she took. "And you said you weren't going back. I believed you. Now stick to it," she demanded, stretching up on her toes to look him straight in the eye as he tried to look away. Finn backed up, looking at Justin for help, his face hopelessly confused.

"Finn, you know the cycle. Going back means using again. Don't do it. You love it here. That's all you talked about, all season," Justin added, trying coercion, hoping he sounded like a friend, not a boss.

"They want your money, and you ought to know that. You're a free ride." Ginny's voice dripped with anger and disgust.

Justin shot her a surprised look and countered her tone with his best voice of reason. "You were a good skiffman. I mean it, and they're hard to come by. I'd give you a good reference if you stick around, but no skipper likes it when a guy takes off."

"Well, I'm not really taking off—"

"Yes, you are. The season's not over until I say it's over," Justin said, his tone hard again.

Finn looked down, away, anywhere but at Justin. "Look. It takes days, sometimes weeks, to get a payout from the cannery. I don't even know what I owe you."

"Ben and Greg said they thought we'd get between five

and maybe eight thousand. If you can give me four or five, you can mail me the rest, right? A check?"

Justin sighed, shaking his head. "So, if I understand you, you want at least four thousand cash right now, and you're leaving?"

"Yeah, man. That's it."

"Let me get the contract out. You'll have to sign off that you're leaving without the bonus. I really want you to stay. It would be worth it to you if you did. We could probably help you find work this winter, too."

Finn shook his head, skirting an immobile Ginny, following Justin into the cabin.

Justin didn't have the kind of cash Finn wanted, but Mack said he did when Justin called him. He said he'd bring it down. They had Finn sign for it, then watched as he left, hurrying up the dock, his backpack over his shoulder.

He'll be broke and living in an alley before you know it," Mack said, taking Justin's check in exchange for the cash.

"We tried. Ginny tried hardest."

Mack looked at them both, shaking his head. "Jitney first, then nets. Tomorrow morning."

"You look at the tides?" Justin asked, grabbing a tide book.

They looked together. "Start on the big nets at noon," Mack said. "Jitney at nine."

"Sure," Justin agreed, and Mack left, walking back up the dock quickly.

"You kinda put the press on Finn," Justin said, watching Mack leave.

"I like him. And I agree with Mack. They're gonna take every dime. At least one will overdose, probably more than one, and he'll be worse off than when he ran away to come up.

He may never get out again," she said sadly, looking into the harbor. "If he lives."

Justin stared at Ginny as she walked out of the cabin and up to the deck. He still had no idea of the life she'd lived, and it rarely ever came up when they talked. His churning gut told him it might be time to learn more about what she'd been through.

He went up on deck, still thinking about what she'd said to Finn. "Now that he's gone, you want to move your stuff over here?"

"Yeah. I'll go pack up. Are we still going back to Aialik? Or somewhere else? It's gorgeous there," she said, her smile growing.

"Let's see how the week goes. I don't want to go before the campfire. Hattie's really looking forward to it. So am I."

44

"Are you seriously letting the kids camp out here? We didn't get to stay out here alone until we were teenagers," Case asked, resentment in every word as he stared at the tent set up next to Mack's gravel mound and the two boys playing on the ground next to it.

"Are you done being thirteen? Of course we're not. By the time we're done out here, they'll be sound asleep. I'll carry them inside. What the hell crawled up your ass?" Mack asked, frowning at Case.

Before Case could think of a good retort, Hattie swooped in, growling, "Whatever you two are arguing about is going to stop," she lowered her voice even more, "right now. Got it?" She spun around and went back to playing with the boys in Mack's gravel pile as they loaded their toy trucks with glacial shale, building a grey road to their tent.

"Okay, look, I'm sorry," Mack said quickly, and Case stiffened in surprise, looking at him warily. "Jesus," Mack sighed. "We all saw what happened here last year." Case looked away, his mouth tightening. "And now this, with Justin. Look, I'm sure it's tough." Case's face softened. "Call one of your two-thousand girlfriends and invite her over," Mack suggested.

Case shook his head, staring into the campfire's flickering flames. "You know as well as I do that any woman I invite here who watches Justin propose is gonna think her day's next. I can't do it."

"Yeah, they tend to do that," Mack agreed. "None of 'em already got a ring on? Or are just friends?"

Case shook his head. "Only Chelsea, and she hates me now."

Mack perked up, grinning. "Seriously? What'd ya do? If it involves sex, I don't wanna know," he qualified quickly.

Case shook his head. "It involves her losing a bunch of weight and me telling her I liked her the way she was."

"Oh, Jesus Christ, you stupid idiot," Mack laughed deeply and shoved his nephew on the shoulder. "How'd you manage to do something that dumb? I'm pretty sure you know better."

"I didn't even *recognize* her to start with—"

Mack howled with laughter, doubling over.

"You're an asshole. There's a reason we don't get along," Case said, his mouth twitching, trying not to smile as Mack continued to laugh uncontrollably.

Gasping, Mack put his hand on Case's shoulder, his deep laugh winding down. Finally catching his breath, he said, "Oh, don't I know it. You should hear the story about Hattie checking my phone texts when we were in a hotel room in Homer, ah, trying to straighten things out between us."

Case instantly remembered exactly how miserable Mack had been when he and Hattie had split up a couple of years ago. He glanced at Mack quickly, then at Hattie. What had they gone through? A twenty-year marriage and it had broken so badly?

And I think I've got it bad?

"Tell me. Don't leave anything out," Case challenged, and Mack took the bait like a hungry silver, leaping to tell the story. When he was done, they were both wiping their eyes, still laughing as they eased toward the campfire, looking for a cottonwood round to sit on to catch their breath.

One of the boys called Mack to come help move a big rock for their road, and Case watched as Mack said something to Hattie that made her laugh as he squatted down to help them. The boys waited, trucks dangling from each of their hands as they cheered Mack on.

Hattie'd loved taking care of the twins and had fostered plenty of other kids. Case wondered suddenly why they'd never had their own and why he'd never wondered about it before. What have they been through?

He kept watching as Mack hefted the rock and rolled it away. Hattie said something to Mack quietly, and he laughed, then sat next to her. He looked at her like she was the only woman in the world, and her face said he was the atmosphere she needed to keep their world alive.

Case stood up, pulled a bottle of beer from the cooler, then went to sit as far away from everyone else as he could get. Pulling out his phone, he tapped out a text, and before he could agonize or delete it, which he'd done multiple times in the past weeks, he sent it.

CASE

I'm sorry. I'm going to text that to you every day

CHELSEA

Don't

CASE

I miss you so much. I miss talking to you. What are you doing?

CHELSEA

Reading a really good book

CASE

Mack made a campfire. Want to come over?

CHELSEA

I can smell the smoke

CASE

It's a good one. Walk over. The creek's low. Justin and Gin are here

He waited for a reply, stood and stretched, paced, checking his phone repeatedly, looking at the signal strength, telling it to vibrate. Finally, he typed again.

CASE

Please

Please come over

CHELSEA

Have you been drinking?

CASE

1 beer that's all, I swear

CHELSEA

Okay. I want to say hi to J&G

Case slid his phone into his pocket, his hand trembling. He walked into the deepest part of the forest, making sure no one was around, and unloaded a full bladder. His hand was still unsteady as he zipped up. Heading for the path that led across the small creek to Chelsea's dad's house, he had to push alder aside. I should have trimmed the branches back first, he thought. They hadn't used that path much since high school.

He waited near the creek, watching the overgrown path on the other side.

I'll push them out of the way for her.

45

Seeing her coming, ducking to dodge branches in her way, Case ran to Chelsea. Wrapping his arms around her, he was amazed by how wonderful she felt before she wriggled free.

"Chessy," he grinned with his best everybody-loves-me smile. "God, I'm so glad you're here. I need to talk to you. Come sit next to me. Want some pie?" he asked, backing up as she continued toward the clearing and the fire.

"I'll hit you," she stopped, stiffening.

"What? Why? C'mon Chess." He inched closer, his face serious for a change.

"I don't want pie. I don't want to eat sweets. When are you gonna realize that I like how I look now? Stop trying to fatten me up. I want to go say hi to Ginny," she said, trying to get past him as he blocked the overgrown path.

Mack nudged Hattie, leaning toward her as they sat on huge cottonwood rounds on the far side of his campfire. "You watching this? Looks like we get a double-feature. This is getting better by the minute," he said happily, staring at Case and Chelsea. "Best seats in the house, if you ask me. It's like I planned it all," he bragged.

"Jesus. You'd take credit for the sun if you could get away with it."

"Awww, honey. Nope, not me. God, I'm getting antsy. Been waiting for this forever." He looked around for Justin or Ginny and saw them in the center of the clearing, inches apart, having their own intense conversation. "You're keeping an eye on them, too, right?"

"Yes, and I'm going to need a neck massage, going back and forth, watching all of them. Good God, leave it to the twins to do this kind of thing at the same time. Case looks like he's getting ready to propose, too," she whispered.

"Propose sex, most likely," Mack said and she spewed laughter, covering her mouth quickly. "If they head into the woods, don't look," he advised, and she laughed harder, pushing his shoulder. He grinned, wrapping his arm around her, pulling her closer.

Pete stood a few feet behind Mack and Hattie, giving him an even better perspective of the clearing and the paths leading into it. He could see both young couples without too much neck twisting, and he was rooting silently for both of his sons.

My twins. My babies—grown men!

He'd heard every word Mack and Hattie had said and had to smother his own laughter. His heart broke as it swelled. He could feel his boys slip out of his life like a wisp of mist, but he surged with pride, love, and respect for the men they'd become and his eyes softened with love for the young woman his oldest son had chosen.

. . .

"Gin, I have something I need to ask you," Justin said, reaching for her hands as they stood in the clearing on the other side of Mack's huge fire circle.

"Right now? Chelsea just got here. I haven't seen her for so long. Look at her! C'mon, let's go say hi," she said, tugging the strong, immoveable, calloused fingers that were firmly entwined with hers. She turned her face up to his, stepping closer. "Besides, everybody's looking at us," she whispered.

"Are they?" Justin didn't look around. He was ready to kneel and reach into his pocket for the ring he couldn't stop touching.

She leaned in closer. "Yes. I hate being watched. You know that. C'mon, let's go." She looked around him again, tugging his hand. "Look! They're almost kissing!"

Case dropped his voice. "No, you can't go say hi yet. Wait! I'm telling you; I *need* to talk to you."

She froze, her voice low. "Not now. You asked me to come here, and I told you it was to see them."

He twisted, body-blocking her, his hands on his hips. Neither was aware that everyone else's eyes were on them, and they were all watching avidly.

"Chessy, please." He tipped his head to one side slightly as she looked at him closely. "This is a big deal." She focused on him, finally, instead of stretching to see around him. "Please don't be mad at me anymore," he whispered. Even he heard the hurt in his voice. "You're important to me."

Justin's heart raced. How could he have forgotten Gin's total fear—panic—at being the center of attention? There was no way he could ask her now. Not here—in front of everyone. *She'll cry.* That wasn't how he wanted her to remember her only marriage proposal. He took a deep breath, re-thinking everything in seconds. They all expected an announcement. They'd been waiting months for it, and he'd said it would happen today—right here at the campfire. No more delays. He looked past Ginny to Hattie, who met his gaze with all the love in her heart, smiling reassuringly. Mack grinned his widest and tipped his beer in a silent toast. His dad nodded, pride bursting from him like a lighthouse beacon.

"What, exactly, is going on? Who's here?" Chelsea tried again to scan the people in the clearing, looking for some woman he probably wanted to introduce her to. She wouldn't put it past him, and she'd deck him right in front of whoever-she-is *and* his family.

"Stop stretching and look at me. You know who's here. Just my family."

She sighed and looked into his eyes, relaxing the tiniest bit. "Well?"

"Can I at least touch you without you slugging me? Please?"

"Where, exactly, do you plan on putting those hands?" she asked, her eyes narrowing.

"Just holding yours, like we always do, okay?" He moved closer and eased his hands onto her wrists.

"Fine. Now spit it out. And you better not hurt my feelings. You're risking your balls."

Justin squeezed Ginny's hand as they watched Case reach for Chelsea. "This is too good to miss. My question can wait. Let's go find somewhere we can hide and watch. C'mon, bunny." Justin led her a few feet away, into the nearby spruce trees, and they turned toward the clearing to watch. He stood behind her, his arms wrapped comfortably around her, resting under her breasts as she leaned back against him, and he looked over her shoulder.

He sighed with the deepest contentment, then bent slightly to whisper in her ear, drawling the same way Case did when he was coming on to a woman—deep throated, smoothly, with more than a hint of teasing amusement. "She's gonna hit him. My money's on it. He may lose teeth. I think she's been working out."

Ginny shook with laughter. "Nope," she gasped. "He's gonna kiss her. You owe me a thousand kisses if he does." They stared, happily watching the scene.

Case gazed into Chelsea's eyes, seeing the pain he'd caused her. "I never meant to hurt you. I swear, Chess. Never. Not you."

"Okay. I believe you," she said, letting each word out slowly, watching his face change from regret to joy as she spoke. She couldn't help herself as she smiled back at him.

He laughed and hugged her tightly, letting her go when she struggled to get free, then saw her pulse beating rapidly near her throat. He wanted to put his lips on it and a groan escaped before the urge even registered in his brain.

"I believe," she leaned back, "that you wanted to *talk*."

"Yeah, talk. Um..." he looked into her eyes and couldn't speak.

"Ha. I'm gonna win. She's gonna slug him. Wait for it," Justin whispered into Ginny's ear, but she shook her head.

"Nope, it's not over until someone's down on the ground."

Justin buried his face in her neck, laughing so hard he

shook. He could feel Ginny twitch as she laughed silently, her hands over her mouth.

"You're fucking with me, Case. Why is that?" Chelsea murmured, more to herself than to him. She gave up trying to look around him, staring up at him instead. Examining him as if he were a stranger, she looked at his chin, stubbled with dark beard, as usual. Eyes bright, his look intense, mouth trying to move, nothing coming out.

"I'm not. I'm just, ah, it's just," he threw his hands up, "Argh!" *Justin.* He leaned in suddenly, grasping her shoulders, pulling her close, whispering in her ear. "My big brother's gonna pop the question. Right here. Tonight." His muscles tightened as she pulled back, her hands going to her mouth in shock as her eyes widened. She grabbed his shoulders and tried to push him, gave up and pulled on him, trying to see where Justin was. "Chess," he hissed, his large hands flying to the sides of her face, forcing her gaze to him. "Don't look. Oh my God! It's a secret, dammit. We can't let on that we know."

They stared into each other's eyes. Case watched her face change from amazement to glowing happiness. His own eyes were wide with wonder, his face inches from hers, Case's chest constricted as he tried to breathe. Keeping his hands on her cheeks, he tipped his head down without thinking, his lips lightly touching hers, then pressing harder as he kissed her. And held her. And held the kiss. Her hands on his shoulders went limp, sliding down his chest across his twitching muscles, warming from the intense heat he was radiating. Reaching his waist, they grasped, tightening, then pulled him closer.

"Never saw that coming," Pete said, stepping up behind Mack, reaching around him to hand him a beer. "My money was on her walloping him." Pete had to tap his brother's arm with the beer bottle, Mack was so stunned.

"Where did Justin and Ginny go?" Pete asked, looking around the clearing.

Ginny spun around and wrapped her arms around Justin. "I win," she sang. "Pay up. A thousand kisses." She grinned up at him happily and was surprised when his smile changed to a look of serious concentration.

"I want to offer you a *lifetime* of kisses. Come sit here." He'd spied the tall stump earlier and backed up, guiding her, then sat down and brought her onto his lap. He put a finger gently on her lips. "I've loved you from the first moment I tried to show off to you, right here, when we first met. I want to spend my whole life loving you, and I'm asking you to marry me. I was gonna do it in the circle, in front of everyone but, you said—"

"Yes!"

She jumped up, and he stood slowly, his eyes looking deep into hers as he reached for and held both of her hands firmly.

"I mean it, Genevieve. Through good and bad, happiness and anger. I want you to be my wife, and I will be true to you." He let go of one hand and wiped the tear on her face. "Forever."

"Forever," she whispered, her eyes never leaving his, her hand going to the side of his face, caressing. "Justin. I want to be with you and only you, forever."

They eased closer, wrapping arms around each other, lips touching, pressing their bodies together, sealing their vows.

46

The hands gripping Case's waist pushed lightly, then again, a long moment later. He ended the kiss lingeringly, barely lifting his head from hers, foreheads still touching. "I really need to talk to you," he barely choked out.

"You're gonna have to wait. If he's proposing, I want to be there. I want to see Ginny say yes." The space between their faces widened slightly as she looked into his stubborn eyes, her face still held securely by his stubborn hands. "Okay," she sighed. "When the celebration's over, we'll talk."

He let her go, backing up but sliding a hand down to grasp hers. They looked around the clearing as Justin and Ginny came out of the woods, grinning happily.

Case's eyes flew to his dad, who shrugged, while Chelsea growled, "If you made me miss it, I'm gonna drown you in the creek with all the dead humpies!"

"I think we all missed it," he whispered, leading her toward the fire.

"She said yes!" Justin yelled, and Ginny spun around, burying her face in his chest as they wrapped their arms around each other.

Like a sprinter off the starting line, Hattie was first to reach them, arms outstretched, hugging them both. "Congratulations! I want to see the ring," she exclaimed. Mack and Pete came next, and Pete enveloped Hattie, Ginny, and Justin in his arms as Mack circled the hugging group and patted Justin on the back, congratulating him. Case and Chelsea were a foot away, both saying, "Congratulations," as questions flew about dates and places and a second request to see the ring—this one from Chelsea.

Ginny finally pulled an inch away from Justin, but he held her within his left arm, feeling her tremble, his other hand on the side of her face, fingers in her curly hair, holding her head to his chest gently as her trembling increased.

"We haven't picked out a ring yet," she gasped, and Justin finally heard the requests through the ringing in his ears.

"Oh, yes, we have," he teased, then tipped her face up to his. "I have had this ring for months, waiting for the right moment to ask you to marry me," he said, and he felt her glowing skin warm even more. He let go of her face and reached into his pocket, pulling the ring out, keeping it enclosed in his fingers, holding eye contact with her.

Nudging the hand she had against his chest, he whispered, "Hold out your hand." She did, her gaze finally leaving his as she let go of his chest only enough to extend the fingers of her left hand.

Rolling the ring within his fingers, he managed to turn it right-side up, but he covered it completely with his large fingers as he wiggled it on, then looked at Ginny, biting her lower lip. She looked up at him as he kept his fingers on the ring, and he impulsively bent and kissed her.

Her hand flew to his face, and Hattie gasped.

"Whoa, nice one," Mack admired, now standing shoulder-to-shoulder with his brother. Case and Chelsea quickly wedged in next to Pete and Mack and shared a glance as they spied the ring. Justin brought his hand up, covering hers as he grasped it.

"Did you even see it?" he asked her, and she shook her head. Her whole body was shaking. Holding her hand and tugging her, he headed for the rounds by the fire, and everyone else scattered, commenting to each other on the ring and their wishes for the couple's happiness.

Sitting down, Justin pulled Ginny onto his lap, then backed up, letting her have most of the round, bringing her sideways between his legs. Mack rolled another round behind Justin.

"There, now you can back up."

Justin scooted back, still holding her tight as he whispered in her ear. "You gonna be okay?" She nodded, but her breath was coming in short pants.

"Gonna look at the ring?" he teased, leaning back, running his hand down her left arm, which was wrapped around his waist. He wanted to see her face when she saw it, but couldn't let go of her. She'd stopped shaking and was merely trembling now.

"You don't have to yet, if you're not ready."

Mack started pushing the fire together with a big staff he kept nearby. Chelsea and Case were chatting with the boys by the gravel pile. The only ones watching them were Hattie and Pete, with occasional glances as they chatted. Ginny took a deep breath, then another, and Justin relaxed.

He whispered, "Nobody's watching anymore."

She slid her arm out while looking at him, then looked down at her fingers. "Oh!" she gasped, and in one fluid movement she swung herself around, straddling him, holding him tight. "Oh babe, I was so hoping you'd do that again," he said against her neck.

. . .

"Pete, you must be so proud. Two fine young men and now a daughter," Hattie practically squeaked.

"Jesus. I know less what to do now than I did bringing them home from the hospital as babies," he blurted.

"Oh, baloney," she said confidently. "You're a good man. They're good men." Switching her gaze from Ginny, who she was watching like a hawk while doing her best to not be obvious about it, she took in Pete's stricken face.

"Peter Emory Nichols. You. Are. A good. Dad. Your father was a good father. How many times do you think of him? All the time? I know Mack does. That's what they need. A man to advise them on being men when they need it or ask for it. And sometimes when they don't."

"Linda always said we'd lose them someday. That's why she wanted a girl. They don't need me anymore, Hat," he said softly, his voice full of longing and loss.

"Bullshit. They need you now more than ever. You're going to tell them that they can come to you any time they need to. And they will, believe me. Don't you remember pouring your heart out to your dad? You should have done it more. Things may have worked out differently. I'm pretty sure," she confessed quietly, "that Mack and I would never have divorced if your dad had still been alive. So tell them. Any conversation, any time, on any subject. How often do you wish you could talk to your dad again?"

"Almost every day. I swear, I feel like he's here right now, and I sure wish he was. I'll tell them. I promise."

Case followed Chelsea as she wandered toward the two boys who were re-constructing a hut for their trucks. Squatting down, she admired their road as they eagerly described the mighty hill they'd made and the tremendous power their earth-movers had. She praised it all, and they explained what they needed to do next, pointing to the moss.

"You probably don't remember me," she said, looking at Robbie, "but I used to babysit you. We used to pretend we were monsters and chase each other all over the house."

"I remember that," Robbie said, looking at her. "You had a good growl," he said, then growled deeply, and Mickey laughed and copied him.

"Ooooh, your voice is getting deeper, like your big brother's," she complimented, as Case stepped behind her.

"I'm gonna be tall, too," Robbie bragged, looking up at Case. "As tall as both of my brothers."

"Me, too," Mickey asserted, his face full of doubt as he looked from Robbie, who was several inches taller than him, to Case, who had just hit six feet.

"Lots of guys don't get tall until they're nineteen or even older," Case reassured him. "You've got lots of time."

Hattie walked up to them, saying, "C'mon guys, we're going inside to celebrate. You can each have soda. We have good news!" They dropped their trucks and took off running and howling along the path through the alders to Pete's house.

After champagne toasts for the adults, soda for the boys, more exclamations over the ring, photos taken and shared, hugs and hints on dates dropped, Justin and Ginny left to spend the night on his boat, something they both insisted they wanted to do. They were taking the boat to Aialik Bay for a week, Justin said, and Hattie sent another bottle of champagne with them. Thanking Hattie and Mack for the cookout, Case took Chelsea by the hand, saying they were going to go enjoy the fire for a little while longer.

47

Justin stood on the bow of the Calypso, looking out of the lagoon and across the bay at the huge glacier running from the mountain saddle down into the ocean. There was a tour boat in front of it and another inching its way closer. He tugged the anchor line one more time, checked the cog to lock the winch, then walked down the narrow railing to the back deck, where Ginny stood turning slowly, taking in the surrounding cove.

The sun sparkled on the calm water, ruffled only by the lightest breeze, barely strong enough to swish the tall beach grasses. The marsh behind the grey shale beach was filled with grasses and short shrubs, backed by low mountains. Ginny thought she could hear a creek but couldn't see it.

Putting an arm around her, he enjoyed the quiet for a long moment, thinking about all the things he wanted to talk to her about.

"We have a lot of stuff to talk about, but a whole week to do it. What do you want to do first?" he asked, and she turned, putting her arms around him, squeezing, then let go. They sat on the hatch covers, and she put her left hand on his thigh. "I guess I want the story about the ring first," she said, looking

291

from him to the ring and back. Justin loved the pride shining in her eyes as she gazed at it.

He ran a finger along her arm to the gold ring. "I went into an older store, smaller, in Anchorage. They've been in business forever, it seems. Anyway, I said I was looking for something that wasn't a typical diamond engagement ring. Something with some color. He asked me what colors you wear, and I said green. You look good in green." He bent over and kissed her quickly, then wrapped his arms around her, pulling her closer. "So, he pulled out a couple of emeralds and then asked his wife something, I think in another language, and she came out. I looked at all the rings while they were talking, then told him that we work on boats. I couldn't get you anything that sticks way out."

His voice lowered, and he pulled away enough to make eye contact. "If you're working the net, and it got caught," he shivered, bringing her close again. "Believe me, people have died from stuff getting caught in gear. Raingear, long hair—" He stopped, feeling her tense up. "Anyway, you need to know that. Always look for anything that could get caught in gear and take it off or cut it off."

She squeezed his leg reassuringly, and he continued. "When I said that, he nodded to his wife, and she brought out a tray from the back. He said the jewelry was from an estate and that he hadn't finished evaluating it yet." Justin paused, remembering the tray of jewelry.

"This ring," he lifted her hand with his, "stood out. He said it was an antique, and it needed cleaning, but I really liked it the minute I saw it."

They both admired the gold band set with five square-cut emeralds, two on each side, framing a larger one in the center.

"Anyway, I said I wanted it, but he said he needed time to check it for excess wear and clean it up. He called me a few hours later and said it was ready. I have a nice box for it—"

"I'm never taking it off," she said quickly, and he squeezed her.

"Do you want a wedding band to go with it? I asked him, and he said it was just this ring, but he could make something up that would fit with it if I wanted.

"I don't think so. I like this. It fits me perfectly. I don't want anything more."

He smiled over the top of her head as she looked down at the ring, as if she was memorizing it.

Wait until you see the necklace.

It'll be her wedding present, he decided.

"What are you doing?" Ginny asked him as he pulled the sleeping bags out of their bunks after dinner.

"We're sleeping up above," he said, his head deep in the bow, pulling up the foam that was wedged firmly in place.

"Whaaa!" She grinned, then grabbed the bags and carried them up to the flying bridge, coming back for the pillows he'd tossed out of his way. Justin carried up one mattress pad and told her to stay up there. He'd hand them both to her. They piled things, sitting on the bench on the flying bridge, watching the sun setting over the mountains behind the glacier.

Lying on their pads, wrapped in sleeping bags, Justin's arm firmly around a completely naked Ginny, he leaned over her, propped on one arm. "I want to ask you some stuff."

"Okay," she sighed, smiling. She was still glowing. Their snuggling while watching the sunset had quickly turned into a passionate celebration on the flying bridge, and she wondered if she'd ever look at the space the same way again. She had no idea where her clothes were and didn't care.

"I want to know how many kids you want," he asked, and she choked, laughing.

"Agh! I dunno. I never thought about it." She scanned his serious face and watched him roll away, onto his back. She turned onto her side, and he did the same, facing her. "How many do *you* want?"

"Two. But, um, not for a while. I want us to have time for ourselves first."

"Okay."

"I want to buy a house." He looked at her when she didn't say anything. She looked stunned, speechless. "We need our own place." Her eyes widened. "Gin, what?"

"You..." Nothing else came out, and Justin lay back, waiting. When she choked up, it took forever for her to say what was stuck inside. He gave her a minute, then tried again.

"Don't you want a place just for us? Your own kitchen? Your own room?" Her face did not change from stunned, and he decided to shut up and wait, remembering that she hadn't even grown up in a normal home, never mind had her own space.

Two minutes of listening to the water lap at the side of the boat, the tiny surf on the shale beach in the background. An eagle screeching, then a loud *thwump-thwump-thwump* as it flew over them. He wondered how they ever managed to catch anything to eat except fish since their beating wings were so noisy. Any prey should hear them coming—

"My own room..."

He turned, watching her face, his brows drawn together as she blinked, looked away, then back at him, completely puzzled. It took another minute for her to continue. "My own room—for what?"

"Whatever you want. Your computer, maybe? Hattie had one for quilting. My mom said that as soon as Robbie was a little older, she was taking the playroom."

"Oh, my God," she blew out, lying back, staring at the sky as a couple of stars twinkled.

"What? Isn't that a good idea? I mean, it depends on the house. It might have to be a kid's room someday, or something like that if it's a small house."

"I thought you were saying to sleep in, like, roommates or something. Separate bedrooms."

He rolled over on top of her, shocked and laughing at the same time, his entire body pressing against hers. "No way. Are you kidding? Jesus, Gin. Not a chance," he laughed and tried not to, sputtering, kissing her neck, holding her arms down as she wrestled, trying to get her hands on him. She was laughing too much to even grip his biceps. They finally settled back down, releasing tensed muscles, molding together again.

"Does Case always know everything you do while you're doing it?" She asked, their bodies still intertwined.

"You mean like this?" He hesitated, then laughed, imagining that. "No," he said quickly, squeezing her tightly as he felt her try to pull away. "I'm not laughing at you. Honest. Listen. We started that stuff when we were babies, according to my parents. We'd hand each other things without asking, stuff like that. When we got older, we saw some comedy show or movie, where they called it ESPN." He laughed again, and she giggled. "From then on, we actually tried to keep doing it. I think our parents hoped we'd grow out of it." He pulled back and looked at her, and they both rolled onto their sides, facing each other.

"It kinda stopped when he went back to Fairbanks. I mean, if he's really upset, I feel funny. Like over New Years, when he was so miserable. I felt sick to my stomach the whole time. Remember? You made soup and kept asking me what was wrong?"

"ESPN," she pushed him, laughing. "That's actually funny. Okay, so he doesn't know every little thing?" Justin shook his head. "No, and honestly, I think it was a lot more of me knowing what he was going through than him feeling anything from me."

"Now what?" Ginny asked, as Justin's face looked pained. He rolled onto his back and stared at the sky.

"I, ah, jeez. Um," he turned toward her again. "Something happened to him when we were around fifteen or sixteen. Something about sex. He wouldn't talk to me. I think he might have told Chess. Maybe even my dad. But he'd never answer me when I asked."

"His first time? That young?"

"I know. I mean, I don't know, but yeah, I think so. Fifteen or sixteen. Way too young."

"Chelsea?"

"No. Oh, no," he said quietly, shaking his head.

"She loves him. You can see it all over her face. I could even feel it, it's that strong," Ginny said, quietly.

"She's always liked him. I thought that, after Nell and going all over Europe, though, she might get over him. But... watching them at the campfire..."

"Does he love her?" Ginny ran her hand over his chest. "Never mind. He wouldn't have fallen for Fake-Face if he did."

"Honey," he put his hand over hers. "I think he loves her and doesn't even know it." They both lay back, watching the first star shine above them, the sky changing shades gradually, a few more stars sparkling.

"So, stay at my dad's house, but start looking for our own place? Or do you want to rent our own place now?"

"I like it there, but what about Case?"

"Let's see. We'll talk to him when we get back, okay?"

"Sure," she laughed, garbling out, "you can always

remodel another mmppphhh," her laugh was muffled by his hand over her mouth.

"No. God, I'm starting to see why Mack bitches," he blew out.

"Awww, c'mon. You did a great job. And it seems to be pretty easy for you. And..." she hesitated, trailing a finger over his chest. "We had a pretty good time when we were both working from home..." His laugh rumbled, and he pulled her close, snuggling her body up to his as she wrapped herself around him.

"I couldn't keep my mind on work, you troublemaker. And I've already decided, I'm not doing another season without you," he said, pulling his shoulders back, brushing curls from her face to see her reaction.

"Yeah, I agree. I wanted to be back on your boat before we even cleared the bay. I just didn't want to change things after we had already decided," she admitted, then put her face into his chest.

Justin sighed, relaxing, running his hand absently up and down her back. This is a good start, he thought.

Better than I'd hoped for.

It's going to be a great week.

48

"Good morning," Al said, walking into the office Monday morning. Connor grinned, repeating the greeting, and Al stopped at Pete's desk. "I saw the seiners coming into the bay last week as I was leaving town. I hope it was a good season for them?"

"They both think it was," Pete replied, smiling warmly, feeling far more relaxed than he had in months.

"Wonderful. I have been waiting to say this, but I'm eager to get Ginny back. Her work with video is truly changing things for us, and I want to ask if she's had any further thoughts on expanding our outreach." Al motioned for Pete to come with him as he headed for his office, putting his brief-case on his desk.

Pete sat across from Al's desk and leaned back, waiting for Al to sit and get comfortable, then said, "You'll have to wait a week, at least, to ask her. She and Justin took the boat to Aialik."

Al leaned forward, his eyebrows going up. "Oh, how nice. I'd have thought they'd be tired of boat life by now."

Pete sat up straighter, beaming proudly. "Well, this trip is kind of special. Justin proposed!" he blurted out, unable to hold it in any longer.

"What! Oh, congratulations, Pete. What wonderful news! I believe that means that you, lucky man, will now have a daughter. Good for him. And good for you. She's a lovely girl. Woman," he corrected himself quickly. "Oh, Lord, they'll always be kids to us, won't they?" he added quietly.

Pete nodded, his smile still full of pride, with a hint of the loss he still felt deep inside. His baby. His first child. The first one he'd ever held in his hands, naked, just born, so fragile, so tiny. Soon to be a married man. The love and pain of it all astounded him, taking his breath away.

"That's not all the good news. I have some too," Al preened just a bit, speaking in his normal quiet tone, leaning back, cautiously watching the difficult emotions swirl in Pete's eyes. "I heard from the village council a couple of weeks ago. The village voted to terminate the enhancement program's proposed hatchery. I promised not to say anything until their attorneys had looked over the paperwork, but that's done now. It's official. No new hatchery."

Pete raised both hands in the air. "Yes!"

"Oh, yes. As soon as we're done celebrating, I want to show you the Board of Fish proposal that addresses dividing the seine district. F and G put one in months ago, and I have a copy of it. The proposal book should be coming out in a month or so, and I want to draft a comment from the tribe supporting the division, then circulate it to see how many more people and organizations we can get to comment favorably as well. I think this might have a broader impact—*better*—than we had anticipated."

Al continued to cover a few of the other proposals he knew were coming up before the Board of Fish, and they moved to the office conference room to be able to spread out, then went to fill coffee mugs.

. . .

Al took a call in his office, and Pete sat at the conference table, remembering watching the seiners return to the harbor. It had hurt as much as watching them leave. He'd thought he'd feel better, seeing them come home, but the ache—he'd actually reached out, as if to put his hand on the wheel, when he'd seen Justin standing on the flying bridge. The pang of wanting to be there was sharp, and it lingered.

What's life if you're not doing what you love?

I need to get back to fishing.

Maybe now... if the area's really going to be split? Aialik's open again! It's a miracle.

The miracle I need? Can I do it again?

Yes, son, he felt his dad say in his chest, in his head, deep in his heart, as if his dad stood right behind him and half-way within him, cradling his heart as Pete had cradled his newborn son.

~

Waiting to have the office to himself, Pete wandered it, touching things, looking out the windows, then sat in the interview room and texted Hattie.

PETE

Can I stop by for a chat?

He stood up and paced. His phone pinged.

HATTIE

Sure. Taking boys to the playground while Mack cooks dinner. Meet us there?

PETE

On my way.

. . .

They watched the kids playing, as they leaned against the fence surrounding the playground at the water's edge, the smooth, glassy bay beyond sparkling in the early evening sun, and Pete poured his heart out. Hattie listened without interruption.

Touching his arm, when he'd finally wound down, she began, "But your heart…"

"My life's worthless if I can't do what I want. I need to try, and I'll keep it easy. I don't need much for money anymore… It's not—"

"I get it. I try to get Mack to talk about retirement, but, well, we both know that's not going to happen. Next year, then? What boat?"

"I don't know. Maybe a small one. Yes. Definitely next season. That gives me time to wrap up at the office, find a boat and skiff, maybe build a net…"

"Find a good time to talk to Justin," Hattie said quietly, "when they get back."

Pete turned to look at her. "Why?"

"He's not as happy as you might think he is. He hides it well. I'm hoping that the week in Aialik will help. Maybe finally getting married will, too," she exhaled. "He craves security. Or, well, he did. I'm not so sure now."

"I… I thought he loved it."

"No. He took over in the skiff to help you when Case quit, and maybe to prove something to himself. Then he had to take over running the boat and finish the season when Linda got sick. That's a lot of change in one year. Last year, well, with your heart… He did what he thought he had to do and bought the boat. I think that was his way of holding on to what was familiar, what he knew he could do. This year, I think he did it just to stay near Ginny, to keep things the same between them."

Hattie felt he'd done it all under pressure. Maybe too much pressure. He'd tried to step into Pete's shoes: helping care for Robbie, taking on the family boat, holding tight to his first love. She thought Justin needed time to find what really called him, and it wasn't seining. Her greatest fear was that he would grow out of love the way he seemed to be growing out of seining. They'd had three years, she reassured herself, of working together and getting to know each other better, but what traumatic years! At least they're not doing what Pete and Linda had done.

Pete looked past the playground, out at the bay, thinking about what his son had been through, regretting the load that had been dumped on him, wondering how to make it up to him.

"Stay for dinner? You know Mack still cooks like he's feeding a hungry crew."

"Sure. Thanks."

"You really think he wants out?" Mack asked, after excusing the boys from the table and sending them downstairs to play. He looked from his brother to Hattie, who hadn't even gotten up to clear the table or clean up the mess he'd made in the kitchen, which had been his first clue that something was wrong.

"I'm only saying that he's talked about buying a tender and then that business that Gabe's trying to start. His heart isn't into seining like yours is."

Mack and Pete shared a look, each of them preferring the roll of a boat on the ocean to the relentlessly flat, hard ground beneath their feet.

"Al's convinced that the division in the district is going to be a real thing. Things are changing," Pete said, elbows on the table, his hands spreading, his face eager. "Aialik—"

"And Day Harbor. I never even made another set there after the first one. Great fish. Natural and plenty of them. Good sized—"

"The monitors reported great escapement—"

"What are the numbers?" Mack asked, interrupting. They talked over each other, going back to the past, naming places they used to fish and how good the catches used to be. Stories they'd told many times before were resurrected and repeated. Hattie stood up, taking plates to the kitchen, completely ignored as the two became skippers again and years floated away like they'd never happened.

"And I had the bay to myself!" Mack exclaimed. "About damned time," he added, and Pete said, "Justin—" but Mack cut him off. "He's no competition—"

"Then maybe you need some," Pete challenged, his eyes alight, one eyebrow raised.

"Bring it on," his brother urged. "I can out-fish you any day. This is *my* bay," he asserted confidently, "and I finally have it back. Next year's gonna be the best ever."

Next

in The Seiner Series

Aurora Bay opens where Aialik Bay ended, following the seiners and their families through an emotional end of the year, culminating on New Year's Eve.

Case, given an unexpected second chance, didn't even recognize his best friend, the only person he's ever poured his heart and soul out to. Now she wants nothing to do with him and this time she means it.

Leaving seining behind, Case is still called by the plight of wild salmon, eager to continue his efforts to protect the species but unsure what career path will have the most impact. Should he stay in Seward, near his family? Or move up, and out, accepting national challenges?

Chelsea has adored Case since they were teenagers, but that secret crush ends when he flirts with her, thinking she's a stranger. Why didn't she straighten him out immediately? Does she owe him one more chance or not? Is she finally over him?

Justin took months to pull the ring out of his pocket and put it on Ginny's finger. Now he wants it official, as soon as possible and he can't understand why she won't even talk about picking a date.

Hattie's Home

Nineteen-year-old Hattie Landers arrives in Seward, Alaska, seeking a fresh start. When fate throws her onto a fishing boat with Rory and his guarded son Mack, Hattie finds herself navigating more than just the treacherous waters of the Last Frontier.

As Hattie proves her worth among the crew, she discovers a sense of belonging she's always craved. But when tragedy strikes, leaving hearts shattered and dreams adrift, Hattie is forced to leave behind the life she's come to love and the man who's captured her heart.

Drawn back to the rugged shores of Alaska by an unexpected twist of fate, Hattie must confront the ghosts of her past. Can she mend the bonds broken by time and grief? Will the wild beauty of the Seward, Alaska once again become the home she's longed for?

Set against the breathtaking backdrop of Alaska's untamed wilderness, "Hattie's Home" is a poignant exploration of family, forgiveness, and the courage it takes to give love a second chance. This unforgettable story will stay with you long after the last page is turned.

Women's Fiction & Romance
by MM Travis

Visit https://inside-alaska.com/romance/

Acknowledgments

I thank the skippers, skiffmen and deckhands who continue to share their experiences with me. Working together and hearing your stories affords me endless laughter and ideas whenever we're together.

I'm grateful to Joan Graham and Nancy Hillstrand for their enthusiastic encouragement and editorial assistance.

Thank you!
Max

About the Author

Max Travis is an Alaskan fisherman who loves salmon and cherishes the opportunity to catch and eat them.

Passionate about protecting the natural resources of Alaska, Max incorporates current affairs with personal stories.

Please sign up for our newsletter at https://inside-alaska.com/authors/ for more about Alaska, the books Max Travis writes, and exclusive content.

www.ingramcontent.com/pod-product-compliance
Lightning Source LLC
Chambersburg PA
CBHW021939120726

47992CB00001B/59